By John A. Williams

FLASHBACKS

CAPTAIN BLACKMAN

THE KING GOD DIDN'T SAVE

SONS OF DARKNESS, SONS OF LIGHT

THE MOST NATIVE OF SONS

THE MAN WHO CRIED I AM

THIS IS MY COUNTRY TOO

AFRICA: HER HISTORY, LANDS AND PEOPLE

SISSIE

NIGHT SONG

THE ANGRY ONES

Mothersill and the Foxes

Mothersill and the Foxes

By JOHN A. WILLIAMS

1975
Doubleday & Company, Inc.
Garden City, New York

PRINTED IN THE UNITED STATES OF AMERICA
FIRST EDITION

Library of Congress Cataloging in Publication Data

Williams, John Alfred, 1925–
Mothersill and the foxes.
I. Title.
PZ4.W72624Mo [PS3573.I4495] 813'.5'4
ISBN 0-385-09454-X
LIBRARY OF CONGRESS CATALOG CARD NUMBER 74-9469

To Eva with love

In the olden days Death was
not among men and God still
lived on earth. If Death
appeared, God chased him
with his hounds. This day
Death was being chased closely
by the hounds. Death ran to a
woman and promised that, if she
hid him, he would protect her
and her family. The woman
opened her mouth and Death leaped
inside. God came and demanded
to know where Death had gone. The
woman said she had not seen him. But
God who is the Seeing One knew Death's
hiding place. He told the woman that
since she had hidden Death, in the
future Death would destroy her and all
others. God left the woman in anger
and from that time Death came to all men.

Wabembe tale

"Sigh not, therefore, neither
be moved; and say not in thy
heart that this darkness is
long and drags on wearily;
and say not in thy heart that
I plague thee with it.
"Strengthen thy heart, and be
not afraid. This darkness is not
a punishment. But, O, Adam, I
have made the day, and have placed
the sun in it to give it light; in
order that thou and thy children
should do your work.
"For I knew thou shouldest sin
and transgress, and come out into
this land. Yet would I not force
thee, nor be heard upon thee, nor
shut up; nor doom thee through thy
fall; nor through thy coming out
from light into darkness; nor yet
through coming from the garden into
this land.
"For I made thee of the light; and
I willed to bring out children of
light from thee and like unto thee.
"But little of darkness now remains,
O Adam; and daylight will
soon appear."

The First Book of Adam & Eve

Part One

ODELL MOTHERSILL WAS flying home, speeding through Washington Square Park, the first dried leaves of autumn, carried on a slightly chilling wind, swirling and scraping on the walk beneath his feet. The arch was lighted and the streetlights up Fifth Avenue gleamed in the dark. Down here it was quiet, the pace more civilized, even, as now, promising excitement. His stomach was filled with spaghetti, and his head buzzed nicely with wine. He touched Shirley's elbow and she turned and smiled at him, nudged him with one of her ample hips.

Shirley, matching him stride for stride, although he was the taller, smiled again at his obvious eagerness. It pleased her to think that he'd been waiting for these two weeks.

He'd come into the bar in the afternoon with that older fellow she often saw there, and she was sure they'd come to see her. Shirley accepted the fact that when she was on duty, the patrons were far more numerous than when she wasn't.

Now Mothersill smiled as they moved quickly past the empty fountain. Gibson had taken him to the Emperor's Bar after the conference. Like most adoption agency conferences, it had been long and dry, with half the white people there scared to death because they were in Harlem. But, since the Catholics had made great inroads to the black population, weaning people away from the Methodists and Baptists—and the people had been eager to break away from these fundamental religious ties—there had come under the jurisdiction of the Church more and more black orphans requiring homes. So it was fitting that the conference took place uptown. Old Man Gibson, long a figurehead in the city's adoption programs, took Mothersill to the Emperor's, his tongue clacking in his mouth, so badly did he claim the need for a drink. "And besides," he'd said, "they got this fabulous bartender, got the biggest tits in the world. Name's Shirley. And,

Odell, I tell you I've done some of everything there is for a man to do, but I haven't been able to get next to Shirley."

They drank their first martinis like they were water, and then Mothersill studied the bar and Shirley. The bar was at least fifty feet long and could accommodate as many men leaning on it and another fifty behind them. There were a hundred pairs of eyes on Shirley, who walked proudly from one patron to the other, moving with a grace and sexuality that Mothersill felt grinding in his genitals after the third drink. Normally gin was not his drink, but the Catholics had driven him to desperation; he was glad he worked for a nondenominational adoption agency.

Mothersill and Shirley walked out of the park and hurried between the old dark garages and factories that were almost indistinguishable from the New York University apartments and office buildings. He slipped his hand into Shirley's and they increased their pace, neither noticing how heavily they were starting to breathe.

Shirley liked the feel of his hand. His taking hers was a gesture she associated with him, like the shyness that came through at the bar that day; or like his smile, which wavered somewhere between the street-wise grimace she was so used to, and a schoolboy's nervousness. One got tired of being hit on by anyone who'd bought a couple of drinks. Just because she worked in a bar didn't mean that she did not want to be treated with consideration. Odell was a stranger in the bar that afternoon; she'd spotted it in a minute. A man of some other cut than she was used to. She smiled again thinking how often she'd wiped the bar before him, leaning way over so he could peruse her breasts. That way, she could look at him and study his expression. Joy. Not that hard, measuring quality of some of the glances—most of the glances—she got. A young, exuberant kind of joy. She had said, "Yes, lover," when he asked if he could take her to dinner, "Yes, lover," to his popped-eyed astonishment. But she had been sure that he wouldn't call, that she'd been talking to his martinis, and they'd been talking to him.

A half block from his apartment building, Mothersill slowed; he had it made now. Earlier he'd plucked Shirley down from the upper floors of Esplanade Gardens and eased her past the big guards who paced in the lobby, their great buttocks jangling guns, keys and flashlights, and A-trained her downtown. He'd promised to show her something of the Village and had told her that of course she could wear her toreador pants and spiked silver heels. She'd been a hit, even in the Village. Now they were heading home and a heavy, warm erection began in Mothersill's pants. But he knew she wasn't one of those women you grabbed from behind while they stared at your bookshelves. Oh, no. With Shirley, you wouldn't do anything until she was ready for you to.

Ahhhhh, he thought when they were in his apartment and he was helping her off with her poncho, the tiddies on this woman!

"It's nice," Shirley said looking around. "Is that color TV?"

"No," Mothersill said.

"Shit."

Mothersill glanced quickly at her. "Sit down."

"Turn on TV?"

He hesitated for a moment. How could he refuse? Could he lie and say it was broken? But if she found it wasn't she might leave. He was suddenly filled with hatred for the object which, until they walked into the room, had been inanimate, without life, a collection of glass, plastic and cheap metal. "Go ahead," he said, miffed. Mothersill was also puzzled. Only moments ago Shirley seemed to have had nothing on her mind save being alone with him. But now she was crouching before the set when, ordinarily, there'd be small talk about the record player, the couch, the carpet; that was the way it was with other dates. (For as shy as Mothersill appeared to be, he was sublimely unaware of it.) The talk would move from one thing to the next, easily, as Romans spoke of stuffed grapes, battles and nubile Nubian slaves.

For Shirley, TV was companion and comfort—and also a

mechanism of defense. She lived alone on 120th Street, just off Lenox; that is, she was currently living alone and enjoying it. She was free to see whom she wished, but at the end of the afternoon shift at the bar and the grabbing, clutching eyes, the softly dropped suggestions, she enjoyed being alone with her TV set. Even when she was away from it the voices kept her company. TV allowed her to enter a world outside her own. Sometimes at the bar she found herself talking like one of the characters in a morning serial.

The set was a defense now because it was approaching *that* time. To be sure she had looked forward to making love with Mothersill; there was something, she thought, so young, different and unstreetlike about him. She did not know that they were the same age, but she did feel that working among men, and having known many of them in many places, including bedrooms, she was wiser about them than most women. But now it had come down to the same old thing. The hand-holding was over; the sweet talk, Mothersill's bashful smile, would vanish. It was bedtime and she wished to hold onto her illusions of TV love and romance.

In the kitchen Mothersill fixed Shirley a strong drink and listened to the sounds coming from the set. TV, he sniffed. Here in Odell Mothersill's crib and wants to look at TV. But her smile was so bright when he gave her her drink that he was encouraged to place her head in his lap.

Shirley fluttered her lashes at him when she felt his penis hardening along the softness of her neck, and Mothersill, also aware of it and pleased that she did not move away, thought a sigh of relief. All was going to be fine, and he raised her to kiss her.

Shirley tossed up her tongue like a piece of warmed-over chitlin; her attention remained on the set. Mothersill cupped one of her famous, large breasts, trying to make her turn away from TV. She made a sound and he chose to accept it as one indicating that, if he mined deeply enough, he'd fine some passion;

he rejected its being a sound of annoyance, which was precisely what Shirley was trying to convey. Mothersill slid his hands beneath her blouse. Wow! These is some tiddies, he thought. He ran his hands around her buttocks, which were encapsulated in a panty girdle, and then back to her breasts. Only then did he become aware that the program she was watching was ending.

Resignedly, Shirley leaned forward, starting to undo her blouse. Might as well get it over with, since it was going to be the same old thing, only with a Greenwich Village setting. "You want to get with it, right?" she asked, sounding as if she was asking a patron to repeat his order at the bar.

Mothersill nodded dumbly.

Shirley undid the blouse, the snaps on her bra. The shoes, stockings, panty girdle panties, and there it was solid, plentiful. She smiled at him as he rushed out of his own clothes. Shirley thought it was cute.

"Oooo," she said, when she reached out and stroked his penis. Sure can't tell much about these quiet ones, all that still water running deep. Mothersill ran his fingers over her broad, sloping shoulders, kissed the breasts which, although large, were firm and shaped, and ran his hands up between her legs and felt her tremble. They first knelt and then lay down on the rug, commercials on the set ending in the background. They kissed, felt, moaned until Shirley, feeling once again a curiosity about this thin, angular man, pulled him to her. Just before he entered, a new program began and Shirley rolled away from him. "Hey! I forgot. 'Cheyenne' is on. That's my man, Odell. I don't miss 'Cheyenne.'" And she didn't. Every week she watched the tall, dark-haired cowboy who spoke as though his tongue was located in his throat. He was big and strong, but there was about him, too, a quality of gentleness she loved in one so capable of breaking people in two. Shirley patted Mothersill on the cheek, her eyes on the set, while Mothersill, astounded, held his melting penis captive by the scruff of its circumcised neck.

For forty-five minutes he watched and listened as Shirley cried:

"Kick his ass, Cheyenne! Whump! Aw, do it, Cheyenne!" She paused between exclamations to smile at Mothersill. He, however, was willing his limp penis to rise, but the flesh was weak, mortified and unable to sustain his imagery. Finally it sulked between his thighs as if seeking a hiding place.

When the show was finally over Shirley turned off the set and lay down on the rug, drained. "Now," she said, waiting, holding up her arms, anticipating his warmth and slimness, him in her.

But Mothersill remained motionless. He wished for the most massive of erections, so he could beat her to death with it, send her into the street on her knees. How was it that she could go from about to making love to Cheyenne and back to wanting to make love again without a change of pace? No niceties. No feel for mood, atmosphere. Just rip off some here, a little there, bam-bam. *Now,* he thought, his penis dangling impotently between his thin thighs, his rage short-circuiting his desire.

Shirley turned and looked up at him, saw his cold eyes and knew instantly, if not frighteningly, that this was not the boy-man she had taken him to be. This awareness made her beat a fast retreat into a kind of barroom toughness. "Whatsa matter, you can't get it up?" she said as nastily as she could. This tone had shriveled up many a man.

Coldly, Mothersill said, "Get offa my rug. Put your clothes on and get out. You and some goddamn Cheyenne."

Shirley met such denunciations quickly and vigorously. She jumped to her feet and began pulling on her clothes. "That's cool, fagot. You can't get it up, I might as well leave."

With a sinking feeling, for he felt himself rising lazily, Mothersill watched her smooth brown muscles flowing and jerking under her skin as she dressed; his mouth dried instantly when he understood that he was not going to kiss or suckle her breasts; she had rejected him, his gift to her. His pleasure would have been drawn from giving her pleasure. Old cracker antebellum term—pleasuring. But Shirley was shouting at him:

"All you cats livin' down here is fagots anyway!"

He recoiled, and almost watched his own words emerge and hang in the air: "Cheyenne is a fagot." He saw that she was stung now; the implications inherent in digging fagots was too much. But, momentarily mesmerized, examining the meaning of his words as intently as he, and noticing for the first time an ominous tone, heavily larded with contempt, Shirley fought back. "No he ain't no fagot, he's a man."

Mothersill backed up and looked at her. This was silly he realized. Didn't she, too, realize how silly it was, arguing about— Now he shouted, "What're you talkin' about, woman? *Somebody made him up and took his picture—*"

"—you're just jealous!" she stormed, watching him narrowly; his words carried an unfamiliar import, and she didn't want to hear any more. Quietly, with the air of finality she had used with drunks a thousand times over at the bar, she said, "I'm ready. You takin' me to a cab?"

Bitterly, but just as quietly, Mothersill asked, "Baby, does Cheyenne have wings?"

He watched her stamp to the door, snatch it open and pull it closed behind her with all her strength. *Blam-lamm!* The paintings on the walls bounced and flapped.

With a mixture of rage and sadness, Mothersill thought, Aw, she'd make a rotten mother anyway. Then, damn, Shirley this isn't the way it's supposed to be.

He thought of Etta Mae then. Why, he didn't know, but smiled, and considered how it must have been for her.

The unusual quiet broke in on Etta Mae and she started guiltily. The kids must be up to something, she thought, and for a moment she felt a searing hatred for the boy and girl. Twelve, Etta Mae had been in one of her frequent reveries. She enjoyed them, they were like candy, and she emerged from them into the real world with heavy, sad sighs, except when that world intruded on her as it had now.

The reveries had come with the first day of spring. The sap had loosened and flowed to some dangerous edge and piled up there, viscous, dark and unpredictable. In closets jammed with clothes Etta Mae burrowed herself smelling the parts that covered the genitals, and fondled her heavy breasts and lovingly stroked her clitoris. She closed her eyes and saw only what she wished to see, not what she had to. Lean, brown boys with long, smooth muscles in their arms and legs raced into and out of her vision, smiling at her with dazzling teeth. She saw them close to her, heard their voices and felt them inside her. They said all the things she knew they'd never really say to her.

For Etta Mae was squat and square-shouldered. Upon her wide face her mouth was a heavy-lipped crescent and her nose was flat. Eyebrowless, her hair was only as long as a boy's. God's final curse was her absolute blackness; in the right light her skin gave off a soft, bluish color. But she was the only one in her group who had real breasts or who had periods and pubic hair.

She lingered on the edges of things. Always anticipating ridicule, Etta Mae stored up a host of anger. Invited to parties where they played spin the bottle or post office, she left after the first fifteen minutes, avoiding the probability of someone refusing to kiss her.

But now she was moving across the carpeted floor of the living room. Mrs. Mothersill sure kept a good house; everyone said that. It was a place Mr. Mothersill beat a quick retreat to whenever he had time between trains.

Etta Mae's eyes swept the kids' bedroom; she'd arrived there silently. Her eyes shot back to what she first thought was a pile of dark clothing waiting to be pressed.

Damn, Etta Mae thought.

Odell Mothersill, nine, was pressed against his sister, Lispernard, six. Her little white panties were down around her thin legs. She held a doll, a blonde with blue eyes, and was stroking its hair while her brother, his tiny penis limply pumping empty air in the vicinity of his sister's private parts, clutched her shoulders.

The little *devil,* Etta Mae thought. With a grin.

She moved back out of sight as a fever rose up in her. She was standing just inside the bedroom door belonging to Mr. and Mrs. Mothersill. She stepped quickly out of her underwear and tucked it inside the top of her dress, smelling, as though it were a breeze quickly come and just as quickly gone, the faint musk from between her legs. She felt her heart racing and now she was overcome with heat, but she knew that if she was to die within the next minute, she'd have to do now what she was going to do.

"Odell, come in here." Not angrily, but with just enough force to make him leave off and come at once.

"What you been doin'?" Softly, with a smile.

"Nothin'."

"What's Lispernard doin'?"

"Playin'. With her doll."

Etta Mae could hardly breathe. She could hear her heartbeat in her ears. On rubbery legs she retreated until the backs of her knees found the bed. She held out her hands to the boy, pulled him gently toward her. She lay back. The boy filled her arms, puzzled by the look in her eyes. Firmly, she lifted him atop her and began to unfasten his pants.

He felt her hand, large, warm and pleasant, encircling, pulling on his penis, and before he knew it, it was straighter and harder than it'd ever been before. She moved beneath him and he looked down and saw the blackness of her legs.

Etta Mae was breathing fast. Odell felt his penis being thrust nervously into a warm, wet place. It felt good. Some great game. He watched Etta Mae opening and closing her eyes, her mouth. She had him by the waist now and moved up and down. "Bump up and down," she whispered.

"Like this?" he whispered back.

"Like this." She pulled him to her and pushed him back. "But from down there."

Really, really *keen!* He moved up and down until Etta Mae jerked beneath him and whispered intensely, "There! That's the way it's s'pposed to be!"

He was so intent on watching the expressions change and merge on her face that he almost stopped. There was at times so much beauty there, fixed in the curl of the mouth, the slightly distended nostrils, the fluttering eyes which gave off a softness—

"Don't stop, that's it, oh, don't stop." Sucking air in through her teeth all the while.

A third party, small and curious, stood in the doorway watching.

Lispernard Mothersill with one glance took in all the fun Etta Mae was having, and, angered at having been left out of this game, flung down her doll and screamed. "Me, too! If you don't do it to me, Odell, I'm gonna *tell!*"

How could she have known it was worth telling, forbidden? Did she know from Odell's little ass curving and humping in the air, his pants and underwear a bundle somewhere near his ankles? Or was it the sight of all Etta Mae's black flesh revealed in its welcoming posture on the bed? Or Etta Mae's sounds? Lispernard Mothersill knew.

At the sound of her voice the boy froze where he was gathering momentum for the bump-down stroke. Etta Mae closed her legs with a whoop, snatched down her dress and came to a sitting position all in a single motion, spilling the stricken Odell into his sister and knocking her down, too.

Oh, sugar, Etta Mae thought, kneeling beside the children. She pushed Odell aside; Lispernard was going to be her problem. "Honey, are you all right?" Hating her and being concerned for her at the same time. Females. Dumb Odell. "There, there—"

"Me, too, me, too," Lispernard wailed.

Close to panic, Etta Mae seized Odell's shoulders. "You do it to her, too." To Lispernard: "But you mustn't ever tell, because if you do, I'll tell your mother that you did it, too!" Dealing on her level.

"Ain't gonna tell," Lispernard said, climbing on the bed with her doll, then remembering to pull up her dress.

Odell looked from Etta Mae to his sister.

Etta Mae said nothing about the pants.

Odell said sullenly, "She got her unnerwear on."

"That's all right," Etta Mae said. "You just go ahead and bump-up and bump-down on her, like you did me."

"I don wanna do her. I wanna do you some more."

"Not now, Odell, not now. Go ahead."

Odell climbed atop his sister and went bump-up and bump-down a few times and got down. He stood next to Etta Mae, awaiting Lispernard's verdict.

"That's not much fun," she said. "Gonna play with my dollie."

As soon as she left the room Odell pulled at Etta Mae, tried to push her back on the bed. "Get away, boy," she hissed. "Get away." He watched as she left to play with Lispernard and wondered why Etta Mae was laughing so hard, cooing so much with Lispernard. Did it have to do with the bumping-up and bumping-down?

He went to the living room and stood looking out the window, thinking. Two years before when his mother's cousin, Retha, was staying with them, Odell, having outgrown that period when darkness frightened him, prowled through it every night. That particular night Mr. Mallory had come to pay a call on cousin Retha. They'd stayed up in the living room until mother and daddy went to bed. Odell fell asleep, but came awake sensing things, and so crept, like an Indian he thought, to the door of his room, pushed it partly open and saw cousin Retha and Mr. Mallory standing in the center of the living room, partly in the soft glow of the streetlight. Mr. Mallory's pants were down around his ankles and there was something around cousin Retha's ankles, too, but he couldn't tell what. Her dress wasn't hanging as neatly as usual; it hung behind and was raised up in a sharp angle in front.

Standing up, they were bumping-up and bumping-down. No, bumping-in and bumping-out. Odell Mothersill marveled. Now he smiled at the sounds coming from the bedroom; he thought he understood them, especially Etta Mae's.

During the months following, Odell managed to touch Etta Mae often, though surreptitiously, on the way home from school. Only when Lispernard went upstairs to play with Barbara did Odell and Etta Mae bump-up and bump-down. Now she made him turn his back to her while she removed her underpants, and she smiled differently at him, and held him familiarly. And she talked to him:

"Oh, Odell, I wish—"

"What?"

"Nothing. Shush."

"What do you wish, Etta Mae?"

"Well. That you were a little older."

"Why?"

"Never mind. You're going to be cute."

"You're already pretty, Etta Mae."

Looking at the expression on her face, he felt himself filling with goodness. Never had anyone responded so to him. Giving gifts at Christmas, birthdays and parties, the response was always routine, thin. "Why, thank you, Odell." His handkerchiefs, toys and drugstore chocolates—his gifts—were accepted with that staged veneer of gratitude. But it did please him to make people smile, to see their eyes brighten and their hands flutter with delight, when they were genuinely pleased.

Like a small god he leaned forward and kissed Etta Mae's forehead, unaware of the pure benevolence of the gesture, and completely ignorant of the girl's purring pleasure.

Mothersill never thought of the times with Etta Mae without thinking of Belle.

She came home with his father during a break in his run. Fall and getting on toward dinner, Etta Mae gone, Mrs. Mothersill a silhouette moving back and forth behind the kitchen window where she was preparing dinner. She had come home smiling, without complaint of how hard she'd worked in Mrs. Lowry's house, changed clothes, reddened her lips and cheeks and began dinner from scratch: no leftovers. Mothersill and his sister romped in a pile of leaves, pausing to run to the street side and see if their father was coming. For their mother's fresh dress and perfume, the frying chicken and baking pie told them that he was on the way.

Coming home for three days, filled with stories to tell about the passengers on his train, the crew and what was happening in the big cities. In another year or two on his vacation they would be able to go places on his railroad pass, and they would see the places he spoke about with such bored familiarity.

As if by magic he appeared beside the pile of leaves, and they, thinking it time to check his coming down the street, ran into him and recoiled, startled by the suddenness of his presence, but they were at once reassured by his laughter. "Scared you, doodley-doo," he sang, putting down his small suitcase in the leaves and trying to embrace them with one hand; he held Belle in the other, a thin, wide-eyed child who reminded Odell of the pictures he'd seen of starving kids. He and Lispernard accepted his embrace, their heads pressing against his clothes to feel the presents in his pockets, but their eyes were drawn to the little girl's and hers were just as questioning as theirs.

"That you out there, Randolph?"

Mothersill heard a lilt in his mother's voice.

"Yep, made that time and now time's mine."

"Oh, just listen to him," Mrs. Mothersill said, withdrawing quickly from the window, wheeling to come out the back door. But she reappeared at the window. "Randolph, what is that, a child?" The lilt was gone from the voice, and it was like the first cold wind blowing off the lake.

"This is Belle, Lulu," he said, laughing uneasily, feeling down for his suitcase. "Leastways, that's what I call her."

"Belle *what?* Randolph?"

Mothersill heard the challenge in his mother's voice. He looked at Lispernard. Then his father sighed, a long exhalation that went through his entire, slender frame. "Don't know, Lulu. We're comin' in," he said briskly. "Sure smells good around here."

"Ummmm," Mrs. Mothersill said, watching them troop up the stairs.

"Hold the door for me, Odell," his father said. "Hold it now."

In the bright kitchen, the chicken splattering and hissing in the number ten iron skillet, they stood, Mothersill, Lispernard, their father and Belle, grouped together, and Mrs. Mothersill alone, standing before them, her eyes sliding from the baby to Mr. Mothersill.

Setting his bag down, Mr. Mothersill tried to shift the baby to his other arm. It was then that Mothersill found her fingers wrapped tightly around his. The movement frightened her and she started to cry, reaching back for Mothersill's hand.

"Somebody left her in the bathroom, Lulu. Some of our people on the last leg north I guess."

"Lord, lord, lord," Mrs. Mothersill said, shaking her head and holding out her arms to Belle. "Why didn't you tell the poe-lice, Randolph?" The baby was shrinking back against Mr. Mothersill, her finger still around Odell's. "She won't turn loose, Odell, will she?"

"I figured I'd go to the poe-lice tomorrow, Lulu. She can stay with us till her folks gets found." He glanced at her. "Can't she?"

Mrs. Mothersill spun back to the stove. "This chicken's 'bout to burn up. You kids get washed, and you, too, Randolph. I need me some time to think. I mean, she's here, now, but I still need thinkin' time."

"She's a real skinny little thing, Lulu."

"I can see that, Randolph."

"Yeah, well, let's get washed kids. Odell, you think you can bring ole Belle to the bathroom?"

He didn't miss Etta Mae those few days Belle was with them. Odell's mother remained home, feeding and fussing over the baby, oiling, powdering and nursing the small, scabbed body, laughing softly at the snatched forks whose ends were filled with mashed potatoes and gravy, or grits, or eggs and finely sliced meats. In a day and a half she began to smile and Odell Mothersill watched a set expression come to his mother's face for she knew, as he knew, that she would not be with them long.

As it was, his father spent his days off trudging around the city to the various agencies, until, on his last day, when he spent so much time whispering to his mother, and casting gray glances at Belle crawling over the floor, Odell knew that soon she would be gone; he'd come home from school and she would have disappeared as suddenly as she had appeared.

"It's a shame," his mother kept murmuring. "A shame. Lord, what is the world coming to? But we can't do no better. Just can't."

"Don't fret, now, Lulu," was the murmured response. "We done our best, our level best."

"Poor child, and Randolph, you can say what you want about those places, but a child belongs with its folks, now, Randolph."

"Maybe I shoulda left her on that train—"

"Hush, Randolph. You shoulda no such thing."

"Where," Odell grew bold enough to ask, "is Belle goin'?"

He awaited the answer with dread. He played with enough children to know that they were constantly threatened with the children's home if they didn't behave. Exiled from the bosom of the family. Abandoned to the care of strangers.

"She's gonna be all right, son," his father assured him, shakily.

"Go play, boy," his mother said, sternly.

But, he remembered standing in their mildly shocked silence, seeing himself as Belle, or a Belle, abandoned on a train, cold, hungry, frightened; saw himself brought to a home with people like his mother and father in it, himself and his sister, a comfortable home, where there was fun and an understanding that there was some kind of future (his folks always talked about saving and bankbooks and a new house and furniture and how much longer his father would have to be away, how much longer his mother would have to work in someone else's home), yes, standing there, Lispernard joining him, curious, but he felt, in support, and hearing Belle's voice happy, chasing a stray dustball, and finally saying:

"Why can't she stay with us?"

He could not meet the looks in their eyes and so turned to his sister, aware then that he had stepped over something, a fence, a barrier. And then his mother covered her eyes and cried; rushed from them into their room, and he heard the springs of the bed upon which he and Etta Mae bumped up and down squeal and stop, and a moan, like a new sentence, began and trailed away.

Odell turned his gaze on his father. He, after all, was used to things, going to places like Chicago and New York; surely he could do something. Toss that thin-haired head, sharp face upward, his teeth giving off a flash of gold, and it would be done. But his father merely stood, touched both their heads in sad benediction and left the room.

Odell Mothersill was not surprised when he came home from school the next day to find Etta Mae there, his mother at work. He had seen his father go in the morning, bearing Belle in a new snowsuit in his one arm, his other jammed with his suitcase and a box full of new baby clothes.

But it is now 1950 and Odell Mothersill is twenty-five. Like many social workers, he has moved far from his roots, the home finally purchased, the new furniture now old, the parents so steeped in habit that running on the trains and cleaning Mrs. Lowry's daughter's home have become a way of life. From Hough, on the run, Mothersill took refuge in the state university.

World War II has been over for five years. During it, he grew up, for men, scattered over the earth preserving democracy, were scarce at home. There was Jennifer, and also the unspoken laws that exist between men and women concerning the ages at which they shall be indoctrinated into grown-up sex were quietly set aside; fifteen-, sixteen- and seventeen-year-old boys were made men in other men's beds. The women of Hough were amazed at Mothersill's precocity; they did not know about Jennifer. They said Odell was sweet. Moving fast and looking over his shoulder, he entered Ohio State, where he became a diligent student for fear of failing and having to return home to, at least, a bad beating. When he finished his studies, it is possible that Mothersill took himself to one of those medium-sized cities where nobody ever heard of the mayor, but the world knew about its football team. Maybe not. Maybe he stayed in Columbus, which is such a city.

Wherever he stopped, he worked in Public Assistance—casework being a job in most cities where only recently a college degree was required. Being a caseworker is a good job; it provides under certain conditions the time to think and make plans, such as taking a higher degree part-time with an eye to becoming a supervisor or a worker in a private agency. Mothersill became a graduate student.

This while for two years he was responsible for the actions and well-being of ninety people, about half of them black. They were—clients. The smell of the service room which he attended once a week—sweat, vomit, stale whiskey, baby shit, cheap perfume, bad breath, flatulence, dirt—became embedded in his clothing.

At first he liked it; it was a chance to help people, an opportunity to get to know more and different kinds of people. But nothing ever changed, except their seasonal budgets. Naturally, he saw over ninety people in the dingy service room or in their houses, which were uniformly gray, filled with the mixed odors of bargain foods hastily cooked (and probably more quickly consumed), stale bed linens and always the bothersome edge of urine dried in clothes. Black and white, native or foreign-born, they were a class: as one, slick, devious, pathetic, beaten, needy of more than the few dollars the county, state or federal government grudgingly gave them. What? His love, perhaps, and often he bought cigarettes for the old-agers, candies for the kids on ADC. As soon as he knew how to, he diddled with the budgets on their behalves, but the supervisors were eyed like eagles and his case cards were always being pulled and sent back to him for readjusting.

They clawed at him without so much as raising their voices or lifting their eyes. He saw their stunted black, brown and white bodies even in his sleep, scribblings by Daumier; their faces leered up at him from the pages of his textbooks, and their smells haunted the tiny crevices in his nostrils. Inadvertently he brought home their little bugs, even from the hard chairs every caseworker as a rule sat in when conducting a home visit.

"Do your job and when you go home at night forget them. That's the way to last on this job."

And Mothersill saw the workers who'd been there twenty years and who told stories of how, when they first began, they used to walk along the railroad tracks at night and pick up coal to take to their clients who had none for heating. Or how, during the Depression, they took their own food to clients. They'd done none of these things for years. "Do your job and go home at night and forget them."

None of them told him about the women, often battered, beaten and completely sexless who nevertheless offered him sex even if he couldn't increase their food budgets three or four dollars a month. Once he came close to doing it, for he'd not been able to provide anything else for Mrs. Donaldson; once he thought he could close his eyes to the filthy bedsheets, her furtive eyes and her clubfoot, but finally he could not, and laughed embarrassedly while he backed away from her outstretched arms.

But he was stuck midway through work on his master's. He

became, then, like the other workers, and failed to visit his clients on time. He fabricated visits and dictated them, hoping none of the people were dead, playing banquet host or hostess to the rats. When he went into the field, he merely went home to bed.

He accepted the offer of a transfer to Children's Protective Service; that division sounded nicer and many of the workers were members of the Junior League and drove little sports cars on their visits. This is not to say that there wasn't much concern about Mothersill's working with young mothers and foster mothers, most of them white; there was. But the officials decided to chance the possibility that Mothersill would be raping each and every one of them on sight.

He had never before seen a battered child nor one eaten alive by rats; nor could he understand children's court judges in tailor-made suits offhandedly dispatching children to reform schools without so much as a blink of their eyes, kids Mothersill *knew* had no business going because they wouldn't be much good when they came out. The sickness began to tug and drag at his guts when he got a rash of cases where fathers were buggering their sons so that, when step-mother hatred, so prevalent in fairy tales was found to be an ongoing reality, the sickness seemed to lessen, a remission perhaps, for there were fathers, many of them, who slept with and impregnated their daughters. In the foster homes the greed for the county, state and federal money often far outdistanced the care the foster parents gave the children placed in their keeping. Were children better off with idiot parents than in foster homes? *Yes* was the opinion and they were handed over to the parents who had found each other years ago in some idiots' place.

Mothersill had always managed to get in touch with the police in the children's division in tight situations with parents, but once he got cut in the calf while prowling into a room where a mother and a lover, drunkenly fornicating on a floor, kept vigil over a baby on the couch three days dead.

In his third year, Mothersill began staying home, trying to understand why he felt so gray, so cold, and he slept most of the time, and the doctors came but found no originating cause for his condition. Better, after weeks, he plunged in again, as in a nightmare, but saying to himself even as he moved through it that it was only that, nothing more, and he was going to wake up and it'd all be gone, the broken babies, rats, the dead babies and insane parents; the judges and courts would be gone, too, and nothing would be left but the children, pure, clean, coming onto the next generation unafflicted by the illnesses of the last.

When he slept at night he dreamed he was Millet's "The Sower" striding across a brown, plowed field, his hat pulled down on his head, his right hand clutching the seed in his bag, about to spray it forward to fall into the furrows. His grain sack, like the sower's, dangled from his left shoulder and his thick right leg, planted firmly on the softened ground, pushed out ahead of his left, already raising behind him. There were many furrows, but all merged into one large, yielding, curving warm slice in the earth, shaven, scented; and the seed passed through him into that large furrow, always warming with the hint of a sun as yet out of sight, and it spattered on the sides of the furrow and into it, silently, a natural movement of ascending and descending, accumulating a glitter from the morning's dew. There was nothing in the sower's manner to indicate that he would not be able to bring forth new life from the earth over whose bosom and bottom he strode. Nothing.

When he finished his studies he was a specialist in child care and adoption, an M.S.W., and he put whatever city he was in behind him and followed the malfunctioning to New York, where there is no end of them. He knows now that the children are blameless. Over the years, moreover, he has dreamed he was the father of a million, zillion children and knew all their first and middle names and loved them. He wishes to make love and produce children so that their laughter and innocent little ways could spring-rain down soft and warm to sweeten the earth and all things therein. He saw (and still sees) himself, Father Odell Mothersill, at the head of their multitude, so many that they cover the hills and fatten the valleys as they move over the land with their brave guilelessness. They believe that because they are children they will be loved; they do not even consider the justness of that belief. In his dream as they move over the world, Mothersill assures and reassures them that they are indeed loved.

So it is 1950 and Mothersill oversees a section of a private adoption agency, the Good Shepherd, in which he works. Charlie Parker is four and a half years from his death, so Bop rules the real New York. The war in Korea has begun. Ginsberg, Jones, Joans and Kerouac are in cocoons. People are grumbling about Harry S. Truman and witches are being hunted from one end of the country to the next.

Living in New York, Mothersill feels that he has come home; the city gives that feeling to many, as if they had been programed to arrive there and mesh with others wired up the same way. In Mothersill's agency, however, the casualty rate is high. What happens outside New York happens in it, and with a special fury. At least three workers a year, unable to digest what happens to the children in their care, wind up in Bellevue for observation and then are tenderly conducted to private sanitariums by Asa McDaniels, the Good Shepherd's resident shrink and M.D., a sometime conversationalist with Mothersill. The workers have not had Mothersill's background, and have not had time to adjust, to tinker with their minds so that they can run smoothly, whatever the situation. In short, they have not learned to dream above the pit, but have stayed rooted in it. Mothersill views these workers as an outpatient might see permanent inmates of the hatch. But, as in war, these casualties are always replaced. Do-gooders are a dime a dozen, especially if they are paid. In two months their saintly expressions give way to bewilderment; in four to stark consternation; in six, to fatigue coupled with anger. In twelve they are either crazy or don't give a damn.

And Asa, who plans to go into private practice in a few months, looks at Mothersill, on the occasions when they drink and talk shop, in the casual way a doctor looks when he knows he has a potential patient.

Mothersill turned away from the window at the sound of the phone. He shifted the cup of coffee to his other hand. "Hello."

"I know it's early, Odell, but it's hard to catch you, so I thought I'd try morning. How are you?"

He smiled into the phone. His sister. "Okay, Lispernard. You? Mason? The kids?"

"Oh, everybody's just fine, thanks."

"That's good. Real good."

"Don't be so grumpy."

"I always sound like this in the morning. It doesn't mean anything."

"Listen. A friend of mine's moving to New York next month. I want you to look out for her."

"Her?"

"Yes. Groovy chick, too. Name's Eunice Potts–"

"What's she do?"

"An actress. Done some nice things at Karamu. Trying to get the break in New York."

"I don't know anything about show biz, Lisp."

"No, no. I mean, show her something of the city, take her out, things like that."

"Trying again to get me married, hey?"

"If you did get married maybe you wouldn't be so skinny. Besides, if the shoe fits–"

"And if it don't, baby?"

"Don't force it."

Mothersill took a sip of the coffee.

"Odell?"

"Yeah?"

"She's comin' off a busted marriage."

"Hummm."

"Her second. I guess she feels that she's just gotta get outa here."

"I see what you mean. Okay, tell her to give me a call when she gets in."

"Good luck."

"Me or her?"

"Well—oh, yeah, I'm pregnant again."

"Damn, girl, when you and Mason gonna quit?"

"Never! Maybe when it wears out."

"You right about that. That's gonna be never."

Mothersill hung up. Ol' Lispernard. Born in Hough, gonna die in Hough. With a smile on her face, looks like.

The sight of Mrs. Johnson in the office completely dissipated Mothersill's chaotic anger in which toreador pants, silver shoes and Cheyenne whirled around and around in red-hot gases. Annabelle, if she didn't stop everything, softened things. How was it that she, too, had arrived early at the agency? Was this some manipulation by fate that she was there, Mount Vernon sharp, bending over her desk, her black, New York Friday night dress riding up above her mid-thighs, her arched calves streaming luxuriously down into her black, patent-leather pumps?

As he stared at her, he thought of her husband. Mothersill called him "Big Mariney," for he was big, and had reddish skin and a shit-brown mustache and blue eyes. Mothersill gave him a bright grin whenever he showed up at the agency, eyes flashing, mustache twitching, sniffing about for hanky-panky. He wore his distrust of his wife openly and Mothersill knew he was the object of special attention.

Only once had Big Mariney caught him talking to his wife. They were standing near the water fountain and Big Mariney had rounded the corner to find them. His blue eyes had flecked suddenly with red, and they'd stapled Mothersill to the wall.

The mustache quivered like a woodchuck plinked from fifty feet away and trying to make it back to his hole. Caught, yes, because Mothersill had been listening for tones in Annabelle's voice and searching for expressions beneath expressions, gestures that meant more than they appeared to mean. And Annabelle's breath had come out in a surprise gust, patting against his face with its smell of lunchtime martini. She, too, had been caught that day.

Mothersill had known men like Big Mariney. They'd worked hard to capture their handsome wives; adored them the way you adore a brand new Cadillac Brougham, even though they had to install alarm devices to keep it from being stolen. They maimed and killed because of their wives, not necessarily for them.

One such man aided Mothersill in his desire to leave Cleveland; had literally run him from Hough all the way to Route 20 and had him sprinting eastward toward Ashtabula. Mothersill still remembered the ache of his legs, the daggers of intakes of breath, the comic but deadly sight of two men wheezing along in the dark down the middle of Euclid Avenue, one of those flasher routines of Buck and Bubbles. The man had caught him dead to rights, in the basement of his home, the washroom. The wife'd been bent over the sink and Mothersill was giving it to her from behind, curve fitting curve, with the water running and suds growing out of the sink like a disease. One heavy footstep on the stairway, a stumble, was all the warning Mothersill got and the seventeen-year-old hot blood curdled right then and the python collapsed and was ejected with a slick, popping sound when the wife, hearing the sound too, contracted with fear. Out the other door, hopping, grabbing down for his pants, securing them just in time to evade the husband's first swipe with his safety razor. He was of the old school, much older than his wife.

It was several seconds before Mothersill realized that Annabelle was looking at him. He smiled back. She hadn't changed her position. Don't do it, Mothersill told himself as he rose. Don't be no fool, now, but he was going. Vision precedes deed, and he'd had the vision of himself and Annabelle.

"Hey. I think it's time we had a conference, after hours. Drinks, dinner, whatever, Mrs. Johnson."

Now she straightened while he waited beside her, licking in the scent of Chanel 22. She'd have all day to make up a story for her husband. This queen, he thought, doth make the waves and all other things quiver in their sockets.

She dimpled. "I was going out with some of the girls tonight, but you've just changed my mind, Mr. Mothersill." Her smile deepened. "Heard a lot about you, sir. Good company and all that. Charming, bright."

Social workers talk too much, he thought, then said, "Why don't we meet at—"

"That's not necessary. We can leave together."

"Uhhllummm," he said, wanting to ask about Big Mariney and the chance of word getting back to him, and not wanting to ask.

"What'd you say?"

"Okay." As he started to return to his office, she called him back.

"I'm not anxious to have this get out, just yet, but my husband and I—"

Joy bubbling. "Yes?"

"Well, we're not making it any more."

"Oh! Too bad, Annabelle. I'm really sorry to hear that."

But she was already laughing at him, her voice soft and knowing. "Odell, you're a jive somethin'."

He returned to his office rubbing his hands. That big dumb Mariney let that fox get away? With all these cunt-hungry cats out here? His reason returned in moments. No, she just went away, was what happened more than likely. And he's probably stalking her more now than he ever was, believing it was some cat talked a hole in her head. He figures all he got to do now is find him and kick the crap outa him for things to get back to cool. Even if they don't, he's got his mad out of his system. As cold sweat started to roll down his body, Mothersill wondered why Annabelle and Big Mariney had no children.

Helped by three mugs of draft beer and a hot roast beef sandwich in a Third Avenue White Rose bar, Mothersill returned to work in the afternoon emboldened but contained, and started to review the files on his desk which awaited his signature.

The Dedham child was being moved again. No good, Mothersill thought, shaking his head. He'd thought the Meadman's a bad pair for the kid. Nearly all adoptive parents wanted their kids good-looking, without problems and malleable. They wished packages already guaranteed. Kids weren't packages. They had problems without love. Chesler defecated on dining-room chairs when he was troubled, and it didn't matter if those chairs were John Widdicomb or not. The kid had got his desire to give feces as a present mixed up with his wish to disrupt. But he wasn't doing it so often now. Too bad the Meadmans wouldn't see that. He'd have to talk to Chesler again, maybe a day in Central Park seeing the zoo and walking. Hot dogs and ice cream kind of thing. Mothersill had always gotten along with Chesler; had in fact a good relationship with all children, male and female.

Mr. and Mrs. Levitas wanted a trial with the child Goldman. Shumel. Could work out. The Levitas were at a good age. Not too old, not too young. Religious, and considering migration to Israel. Mr. Levitas, it was obvious, was all for spoiling the kid to hell and back. But, Mothersill reasoned, that was better than no spoilage at all. He signed his name with a joyful flourish.

Adoption completed for Mavis Howe. Good. Mothersill liked the adoptive parents, an interracial couple. Okay, for Mavis was a product of interracial coupling. The Terrells understood that no matter how fair Mavis was, she would always be black and that she would suffer the corresponding wear and tear. The Terrells knew, and had specifically asked for such a child, of which there were many available, although at the moment, not very desirable. Mothersill wondered why it was that so many children of mixed parents turned out to be girls. Nature had a plan, not only for Mavis, but for all of them.

In Public Assistance, workers automatically assumed that foster parents were at most as concerned with the money they got for the children they kept as they were for the children themselves. The majority cared more for the money. There was a certain rotting honesty about the arrangement.

But in a private agency it was often difficult to perceive the genuine reasons why people wanted to adopt, so many of them returned the kids after trial, like furniture that had suddenly gone out of style. For many would-be adoptive parents, having a child was nothing more than being in style; for others it was simply a matter of having someone to oppress in one manner or another, and for still others adoption concealed a strange and devious guilt, and perhaps an unfathomed need.

The private agencies were still mired in an ancient puritanical Anglo-Saxon bog of rules which were not as religious as they were racial. Jewish kids had to go to Jewish couples; Catholic kids had to go to Catholic couples, and Protestant went to Protestant, black to black. So snarled and wrapped in red tape were the rules that it was infinitely easier for a couple hurting for a child to buy one on the Canadian black market. Any kind they wished.

And couples, Mothersill mused. Who said couples were the answer, even if matched with the correct child as the law dictated? Couldn't a single person provide as much, if not more, love as a couple whose views were often in conflict? Oedipus/Laius and all that. Sooner or later agencies both public and private would have to get down to considering the single, male or female, as a proper adoptive parent. And all the racial rules would have to go out the window too. Love was better than race, religion or rules.

Much later, after the office had closed and they'd had dinner, Mothersill guided Annabelle through the Village Friday night crowd toward his apartment. He had no doubt that she'd spend the night.

"Mount Vernon seems like Hicksville after this, Odell."

"Yeah, I don't guess there's much action up there." She could have a *mess* of babies with that body, Mothersill thought. In the elevator of his building, she smiled at him. "What's funny?" he said.

"You, Odell."

"Is that so?" She'd peeped his eagerness then. "Anyway, you are one real, fine thing, Annabelle."

She pecked him on the mouth.

"Oh what a lovely apartment," she said when they were inside. She didn't even glance at the television set. Shirley seemed like a month ago instead of only twenty-four hours. Annabelle kicked off her shoes and dug her toes into the rug, then she curled down upon it, looking up at Mothersill challengingly. He piled down beside her and kissed her, Annabelle's tongue attacking his mouth like a school of minnows. "I want you to make love to me," she whispered. "Make love to me."

"Yes," he said, wonderingly. Why did she need the words?

Suddenly, laughing softly, she sat up. "The wine was great, but I like my drinks a little harder."

"Sure," he said hoarsely. "What?"

"Bourbon. Rocks."

Mothersill hummed in the kitchen. It was, after all, kind of nice that she'd said it. There'd be none of the games then, none of the pleading or retreating coyness.

Three hours later, the bottle of Bourbon empty, he eased her into his bedroom, where, leaning against him for support, she undressed. Annabelle sat smoking on the edge of the bed as Mothersill stripped. "Mmmm," she said, "you pretty well hung there, Odell. I never would've guessed it." She took his penis tenderly in her hand and kissed it and they slid into the bed.

The records, which were still playing, underlined their small languid movements, their pleasurable explorations of each other's body, until it was time. Annabelle began to shake beside him and she whispered over and over again, with a strange ferocity, "Don't hurt me, baby, hear? Please don't hurt me!"

Mothersill paused momentarily. Hurt? He'd never thought of hurt together with making love. He believed he was most tender then, considerate. Happy loving made happy children; what went in came out. Joy in, joy out, what was all this talk of hurting?

Then he remembered the first time he saw love-making and heard the word hurt at the same time.

He sat tensely in the heat-filled attic, enwombed in the comforting, secret smell of hot rafters and tar oozing from the shingles. He was hidden behind the box of watermelon rind and peach preserves, and he stared hotly in the dim light at the opened *Esquire* in front of him. An air-brushed blond Petty girl, clad in black chiffon, smiled fixedly at him, urging him on, and his right hand, clamped brutally around his penis, moved so rapidly up and down that it was a blur. His eyes bored into the face, the pink carnation-colored body, tried to remake it into a four-dimensional creature.

Oh, do it, Odell, he made the Petty girl say. *It's so good.* He was sweating. Thoomp-thoompthoompthoompthoompthoomp. *Do it, Odell!* He pounded faster. He closed his eyes and pictured the Petty girl positioned like Olive Oyl, Tillie the Toiler or Dale Arden in the dirty books, with Popeye, Mac and Flash Gordon. *Oh, man, you sure feel good.*

Wearily, Odell pounded on; his clothes were soaked with sweat. He no longer knew just how long he'd been in the attic. But once again, nothing special had happened. Then he felt a thin, sticky liquid warm on his hand, and he stopped. His member, released from his desperate clutch, ballooned from the pumping. Odell slid his thumb through the liquid, caressed the meatus of his penis in wonderment. He took a deep breath and shakily let it out. Guess this is what makes babies, he thought. That's all there is to it? This is all that happens? Not at all like those dreams he'd had.

He forced his still-hard penis down into his pants and slammed the magazine shut. He slid it back farther in the dark, to its usual place. He listened closely for any alien sound and then climbed out of his corner, pausing to check the jars of preserves to make sure that the ones he'd already secretly emptied were at the bottom or back of the box. That way, he hoped, his thefts wouldn't be discovered until he'd grown up and moved away.

Sneaking down from the attic, he felt no great satisfaction that he could now make babies. He felt unfulfilled, cheated. How could such a great thing—everyone talked about it, in whispers—be so dull, so hard on your dick? Safely down he passed through the house and gained the street, wondering just which people knew all the time what he'd been doing in the attic.

Don't know nothin', he thought moodily. He fished out his last nickel and went into Clark's Ice House next door and bought himself a soda. "How you today, Odell?" Reverend Clark asked. "Y'momma need some ice?"

"Okay. I dunno." Odell moved outside and sat on the rickety porch. He saw Miss Wilkens emerge from the corner store she owned with her brother. They both had long faces and big noses; both were tall and thin. But often this summer, his twelfth, he'd watched Miss Wilkens walk by. Once in a hot and choking voice, when dreams of love-making possessed his being, he'd asked if she wanted him to come and empty her trash on Tuesday afternoons. He had a trash route. In his heat, he'd not only take out Miss Wilkens' trash, she'd give him some while her brother was still in the store. She'd meet him in the cellar where everyone kept their trash until Tuesday afternoon, when Odell Mothersill, that nice little colored boy, came and took it out. On Wednesday, he brought the cans back in and was paid. She'd come slowly down the cellar steps, without underwear on, grab hold of it and slip it right up into her. Of this he had no doubt, so feverish was he when he asked her. Her refusal left him in shock. "Oh, I take it out myself or Harold takes it out." And continued on in her long, thin-legged walk. He equated her refusal with a rejection of his affection. Surely she knew (hadn't she seen, hadn't she felt that he had the hots for her?) what he'd really meant? In vengeance then he thought of the women on his trash route, women who, out of his pure thing for Miss Wilkens, he'd not even condescended to look at.

But alas. So many of them talked to him through doors that they kept locked (the neighborhood was changing and they, thus far, had not been able to flee with their more fortunate fellows) and those who didn't were fat, gray and smelly. Those who weren't fat, gray and smelly were thin, gray and smelly.

Now Miss Wilkens, a jack-o'-lantern smile under her nose, approached.

"Odell, how are you today?"

Was today to be the day? Had she thought about it after all, realized, Odell wondered, the real me? "Okay," he said. He followed her with his eyes as she stepped inside Clark's Ice House. He thought he heard—but who could tell, what with the sparrows chirping, little girls playing jacks down the street, screaming and yelling—quick, intense whispering, and then Miss Wilkens' voice, too suddenly and too loudly saying, "Reverend Clark, will you bring me a fifty-pound piece of ice, please?"

And Reverend Clark, old, yellow-eyed, pipe-smoking, fat and flabby, answering just as loudly, "Why certainly, Miss Wilkens. Right away."

Miss Wilkens flew off the porch without speaking to Odell again, and rushed up the street to the neat cottage, in the middle of the block, that she shared with her brother, a strange look on her reddening face, her legs slicing the air like scissors. Inside, with a slamming of the heavy door and a clanging of his tongs, Reverend Clark was already dragging a piece of ice out of the ice chamber. "Odell," he said, breathing heavily, as if overtaken by some secret exertion or excitement, although he hadn't yet hoisted the ice to the pad on his shoulder, "watch the ice house for me. Help yourself to one more soda pop. I'll be right back in a few minutes. God bless you, son." And he, too, flew down off the porch, the fifty-pound piece of ice sliding on his shoulder pad, and made his way up the street to Miss Wilkens' house.

Odell finished his soda pop just as Reverend Clark turned into Miss Wilkens' walk. The boy glanced up and down the street; no one appeared to be on his way to the ice house. With a few steps he was behind the ice house and then, over fence and around garage, he made his way to Miss Wilkens'. These backyards, the plum, pear, apple and cherry trees therein, his territory; bedroom, bathroom and kitchen windows all his to view from a tree limb, garbage-shed top or house roof. Odell knew the neighborhood like he knew the veins on his penis.

Crouching on the top of a garbage can, he peered unseen into Miss Wilkens' kitchen and heard low, hurried voices: "Don't hurt me! Don't hurt me!" Odell's eyes grew accustomed to the minute squares in the screening. The ice-box door was still open. Miss Wilkens sat on the kitchen table, her long, red-splotched legs wrapped tightly against the black flab of Reverend Clark's behind. The preacher's pants lay in a gray, sodden lump down around his ankles. His behind, waffled and burned, pumped heavily into the center of Miss Wilkens, whose arms were wrapped around him as though she were drowning. Miss Wilkens' eyes bugged; her wide mouth flew open from time to time to whisper some savage thing —Odell felt it was savage from her expression—and Reverend Clark pumped harder. "Don't hurt me," she said aloud, again. Odell's own penis from a swollen, beaten acorn to an oak did grow. Suddenly Miss Wilkens' eyes shot open, her tendrils of fingers clutched and beat at Reverend Clark's shirt and she began to slide back and forth on the porcelain-topped table, her behind making squeaking noises. Then she buried her mouth in

Reverend Clark's shoulder and let out a moan that could have come from the suddenly broken transmission of a Mack truck; the Reverend Clark at that moment thrust inward, stopped and, as if mortally wounded in midflight, crushed Miss Wilkens backward so hard that her sharp chin pointed directly toward the stamped-tin ceiling. Shuddering, Reverend Clark said clearly, "Jesus, sweet Jesus."

Miss Wilkens scrambled from the table, stopped, wiped it with her skirt and fled toward the bathroom while Reverend Clark hurriedly pulled up his pants and spoke to the bathroom door. "Miss Wilkens? Miss Wilkens? The ice is a quarter."

She burst out of the bathroom in a crescendo of flushing water, digging in her pocket for a coin, gave it to him and watched him leave. She didn't look hurt to Odell.

And then he knew. But of course! What a dummy he was. People like Annabelle were everywhere underfoot. Women who giggled at times like this he knew, or women who cried or screamed. Mothersill said, accusingly, because he felt the sudden, irrational heat of betrayal, "You *want* me to hurt you!"

"No!" she said. He felt her face contorting.

Mothersill withdrew and, placing both hands under her buttocks, forced back her thighs with his shoulders, then hoisted her legs over them.

"*No!*"

Later she slid ever so carefully away from him, turned her back to him and, before going to sleep laughed softly, contentedly, like a person whose plans have gone off as originally desired.

Baaamm! Bam! Bam! Mothersill came quickly to a sitting position. *Big Mariney!* He knew it without a wasted thought. He reached out for Annabelle in a panic, but his hand encountered only space, rumpled sheets. Hiding in the closet, the bathroom, the kitchen. In panic, Mothersill jumped from the bed and searched all three rooms. No Annabelle. Rushing to the door now, his eyes sweeping the living room, he called, "Who is it?"

"Open up, Odell. You know who it is."

"Who, man, who?"

"Bert Johnson, Annabelle's husband."

"Oh! Hello there!"

"Open up!"

"Let me get my robe on, man, it's chilly."

Bam!

Robed now, Mothersill rushed back to open the door. Big Mariney filled the doorway, easily six-four, 235 pounds. Mothersill, built like one of those graceful half-milers, six feet exactly and thin, 160 pounds, felt dwarfed. He backed up as Big Mariney entered, reddish-blue eyes quickly gouging out possible hiding places in the room, his breath reeking of something cheap, maybe, Mothersill thought, Pete Hagen.

"Where's my ol' lady, man? I want my ol' lady or I'ma bust your fuckin' head in."

Bad now, because Annabelle was gone, which at this moment was pretty much like her never having been there in the first place, Mothersill got hold of himself. "Lissen, you big, red, sonofabitch, what's wrong with you? I don't know nothin' about your ol' lady. Ain't she with you? That's some bad shit, B–Bert, you come to tear up my crib at seven in the morning, thinking your ol' lady's here–"

Big Mariney was walking heavily through all the rooms, slamming doors, and when he was through he returned and sat down in the living room, fluffed his mustache wearily with his fingers and said, "Give me a drink, will you, man?"

"If you're gonna get outa here."

"Yeah, I'm goin'. I just need a taste to get me started."

Quickly, Mothersill poured him half a tumbler of scotch and gave it to him. At that moment, glancing at the rug, he saw laying there, nestled cozily in the twisted fibers, one of Annabelle's earrings. Ice crept up his legs, slid across his heart. Nervously he said, "Now, Bert, you got to get up outa here. Take hold yourself, fella. Maybe Annabelle's with those two chicks from the office, you know, Marilyn and Marj. Go on over there, baby."

Big Mariney glared at him. "Have you lost your goddamn mind? Can you see me kicking in that door, with two white bitches there. Shit. They'd have me hangin' from the nearest lamppost, now wouldn't they?"

"I'm sorry about that, Bert, but you got to get outa here. Finish up and get out, man."

"Okay, Odell, okay. Thanks for the taste, man, and I'm sorry. I sure was gonna clean up the block with your skinny ass."

"Things ain't goin' so good at home?"

"Fuck you." Big Mariney stood, stepping on the earring, which crunched beneath his feet. He looked down, but didn't see it.

On Monday morning, still shaken by Big Mariney's visit, Mothersill sat subdued in his office. When Annabelle came in and fluttered a girlish wave at him, he smiled weakly. Get killed behind that chick, he muttered to himself. Marj Press and Marilyn Garrity came in, smiling broadly, and Mothersill knew they'd been conferencing with Annabelle on her visit to his apartment.

All morning long, whenever he looked up from his desk and out to the room where the workers pored over papers or lingered on their phones, the three of them smiled at him. He wished them out of the office and into the field, but Monday morning was not a good field day; everyone was recovering from the weekend. Annabelle, he guessed, was hanging out with Marj and Marilyn pretty steady now.

Gradually, he immersed himself in his work, the checking of dictation of home visits and the workers' impressions, the progress of the kids, plans for the future. And when these were finished, as always, there was the stack of applications from people seeking to adopt children, of whom there were always fewer than needed.

All that irresponsible fucking, he thought, creating all those kids hungry and aching for love. He thought then of the red-headed brother and sister he had placed the year before; they hadn't been hard to place, of course. Everyone wanted light-haired children. But they'd started calling him "Daddy," because, for a while, he'd been the only male to visit them regularly. Even after they were settled, when he made the finishing home visits, they, to the discomfort of their foster parents, still called him Daddy.

The scent of Chanel 22 penetrated his sense almost as an after-thought and he started. Annabelle had eased into his office and was smiling down at him.

"Hello, Odell."

"Oh!" he said, and then, chagrined that he'd been so wrapped up in his thoughts that he hadn't heard or seen her come in, he reached into his pocket and tossed her the crumpled earring.

"You lost this the other night. Also your husband. Found him in my place."

"Scare you did he?"

He rolled his eyes up at her, but couldn't help responding to her teasing smile. "He did upset me a little."

"Bet you were glad I was gone."

"How'd you guess?"

She covered her mouth as she laughed.

He asked, "Where did you go?"

"I moved in with those two dizzy chicks, Marj and Marilyn. They've three bedrooms, so it's all pretty cozy, and Bert won't tear down their door—"

"I know. He's scared of white folks."

"We're having a big party Saturday. You'll come won't you?"

He said cagily, "Will Bert be there?"

"No, of course not."

Mothersill looked at her hips, flaring gently down from her

waist. He glanced up quickly and saw for the first time, behind the radiance of her smile, an expression of deep mocking. Instantly he knew he'd trapped something, and also knew that she was aware of it, however fleetingly it had shown itself. But the smile, broad, open, she now transposed over that expression framed her lowered voice. "I wish I could get it now, Odell. I mean *right* now."

He shifted his gaze slightly so that he didn't meet her eyes directly. "Baby, I'd like to. Lunch hour? We can cab to my place and back."

Now her eyes shifted quickly. Took this bitch by surprise, Mothersill thought. Confused and upset her. Responding by an instinct he did not understand, he moved to take her off the hook. "Not such a good idea," he said. "Cleaning lady's day." As if he'd ever had a cleaning lady. Shit, he kept a neater, cleaner crib than most broads he'd ever met. He saw relief slowly filling her eyes, and the smile that'd slipped was lifting. "But tonight?" he asked.

"I have to see Bert tonight, Odell. We've got some business to straighten out."

No longer able to take his stare, she dropped her eyes.

"Well," he said in dismissal, "I'll see you Saturday at the big bash. Eight, nine?"

"Nine? Okay. I'll see you." She smiled again and eased back out of the office.

A tease, Mothersill thought. Cock-teaser. Girl-woman. Make me think you love me before I lay it on you. This much. This much. This much. Love me some more and you can have this much more. If you want, you can die for me. Oh, not physically, that's forbidden, isn't it? No, die for me inside somewhere, so I won't be able to *see* the hurt, only imagine it. Sure faked me out, Annabelle, and all the time I thought *you* wanted to be hurt. But I guess you can have it both ways.

From his office Mothersill could see Malone Lincoln explaining his cameras to Barbara Kramer. Before Lincoln was finished,

Mothersill knew, he'd have a date with Kramer to take some pictures of her with his Hasselblad or Nikon. That was his hustle. Mothersill had seen some of the pictures, hundreds of bad over- or underexposed photographs, as if Lincoln had been too excited to concentrate on the proper settings. Lincoln photographed women, all white, in the nude. It seemed, however, that they just made him work for what they were willing to give him anyway. And in some cunning way Lincoln knew precisely that, for his laugh was the last and the loudest. He told the women he was sterile—a battle wound—and that they need take no precautions. Lincoln laughed when he told this.

Mothersill shook his head, glad that he did not have to supervise the man, and relieved that the friendship, born at first because they were the only two black males in the agency, had quickly dissolved. Why in the hell didn't the man and his wife, Phyllis, rush to the top of the ladder and pause and have kids? Mothersill knew, or thought he knew the answer: Lincoln hated kids. Working in an adoption agency, near them, gave body to that hatred; away from them he'd probably become a child molester.

The phone rang softly at his elbow, jerking him out of a cursory examination of the sicknesses of the people with whom he worked, and even, gingerly, his own.

"Would you be going into the field this afternoon?" She was very careful not to make it sound like a demand or a plea, and her voice, therefore, seemed oddly detached from the meaning behind her question.

Mothersill responded with sudden, grateful pleasure. With Cathleen there was always purpose; being with her made his kind of sense. "Hey," he said. "That's a great idea." He felt himself growing warm.

"It'll be good to see you," she said.

"I won't be too long."

Mothersill edged through Manhattan to the Westside Highway and gained the bridge. Spurting between the growling trucks, he felt the wind nudging the car as he raced to the Jersey side and then over the Palisades. He wondered how the kids were. They'd be in school now, of course, and Mr. Hanrahan would be hard at work on Wall Street. The Hanrahans had been Garrity's case. Irish and Catholic. They'd wanted two kids, the quicker to make up for Cathleen's barren womb. Garrity's visits became fewer, but Mothersill, the case supervisor, had filled in the gaps with his own. His visits, however, had not been official for almost a year.

"Hi," she said, standing in her doorway in the sunlight which reflected the blond of her hair. She wore a little blue thing and it occurred to Mothersill that blondes always wore blue to match their eyes, to offset the gold of their hair; blue or some kind of deep black.

Mothersill answered, "Hi."

She stepped back and Mothersill stepped in and closed the door behind him. They kissed. With one hand he unzipped his fly, then hoisted her up; she wore nothing under her garment. He cradled her bottom, she opened herself, and he went into her. She whispered, "I missed you." He carried her across the floor and eased her down before the picture window where they could, like gods, see the Hudson and Manhattan, view the panorama while they made love unobserved.

Cathleen tugged at his jacket, and he, twisting from side to side, slid out of it and then struggled with his shirt and tie. With soft, woofing sounds she began to twirl and rise under him, and he felt her opening and opening as if creating the warmest, richest soil that might close around seed, nurture it and have it finally bear fruit. And always Mothersill recalled when he felt her deepening around him the time she said mournfully, "I couldn't have a baby if God slept with me."

But now she was moving her face away from his, as she always did at this time, beating up to her climax, to study his expression. And he let her for just a moment before taking her mouth with its thin, barely drawn lips into his own. The faster she moved, the more deliberate he became; her little woofing sounds came more rapidly and her back arched off the floor and she stilled. Then Mothersill took her round again, carried himself now into swirling warm symbols of loam and fine seed, of a hybrid mix of winter and summer wheats, of nature's edge of the universe, machinations that leavened everything.

After, lying on the floor drinking coffee and eating toast with marmalade, Mothersill looked out across the river and wondered what Manhattan looked like at night, with its millions of lighted windows and behind them people making love, some of them, others just plain fucking.

"Why don't you want me to look at you when we're making love, Odell?"

Mothersill continued chewing his toast.

"Shy?" Cathleen offered.

"Something like that, I guess."

She giggled and then he said, "No, it isn't shyness. I just don't like to think of what you might be thinking when you look at me like that."

"What do you think I'm thinking?" she asked softly.

"Why don't you just tell me."

"How good it is?" she said tentatively.

He said, "No. Not when you look at me like that."

"You think it's something racial?"

Mothersill sighed. "Isn't it?"

"Can't there be something racial that's good? I don't think it fair that it always has to be bad." Now she turned and looked at Manhattan. "I know I'm not thinking bad things then." When she turned back to him she said, "And you're not so pure, Odell. I mean, I know why you come to me."

Mothersill turned quickly. "Why?"

She smiled at him and tried to draw a finger around his jawline. Mothersill moved his head away. "Oh, it's not because I'm white," she said.

"Then why? C'mon. Stop. Why?"

"Because you feel sorry for me."

"Feel sorry for you?" he almost whispered, feeling ghosts starting to dance out of the walls.

The parties at Marj and Marilyn's were legendary around the office. They were whispered about and invitations to them sought. For they—Marj and Marilyn—walked a line between being crazy and not giving a damn and were considered to be swingers. Mothersill guessed that their parties were also famous outside the office. He'd gone to one and had not recognized most of the people.

This time there would be a known quality besides the hostesses: Annabelle. He wondered how many other black people would be there; not many he guessed. There hadn't been any the last time, white girls and white guys trying to outwait and outwit each other, with Marj and Marilyn overseeing it all.

Ready to leave his apartment, Mothersill paused at the door, strangely depressed by the evening before him. As he was examining his feelings, the phone rang. He remained motionless. Who? he wondered, and then, Why? He left before it stopped ringing.

Marj Garrity and Marilyn Press shared a large apartment in the East Seventies close by FDR Drive. The Irish and East Europeans still bossed the turf, so Mothersill cabbed to the place hoping that when he left it he wouldn't have to wait long on one of the neighborhood corners and have to tackle one of the Irish or Hungarian gangs. He passed muster with the elevator operator and was lifted upstairs where, on the opening of the doors, he heard music and voices filling the hallway. He didn't think anyone inside would hear either a knock or a doorbell, so he opened the door and the noise battered at him like a gust of wind.

The instant before he closed the door he saw them, Marj, Marilyn and Annabelle holding three separate little courts, surrounded by guys who were sweating a lot and grinning a little. The few girls who'd come with some of the guys were standing in a corner, talking and smiling to each other, a little bravely, Mothersill thought, guessing that each was determined to lay so much body on her man that he'd never look at another type like Marj, Marilyn or Annabelle; or not give him any at all to punish him for even being so close to such whorey stuff. Mothersill smiled as he closed the door. The fact was that Marj, Marilyn and Annabelle only complemented the less aggressive types who haunted the corners at parties. Between the aggressive and recessive babes they gave away so much in New York, at least, that Mothersill hadn't yet figured out how any self-respecting, honest-to-goodness, Times Square-type whore, heart of gold or not, ass of brass or not, could make a quarter.

He stood, back against the door, detailing the scene set out before him. Annabelle had the largest crowd, sitting, crouching or standing before her. He had an exploded vision of thousands of Elizabethan sailors, whipped out of England's jails and onto ships deviously owned by Burleigh, Cecil and Elizabeth, landing in Africa, cock-crazed and cunt-conscious, quickly dispatching by blunderbuss, arquebus and musket, puzzled and angry black men. Above the music or maybe in it, a muted, high-register note on a trumpet, crying children, and then wailing women, overflowing with the instinct of their sex that death, capture and slavery was not all that sailed into the channel with these ships. Mothersill thought of the sailors, despised in their own lands where pussy, all of it, from the basest member of the servant class on up, belonged to the moneyed, the powerful, for *droit de seigneur* still waited upon the Revolution to pretend to die. Now they were free, these sailors, league upon league away from home, and these black people were despised as the basest chemical in the alchemy of capitalism, still a fetus. There were no restraints; commanders approved, for fornication drew off energy, gave reward to the loveless seamen and made them leave off for a time the punking of cabin boys not already assigned to do the bidding of the ship commanders. A freedom to fuck at will, with only the conscience of a stiffened penis to attend, and with all the blessings of those who remained back in Merrie Olde England. For a moment Mothersill envied the sailors that freedom and wished that black men had had it for a time as well. That, however, might've produced another kind of black man, one who, like the whites gathered before Annabelle, would be more restrained by time than by law, and afflicted with the disease of remembering free-time fucking, and sweating with that remembrance, for things weren't at all what they used to be.

"Odell!" Annabelle called, waving cheerfully over the heads of her supplicants. The eyes turned toward him, the only black man there, seared him, and he felt their combined surprise, instinctive hate at his coming to collect his own. Annabelle, he knew, was aware of this as she moved through them toward him.

His first words were, "Let's get the hell outa here."

But she blithely ignored them and led him to her group and tried to introduce him, and Mothersill got the message: right there, all about him, were white men, a number of them ready and willing to service her even more eagerly than Marj or Marilyn; for the thing of which they accused black men was theirs in origin, flipped. Perhaps Marj and Marilyn knew it, and behind a twisted, avant-garde liberalism, at that very moment slipping through the crooked streets of the Village, utilized her as bait, the yellow-tailed fly on the swishing, curling line. Annabelle placed before him this challenge of time, race and sex, and by her manner demanded that he best it. Show how much man was left in the black shell. Mothersill glanced at Marj and Marilyn, both big girls, classically American, the Russian Pale and Irish bogs bred out of them: *Dionaeae muscipulae*. There was that look about them, shared, radiating. Did he see relief in their eyes that he had come to match off with Annabelle, or did he only imagine it?

The good jazz music made Mothersill feel at home. He was not, after all, the only black soul there, excluding Annabelle; various black quartets, quintets and sextets played to him, and he conjured visions of musicians crouching over chord changes, smoothing out fifths and ninths, getting back to an old thing, but on a higher level; roots coming green above ground.

"C'mon," he said to Annabelle. People were dancing around

them although it was not music you danced to; the dancing was an excuse to press body to body. Although he'd never danced with her, he knew she could dance. It was like high school back in Hough, when the white kids backed off the floor to admire the coloreds because they could *really* dance. They found one of the interior beats and moved to it, conscious of the eyes on them, and Annabelle grinned and whispered, "Work, Odell!"

Does one make love the way he or she dances? Mothersill wondered, and was that why the women looked at him? The reason why guys drilled their eyeballs into Annabelle's smoothly rotating behind?

On the slow pieces he felt buttocks and breasts passing briefly over his body as he pressed close to Annabelle. Once he felt a hand pressing possessively but fleetingly against his behind and when he turned Marj Garrity winked at him.

Annabelle whispered, "These guys are sure wearing my buns out. Can't keep their hands off them."

"This is no place to be making it, Annabelle. Too many crazies."

"I know, but I have to stay a little while longer."

"That's cool, but not too long."

She said, "Believe it, baby."

After a pause she said, "What'd you do Monday, go into the field?"

"Monday? Oh, I went home."

"Ummm."

"I did."

"I called you."

"Well, I went out for a few minutes, and the rest of the time I just didn't answer the phone."

"So you say, buster."

Mothersill ground his pelvis into hers. "Did you call Monday night?" He'd returned from New Jersey by then and knew she hadn't.

"No."

"Why not? You were in a big hurry to talk during the day."

"I told you I had to take care of some business with Bert."

"Yeah."

"Business is business, baby. Let's sit down and watch."

"Yeh, see how they move."

Mothersill grunted as they squatted on a large, empty floor cushion. He said, "The way you were carryin' on when I got here, I thought you were the main attraction." He grinned. "I guess I changed that, huh?"

"Never mind. You're the main attraction for Marj. She talks about you all the time. I think she has something she wants to give you."

"You know I don't mess around the office."

"No," she said. "Just me and all those mothers you diddle out in the field."

"Who, me?"

The bantering and another drink relaxed Mothersill. It was going to be all right. Annabelle was not going to go through all the phony changes, the coy advances and retreats, just because there was a room full of paddy boys. Some black women did. But now it was only a matter of catching a discreet wind to his apartment.

"No, no," Annabelle said, good-naturedly waving off a young man they'd seen bouncing and jumping over the floor with a variety of unwilling partners. On one of slow pieces Mothersill had been startled to hear him breathing heavily as he danced; staring at him he'd seen his eyes glazed as if about to have a heart attack. The man shrugged and moved on to the next woman.

Annabelle frowned. "Strange guy. I wonder where they found him. I don't understand Marj and Marilyn. This isn't what I'd call swingin'."

Mothersill caught sight of a woman he'd been introduced to in the first flurry of greetings when he entered. She smiled briefly at him, her eyes lingering momentarily, a palpable sadness in them. He hadn't looked at her closely then. He smiled back brightly, trying to say *Don't be sad.* She neither smoked nor drank and this too made him curious. Ellie was her name.

"Stuffy in here," Annabelle said.

"Let's get some air then."

"Not yet, Odell."

"No, no. I mean just down in front for a moment or two."

"Be right back," she said, as they rose and headed for the door. She was speaking to no one in particular. In the hallway Mothersill walked determinedly to a mop closet he'd passed on his way to the party.

"Odell," she whispered, but not pulling back. Then, "O-ho," as he pulled her inside and closed the door. Their nostrils were filled with the odor of rough soaps and damp cloths, of dust and dirt barely caressed with water. Without a wasted motion Mothersill pulled up her dress and pushed down her pants.

"*Odell!*" But spoken softly, as if in admiration of his daring. He heard her shoes scuffling on the floor, enabling her to widen her legs, which'd already begun to tremble. Mothersill crouched lower and felt his own legs tweak with the strain; under and up, rising slowly on the balls of her feet as she now raised one leg, a ballet movement felt rather than seen. His breath came in bursts and she clung to his neck, whimpering.

"Awwah," he said. The bottom of her pelvis was rotating on his straining groin. "Annabelle," he whispered in amazement. "Ease up, *ease up!*"

But Annabelle, like most women, sensing she was close to bringing him down before he took her off, began rotating more furiously, twirling.

"Tell Momma how good it is. Like it like this?" Twirling all the time. Mothersill turned his head into a damp mop and bit it.

"Wait up," he said trying to hold off.

But she put a supertwirl on him and felt him snap up with trying to hold back. Ready herself, her head rocking a can of cleaner on the shelf, she hissed, "Now!"

Mothersill clutched and raised her, aiming her, as it were, in the darkness, all strength, all god for the moment, then, mortal and weak again, he set her down and they leaned against each other panting, their faces draped under the mops and cloths.

Outside the closet they brushed off and re-entered the apartment. Tired, they eased past the thinning crowd into Annabelle's room, where they lay on the floor and went to sleep.

Two hours later Mothersill woke with a start, puzzling over Annabelle's absence. The music was now low, hanging in corners. He heard it clearly, for although he heard soft voices and even softer laughter, he thought most of the people were now gone. Annabelle, shoeless, came into the room and sat down beside him.

"Odell, let's go now, right now." She reached for his hand. "C'mere." Mothersill removed his shoes. They passed through the empty living room, still heavy with smoke. The voices were nearer now. From one of the bedrooms a cold blue light merged with the blackness of the apartment.

"Lick it, lick it." Mothersill recognized Marj's voice. "Catsup, catsup, red like blood, but sweet, oh, do lick it."

A sigh of pleasure told Mothersill the catsup was being licked. He did not have to look, and yet he did; words create pictures; pictures often make words unnecessary. There were things he didn't know or wish to know; maybe they were too far away for him to take the time. But this was just around the corner. He felt Annabelle pushing him to the edge of the door. Marilyn spoke coyly, challengingly: "Strawberry jam is better than catsup. Jam, anyone?"

There'd be no thrills, nothing comical once he looked around the door. He'd be like the kid at once horrified and attracted to Frankenstein films; like the young man thinking *ugh!* while reading de Sade, but envying him, too. If what was in that room upset Annabelle, he knew it would upset him, also. But, Mothersill thought, I ought to *know* about these people I live and work with. And he looked.

He saw five figures, whose whiteness was heightened by the

blue glow of the lamp. None were facing him; they were a frieze brought to life, complete with small sounds, of sudden sibilant utterances, *Greeks or Romans Busy at Orgy;* they moved slowly upon the entablature of bedroom floor prolonging their pleasures.

Mothersill drew back from them, the high, vinegarish odor of catsup, and they tiptoed back to Annabelle's room. Quickly they drew on their shoes. She pulled on a short coat and they went out, not speaking until they were in Mothersill's apartment.

After her first half glass of Bourbon, Annabelle shook her head and said, "Goddamn, I didn't know they were into that. I mean"—she fluttered her eyelashes at Mothersill—"I dig a little lick-a-my-split myself from time to time, but I don't need any catsup or strawberry jam on it for me to like it. I bet they put that damn jam on the breakfast table tomorrow morning, too. Those chicks are somethin' else, and I'm getting my hat next week because they're bound to turn up someone even more screwed up than they are." She started to laugh. "Odell, good thing I'm around, otherwise you'd have been down there making that catsup and strawberry jam scene, the eyes Marj's got for you. Maybe she'd be taking it off you! Damn. Going through all that just to get some new kind of laid. Whoooeee!"

Mothersill had disdained his usual stiff scotch, preferring instead half a tumbler of pure gin. Gin made him do crazy things, foolhardy deeds; he became all id when he drank it, Bacchic, superhuman. He drank it on those rare occasions when some untoward event unsettled him. He had listened to Annabelle's mutterings and now he spoke:

"Listen, Annabelle."

"Yassss, Poppa?"

"You think those people gonna get into peanut butter too?"

She was gone in the morning. Mothersill rolled over for his morning taste and clutched emptiness, but his hangover drove him back to sleep, and it seemed that he'd been out hours and the doorbell'd been ringing all that time, insistently, in dots and long-time leaning dashes. He staggered to the system. "Hey," he mumbled.

"Odell, Odell! Let me in, quick, quick!" Although her voice sounded tinny and fuzzy over the intercom, he recognized the near panic in it. He pressed the buzzer and staggered to the bathroom to splash cold water on his face, and then into the kitchen to get the coffee on, his mind racing, or trying to, around the reasons for her return. Ole cool Annabelle vanished from your bed to be seen neat and well-poised on the job the next day; it was like the closeness of the night did not, could not, carry over into broad daylight. He was back at the door by the time Annabelle got upstairs. She brushed past him, heading for the kitchen and the Bourbon. She drank from the bottle, long gulps that filled her cheeks before flooding down her throat. Mothersill wondered what all this had to do with him, but he could not avoid asking, "All right, baby, what is it?"

"Marj and Marilyn. They're dead, cut from their throats to their vaginas, laying in six inches of blood, catsup and jam—" She broke off and ran for the bathroom. Mothersill heard her vomiting.

I'm having a nightmare. The gin did it. I'm still asleep. I'm dreaming all this shit. It hasn't happened. No way it could've happened. When I wake up it'll all be gone and man, will I be relieved.

But he heard the water running and the coffee smell filled the apartment, and then he moved to the bathroom and watched Annabelle washing. "What'd you do, Annabelle?" She gurgled emptily over the toilet bowl, shaking her head and finally saying, "Nothing. I ran out."

This happens to people you read about in the *News*, Mothersill thought. "You didn't call the cops?"

She shook her head again, and gulped water into her mouth with her hand.

Why didn't they stop looking for kicks and look for kids instead?

"They'll be looking for you," he said. "You're a roommate. They'll look for you first."

She stopped drinking.

"C'mon, have some coffee, then we have to call them." Mothersill drank gin with his coffee. Dizzy, dizzy broads, bathed in blue, nude, a standing streak of light, the knife, standing in the jar of jam, the breasts smeared with it, the falling hair shrouding the profiles, the bent taut muscles, the languidly widened legs, the glinting eyes reflecting some inner triumph, perhaps the deflection of seed. Mothersill got another gin.

"Maybe it'd be better if you just went to the cops," he said.

"Will you come with me?"

No, hell no, Mothersill wanted to shout. No. I want nothing to do with it. Annabelle's question echoed around and around in his head like a distant, barely heard scream. She was afraid of more than the cops. Fucking would not be fun for a while. She'd look for the psycho behind every man's eyeballs from now on. Now, *now,* she realized that not every nut needed catsup, strawberry jam or even peanut butter. But she knew him and trusted him, like the children, in a way. He stroked her neck, sighed and agreed to go with her. Then she broke down, trembling, crying; the delayed reaction had set in.

They rode in the police car from the Nineteenth Precinct Station where they'd cabbed to report the murders. Mothersill held Annabelle, pressing hard when her shudders came, and stared at the backs of the heads of the cop and the detective in the front seat. Two other cars were with them, one in front, one in back, both cruising through lights, their flashers and sirens on.

Almost noon, Mothersill thought, the gin slithering through his stomach, up to his throat and back down. On a normal Sunday morning he'd just be sitting down to breakfast, the mound of Sunday papers at his elbow, his building almost silent, at peace with himself. But here he was, hung over, from time to time patting the woman beside him, rather automatically, as one pats a baby who stirs under hand. And two cops in the front seat. A bad dream, a nightmare.

When they arrived at Annabelle's building there were already police cars there jamming the street, and people huddled together, whispering, looking up and down, judging the size of the crime by the numbers of policemen present. "You okay?" Mothersill asked Annabelle, helping her out.

"No," she said thickly, looking at the entrance fearfully.

"Mrs. Johnson?" The small man waved his finger in the general direction of the brim of his hat. He looked at Annabelle without expression, then glanced quizzically, briefly, at Mothersill. "I'm Detective Elson. You'll make it all right."

He took Annabelle's arm and led her inside, Mothersill and the horde of uniformed and plainclothes cops following.

"Goes my afternoon at the stadium," Elson said in a low voice. "Conerly'll have to do without me."

"There's always next Sunday, Teddy," someone said behind them.

"Yeah, but maybe there'll be another one of these."

The elevator hummed to a stop and Annabelle led the way out, looking around for Mothersill, and clutching his sleeve. She had to let go to get her key, then her hand trembled as she sought the keyhole. Mothersill took the key and, after a few seconds jiggling, opened the door.

No one moved. Annabelle was standing in the way. "I'm not going back in there," she said, shaking her head for emphasis and reaching for Mothersill again.

Elson spoke calmly. "It'll be all right, Mrs. Johnson. You and Mr. Mothersill just step right inside. That's all we'll ask you to do."

She looked at Mothersill for assurance. He put his arm around her waist. "Just inside," he muttered. He felt the cops bunching up to move forward behind them. "Just a second," he said to them, barely turning his head.

"C'mon, baby. Just inside," Mothersill said again, squinting at the sunlight which revealed the detritus of the party in the living room. She moved inside and pressed against the wall. "That's my room on the right side of the hallway," she said, pointing. "The first left is Marj's. They're in there. The next left is Marilyn's."

Detective Elson said, "Okay. You just wait here with Mr. Mothersill while we have a look." At the door to Marj's room they bunched, backed up and then flowed in. Mothersill heard a low whistle and there was silence. Elson's voice carried out to them: "Quite an orgy. Everything but the toast and hamburger buns. Jesus. Fuckin' kids, beatniks, what they won't do for kicks."

A smaller group of men passed Mothersill and Annabelle, followed the sound of the murmur of voices and vanished into Marj's room. Voices rose again.

"Hey, Tom-O, shoot up this mess will you, so it can get cleaned up? Arnie, dust every fuckin' thing you can lay your hands on. Doc, I know you'll give me your best time on the report." Elson's voice became louder as he left the room and approached them. "Bet they came from good families." He looked at Annabelle. "Right, Mrs. Johnson?"

"I guess," she said quietly.

"You coulda been in there too," he said.

"No," Annabelle said primly. "I don't go for things like that."

Elson looked at Mothersill. "You wanna see them?"

"No." Now that they were dead, it was all right to look at them nude, Mothersill thought.

"Okay," Elson said. "You're both gonna have to come with me until we get some reports in. Shouldn't take long. No charges, we'd just like your help."

Four hours later, after alternately dozing and looking out of the chief of detective's window at the view of Center Street, the reports were ready. The coroner's report listed time of death at between three and four. The night elevator man said Mothersill and Annabelle left at two. "He remembered," Elson said with a crooked smile, "because he wondered what two colored people were doing leaving at that time. I guess he didn't know you lived there, Mrs. Johnson."

"Guess not," she said.

"Good thing for the both of you," he said.

"All right, where does that leave us?" Mothersill asked.

As if he hadn't heard, Detective Elson went on. "Two young men left about forty minutes after you, and a single man about three. Your descriptions match the elevator operator's." He placed the reports on the desk. "That leaves you, for now, material witnesses. You're free, but we'll be around to talk to you at your office tomorrow. Mrs. Johnson, uh, will you be staying with Mr. Mothersill for a while now?"

"No."

Mothersill stared at her in relief, the detective in surprise.

"I'm going back to my husband."

"Oh," the detective said. "Good idea." He arched an eyebrow at Mothersill. "Better give us the address." As he was taking it down he said, "Let me tell you something: that really could've been you, too, Mrs. Johnson. It's your own business, but I've been on the force twenty-two years, and I've never known you people to do this kind of thing. Stick with your own kind. That's advice, nothing else. You know the rules about leaving town; they're in all the movies. I'll see you at the office tomorrow. Better get some sleep now."

After putting Annabelle on a train for Mount Vernon, Mothersill went home where, waking and sleeping, he tried to recall the faces of the men at the party, one that would reveal in its features the guilt of the murderer. Once he started, thinking about Ellie, who'd come walking sadly across his mind; she could have been one of the victims. He sat back. No, too shy. But who really knew what one was unless chosen to share?

When his sleep finally came and carried him restlessly into the next morning, the questions began again and the news stories broke. Mothersill took out his baseball bat and placed it near the door, waiting for the inevitable arrival of Annabelle's husband, Big Mariney. But he never came.

Weeks later, after round upon round of questioning in the office, at home and in Elson's headquarters, a composite picture of the murderer was published. It was the man who'd wanted to dance with Annabelle. There were periodic reports that progress was being made in the search for him, and it was true that people were picked up, accompanied by headlines, only later to be released for lack of evidence unattended by a single line of copy anywhere.

Meanwhile, vestigial, like the appendix or the coccyx, Mothersill's penis hung limply, serving only as a spout through which the vessel was emptied. It rose to no occasion, was enticed by no movement or thought. And when he dreamed of "The Sower," he dreamed the grain sack was empty.

Part Two

THREE DAYS BEFORE Thanksgiving, Mothersill answered his phone.

"My name is Eunice Potts."

"Eunice Potts?"

"Yes. I know someone named Tuberosa Begonia Jones. Would that be better?"

Mothersill laughed.

"I'm from Hough." Black people always said Hough if they lived in that section of Cleveland; never Cleveland. Now Mothersill knew who it was.

"Oh, yeah. My sister told me about you. How's show biz?"

"Show biz. Yes. Well, I'm still making the rounds. I called you a couple of months ago. It was Saturday and New York was getting to me."

Ah, he thought. Was that the call that came the night of Marj and Marilyn's party, when he was on the way out? On impulse, liking her voice, he said, "Why don't you come and have Thanksgiving dinner with me?" If she accepted he'd be off the hook for several other invitations he held tentatively for the same day. Lispernard would be pleased that her brother and her friend got together.

Mothersill felt Eunice Potts's gratitude coming over the line, even as she tried to hold it in check by saying, "Can you burn?"

"Can I burn," he laughed. "Eunice, I'm the *front* burner. The chef's chef."

Then she laughed and he liked the sound of her voice even more. "I'd like that very much," she said.

"Good. I'll pick you up."

"Oh, no," she said quickly. "Don't bother."

"No bother at all."

"I'll just come over. No problem. I've got your address and I know New York pretty well now. Any word from Lispernard?"

"Naw. But she's about due to call me up and see what's happening."

Her voice became cautious. "What do you mean?"

"Oh, just to see if I'm alive. She's not much for writing letters and neither am I."

"I see. Listen, can I bring anything?"

"No. Everything's cool. Is there anything you don't dig?"

"No."

"Then I'll see you about two, say?"

She said, "Yes, and thanks. It's been kind of—well, not like Hough, you know."

"It takes a little while to get used to this place, Eunice. Don't worry."

"Okay. I'll see you then."

Eunice Potts, he thought, shaking his head. What does a Eunice Potts look like? The name's as silly as Odell Mothersill. He wondered what kind of names they would have had in Africa—Kenya and the Mau Mau rebellion were much in the news these days, and now and again in a bookstore Mothersill saw a book on African sculpture. These factors had set him to wondering how Africans dealt with orphans, and considering the plight of orphans of black slaves on these shores.

But then his mind wandered back to Thanksgiving. He'd serve duck in a mix of orange and cherry sauces, a little stuffing. It'd be nice.

At close to two on Thanksgiving Day, already feeling good from tasting while burning, he paused. Hadn't he dreamed the sower back in motion last night? Could he now forget about those women now decaying under six feet of earth, gone to their maker savaged as hogs? The ball had taken its bounce and it'd had wild English on it. He, Odell Mothersill, was still cool. He was alive. The downstairs bell rang, and he was feeling so good he finger-popped all the way to the system and rang back without asking who. Who? Eunice Potts, show-biz divorcée outa Hough, lonely in the big city, weary of the casting couch and looking for– Hey, baby! You soundin' like ole times. He was still at the door for the second ring, and opened it.

He liked what he saw just that quickly. Small face, eyes so heavy with lashes that they looked hooded. Her smile was open as she thrust a bouquet of golden mums at him. "Hello, Odell."

He smiled stupidly, he would think later, and accepted the flowers. *She is fine*, he was thinking. *She is tough!* "Thanks, Eunice."

"Everybody calls me Potts," she said.

"Well, walk on in, Potts."

She stood looking around the room as she unbuttoned her coat. "Nice," she said.

Mothersill stood a little behind her taking in the softly rounded shoulders, the smear of brown neck that flashed when she removed her coat, and her legs. It was all done quickly with, not the connoisseur's glance, but the student's. When he had her coat, cradling the flowers under one arm, she turned and said, "Here, let me do the flowers."

Their hands touched and a spark flew between them. "High-voltage stuff, are you?" she asked.

"Not me," he began, but realizing that his voice had gone off somewhere, started again. "Not me. The rug, and it does get awfully dry in New York when the cold weather comes. Here, this way."

"Wow," she said. "Does it ever smell good in here. You weren't lyin', were you? If that food tastes half as good as it smells, it oughta be somethin' else."

Mothersill found himself grinning foolishly. "Can I get you a drink?"

"Vodka on rocks."

As he poured, feeling a small excitement beginning as they

stood next to each other in the small kitchen, he said, "I guess you'd be an ingénue type, huh?"

He found her bright smile so disconcerting that he splashed the vodka. She said, "Oh, sure. I could've had twenty husbands instead of just two, but that's my thing, I guess. Mine and Ruby Dee's."

He gave her her drink and made another for himself. She'd been in town only for a couple of months, true, but a thing as fine as she was, how come no cats hanging all over her? How come Thanksgiving with a stranger instead of one of those jive producers?

"There," she said with a one-handed flourish. "Where do you want them?"

"In the living room and we can sit down."

She glanced into the bedroom as they passed through once again. He thought, and wondered why, her glance was briefly apprehensive. As she sat she said, "This is smooth stuff. I like it." She made motions meant to convey how much at home she felt. Mothersill, bent over the phonograph now, his back to her, said, "Relax." He felt that she wasn't; he wanted her to.

"But I am," she said quickly.

"Okay. I'm glad you called, and I'm glad you came."

"Me, too." The smile again, and he studied briefly the lean, well-carved wrist and hand rather than the drink she was holding in a mute and fleeting toast.

"It'll be ready in a few minutes, Potts. We'll have time for another."

"I'm starved, but another drink would be fine, when I finish."

He asked, "How was Lisp when you saw her last?"

"Fat with child, as they say."

"And Mason?"

"He's a very groovy man, you know. Really is. And fine. Lisp could lose him in a minute if he didn't have so many eyes for her."

"Yeh, he's all right. Where'd you live in Hough?"

"Hundred and Twenty-fifth Street."

"I used to hang out around there." He rose. "Let's get another and dinner should be ready." She passed her glass and again their hands touched. He winked at her. "See, no shock that time."

"So, you've never been married?" Potts was saying. They were now near the end of the meal, which Mothersill thought extraordinarily good. Every once in a while he reached new highs in the kitchen; this was one of those times. Years of plying dates with dinners he'd culled from exotic cookbooks had lent him a skill at the stove which was still improving. In fact, the seat in which Potts was sitting had been polished by almost countless other female bottoms, some of whose names Mothersill could no longer remember. For, to Mothersill, cooking and eating had become subconsciously a part of the ritual of love-making, and now, finally, the urge was back, and he wanted to make love with Potts.

"No," he said in answer to her question. "And you've been twice?"

She laughed a small laugh, a sound filled with secrets, pain and wry memories. "Twice. But you. Lisp says that if polygamy were the style, you'd have married long ago."

"No. I can't handle more than one woman at a time. How about you?"

She shrugged.

He pursued it. "No? Yes?"

"I don't know. I suppose." Then, "Odell, both my marriages were very brief. I never knew what happened. Neither guy said anything, just left. No arguments or fights. It took me a long time to get over the first one, and I'm still getting over the second. So I haven't been what you'd call a swinging chick, and basically, I just don't know how I'd react to having to make choices."

Mothersill felt uneasy, as though he'd just entered an unfamiliar place which, bright at first glance, held somber shadows at the second. Things seemed to move suddenly at his discovery and then draw still, motionless, waiting.

Darkness had come. The duck was a skeleton, its air-whitened bones stark in the soft lights Mothersill had turned on. Sipping his coffee, he reflected that not only hadn't Potts issued one tiny signal, she was trying very hard to make sure she didn't.

"What're your prospects for work?" he asked.

"There're always prospects. I'd have better luck if I were a dancer, too. Then all I'd get would be dancing parts, or chorus line. If you're thinking about my notices from Karamu, they're great in Cleveland, but there aren't too many folks on Broadway who know about Karamu."

Mothersill had been half listening. He was thinking that it'd be cool to go somewhere with her, for a walk, a movie, to see if she moved the way he thought she should, or would. Perhaps even to see how other people looked at her, or even how she would look after a brisk walk in the cold air. So, he spoke: "Hey, why don't we take a walk and find a movie or a brandy?"

"I'd like that," she said. "Let me clean up first."

"Many hands make light work," Mothersill said, rising to help clear the table.

"You sound just like your sister."

"I can't help that. Didn't have nothin' to do with it."

In the kitchen he watched her hands plunging in and out of the soapy water, quick with plates, bowls, silver, pans, glasses, cups, and he wondered what her reaction would be if she knew that that pot, for example, had come to him steaming hot and filled with chicken and dumplings, a gift from a young woman with marvelous big legs whom he'd met at an NAACP convention.

His entire apartment was filled with mementos, like the confetti on the floor, the dancers gone; furrows from half the world seeded. But why, he wondered, was he perusing these things, flipping the pages of what seemed to be a scrapbook, as if reviewing the old life in preparation for a new one?

Mothersill managed to brush against Potts, interiorize her softness. Her face stiffened, then softened into a smile that was only slightly wary around the edges. When he was close to her she smelled of crabapple blossoms.

"There," she said, smiling a pleased smile and edging around him, aware that he stood where he was to intercept her. Imperceptibly she averted her face and he could see a plea in her eyes: *Don't.*

Chesler Dedham, wearing gloves, hoisted his kite into the early December wind in the Sheep Meadow in Central Park. He did not seem to mind being the only kid flying a kite. He has all the right attitudes a rich kid should have, thought Mothersill, who was watching him. But Chesler was no longer rich; his parents had just left him as well as each other, in opposite directions as fast as they could. Chesler was brought to the agency by the maid who herself was owed wages, and who could not care for the child any longer since it was clear that the parents were not coming back.

Maybe Chesler had had five or six years of being rich, but the last three or four had been pretty much hell and at best lower middle class. Mothersill came up behind him. "Chesler, you never answered me. Tell me about this crapping on the dining-room chairs. You're a big guy now. How do you feel when you do it?"

"I told you, Mr. Mothersill, I don't know just how I feel."

"No, you didn't tell me that. Anyway, Chesler, Mr. and Mrs. Meadman don't think they can keep you past Christmas. I thought you ought to know that. Maybe there's something you can help us do to change their minds."

The boy had his eyes on the kite, which was now dipping in a changing wind. "I don't like them so much, Mr. Mothersill. Not really."

Mothersill sighed. "Chesler, this is your third home. I'm starting to believe you don't like anybody, man."

Chesler ran forward a few paces and, as the kite began to soar again, the spool in his hands spun off the string. "It's not that I don't like people. I don't think they like me."

"Well you got some ways you'd better get rid of. Maybe that's why they don't like you."

Chesler said, "But I never shit in chairs until I'm sure they don't like me." He glanced behind him at Mothersill. "I wouldn't shit in your chairs, Mr. Mothersill."

"Damn it, Chesler. We've gone over that. I'm a bachelor and bachelors can't adopt kids. Besides, I'm a Negro and you're white and we've got rules about things like that." Mothersill watched him run the kite deeper into the Meadow, then followed him. "Hey, what's so bad about the Meadmans?"

"Aw, he's always talking about how my father had those sailboats and raced, and the horses we had, and the house, and how my mother and father weren't any good because they ran off and left me, but how he and his wife are really good people because they've taken me in."

"Makes you mad, huh?"

"Not really. Just makes me want to shit in dining-room chairs."

"Chesler, how about the other people you were with, the Popes?"

"Before I answer that," Chesler said, "how come you can't find my folks? The workers always say you can't find my mother and father."

Mothersill watched the kite, purple and white, hanging majestically in the graying sky. Then he said, "Big-guy stuff?"

Chesler gave him a frightened look, then nodded. "Sure."

"Most of the kids we handle, their folks are dead, so we don't have a lot of trouble looking for them, you know what I mean?"

The scared look remained on Chesler's face. But Mothersill reasoned that the truth would bring up a little hate and the kid would stop defending his parents by shitting on dining-room chairs. Or, to be sure, he hated them already, because he suspected things. "Well, in your case, we know where your folks are, and your father, in fact, paid your keep in that nice private orphanage. Chesler, you should see some of the places they keep kids."

Chesler was holding more tightly to the kite string than he had to.

"But, your father doesn't want you and neither does your mother." Mothersill shrugged. "Look, man. It's one of those things. They made a mistake. You're a mistake. I may be a mistake. I bet half the people in New York are mistakes, but they make the best of it, maybe because they didn't have the dough your folks did—"

"People just don't run off from children!" Chesler screamed.

"Shut up, Chesler. Sometimes people kill children." In a gentler voice Mothersill said, "What about the Popes?"

Chesler was winding in his kite. "He was always touching me."

"Where?"

"You know."

"I wasn't there. I don't know."

"On the penis."

"Oh yeah, why didn't you tell the worker?"

"I only saw her with them. She never talked to me by myself."

"I see. Getting hungry? Want to go to a restaurant or go to my place and have hot dogs and watch the football game?"

"Hamburgers and football?"

"Okay."

"You know," Mothersill was saying, his mouth filled with hamburger and bun, "I'll bet Mr. Meadman only talks about your folks the way he does because you've got funny ways, Chesler. Like a lot of rich people. And he's worked hard, as far as I know. He couldn't afford to run away and leave you. How's about another chance? I'll talk to them."

Mothersill watched the blue eyes roll toward him.

"Can't I stay with you?"

"Nope. But you can visit. I like to have you visit."

"I don't care if you're colored. Madeira was colored."

Mothersill shook his head. Maybe now he didn't care. "I'd like to see you give the Meadmans another try." He couldn't tell him that he'd have to get the worker started on finding another couple.

"You could get married," Chesler said hopefully.

"That wouldn't help, buddy."

"Marry Madeira."

Mothersill started to laugh but stopped. Madeira was twice his age and by now was a maid for someone else, maybe even out of the city. For the first month or so after she brought Chesler in, she visited the orphanage every week, then stopped.

"No. The Meadmans, okay?"

"Do I have to, Mr. Mothersill?"

"You have to, Chesler, and that means no more crapping around in the chairs. Shall we shake on it?"

Chesler's eyes brimmed with tears. "You mean my folks are *never* coming back to get me?"

"No," Mothersill said. "You are going to have to make a new life for yourself, man."

Some life, Mothersill thought. His shitting in chairs would turn to shooting people in the head. He'd get even with his folks, with the world. He might turn up at a party one night when he became a young man, cut up two girls and vanish leaving a trail of catsup, strawberry jam and peanut butter; most certainly peanut butter. He might have a special little affinity for niggers, thinking back on old Madeira and me. Unless he got it all mixed up and then believed we caused the whole thing. Maybe that's why we're in such a mess now, these people out here seeding all this sickness and laying the blame on us.

"Time to get you home, Chesler. Gotta go to the bathroom or anything?"

"No. Maybe. Yes."

"Okay, hurry up. We'll pick up my girl on the way."

On the way to Potts's, the boy asked, "When you get married and have boys, Mr. Mothersill, will you go away and leave them?"

Instantly, Mothersill pictured himself walking out on Potts, two little boys clinging to her legs. He said, "Well, I have to tell you, Chesler, I don't know. Nobody knows. I bet your folks didn't know they were going to have to leave you. I'd try hard not to leave my boys, but some things happen and you can't help them, like a fumble, see, or an intercepted pass. Grownies have a lot of trouble. Sometimes they cry at night so no one can see or hear them. You just can't tell. You do the best you can."

Every time Mothersill left Potts or she him, he told himself that was their final date. She wasn't giving up any leg. Something was wrong. But he always called her again, cursing himself after he'd hung up, but pleased that another date had been made. Was she a throwback to those church-bred babes who feared fire and brimstone more than they did good groovy lovin'? In another time, maybe. There weren't many church ladies he'd known who wouldn't take the fuck first and worry about the fire next time. Something else. Mothersill shook his head. Lesbian. Was that what had caused her husbands to leave? No. I'd know. She would've split.

Up until she heard the doorbell Eunice Potts had decided it was time. But when it rang her resolve collapsed; she could not. Yet, she knew she faced the possibility of losing him; she needed more time.

She managed not to tremble when he came in with the little white boy, turning her cheek to him to avoid his lips, but clutching warmly at his arms. Momentarily she enjoyed the pressure of his body against her breasts, but stiffened and drew slightly away. Brightly she said, "Hello, there. Are you Chesler?"

Chesler nodded while searching her eyes. She liked him, he decided. Indeed, the warmth she could not show Mothersill, she extended to Chesler, hoping in some way that it would be directed through the boy and onto Mothersill.

Chesler responded all the way home, babbling joyously, pleased with the way the woman, so pretty, talked and joked with him, teased him. Mothersill drove through the late Sunday afternoon traffic listening, glancing at Potts, smiling to himself at their talk.

When he had returned the boy to the Meadmans, Mothersill climbed back into the car and said to Potts, "I'd like one, baby, just one real kiss."

Potts heard a little sound escape her, but she closed her eyes and leaned toward him, her mouth partly open.

And Mothersill kissed her, uncaring of the Meadmans and Chesler silhouetted in the window watching them. "Relax," he said, to still her trembling. "Was that so bad?"

"No," she said with a shaking laugh. "It was nice."

He looked at her a moment, pleading with his eyes until her own fluttered and then turned away.

"What *is* the matter, Potts?"

"Time," she said weakly. "Just time."

Mothersill punched the car into gear and snarled, "All right. Let's get to the movies."

They sat without speaking or touching, and after, Mothersill drove her home. A few blocks from there he stopped at a phone booth and, when he hung up, his penis was already hard and he hurried to his car and drove uptown. Fuck you, Potts, he thought.

All week he had been hell on wheels in the office, beginning with Monday when he reamed out Kramer for not managing to get alone with Chesler long enough to discover that Mr. Pope was feeling the kid up. And he got her started on the search for other prospective adoptive parents for the boy. Soon Chesler was going to run out of parents. The legal steps to make one or both of his parents return and claim him were long and filled with red tape. The end of the matter would be as in the beginning: they wouldn't respond to court orders anyway.

Glancing out of his office now he saw Malone Lincoln talking to Annabelle, holding one of his cameras in the palms of his hands. Mothersill smiled. Lincoln was wasting his time. It was true that in certain light Annabelle could be mistaken for white; she was that fair. But she was still a subdued and shaken woman, hanging onto Big Mariney with all her might. If he was crazy, he was crazy about her; if a little madness crept into his behavior, at least she could understand it. She, Annabelle knew, was one person her husband would never hurt.

He turned his attention to the Cohens. Mrs. Cohen dominated her husband with precise cuttings of her eyes and the tones and volumes of her voice. Mothersill thought she drank a lot. (The Listerine on her breath was always tinged with the faint hint of good scotch.) She loved her husband, she repeated ad infinitum, or rather, Mothersill thought, ad nauseam. She, a small, plumpish, just over thirty lady, therefore had never considered leaving him even though he could not, according to her interpretation of the medical reports, make babies. But Mothersill had seen the reports and he knew there was nothing wrong with either of them. Maybe some little psychological bug blocking channels or something was all.

The Cohens wanted to adopt. Mr. Cohen would take any boy available, but she wanted to consider only light-skinned boys. The Cohens were black; he was real black and not much bigger than she. Mrs. Cohen was the color of dark gold. Mothersill was intrigued by her shape: a full torso, a neat, nipped waist and hourglass-shaped hips. A perfect cradle, he imagined, for rocking.

Elisabeth Cohen disturbed Mothersill, too. It was in the way she looked at him when he made home visits, not because he had to, but because he wanted to. He understood the signals well, the eyes, the way she moved her body when he was near. Much later someone would call these ancient movements body language, for white people had a fear of not possessing names for things, even those that were and must remain nameless. To name them was to strip them of their mystery, sort of—because most of the mystery was left anyway—and thus one named only shadow, not substance.

During his time at the agency Mothersill had met many women like Elisabeth Cohen. (She changed the z in her Christian name to s.) He believed she wanted to give it up. To him. And why not? As he saw it, she could not have a child and therefore was as free to fuck as if she'd had her tubes tied and felt like it every minute, twenty-four hours a day. She was afraid, basically, and quite naturally, to go out and get the grits she hungered for; she was bound by her Baptist upbringing (and a transfer in her twenties to the Episcopalians) and her schoolteacher, class-conscious parents. But if there were icemen like Reverend Clark, or even icemen unlike Reverend Clark, ones who'd rape her (though black icemen, as Louis Jordan says, have not been known to rape but to diddle), Mrs. Cohen would have loved it. The matter would have been out of her hands.

The Cohens had seen a number of boys, mostly children of interracial unions. Bagel-babies and A-trainers who slipped their leashes in the Bronx and Harlem and converged in the Village, stretching out to touch lives other than their own. Mrs. Cohen had no idea how fitting it would be for them to select their son from the offspring of that group, although Mothersill had not the slightest idea where Mr. Cohen had got his name from.

Mrs. Cohen shunned the fair boys with kinky hair, and the dark boys with straight hair. At the moment they were considering a light brown child, Jeremy Dennis Gregory, who had curly hair.

Mothersill reached for the phone and dialed Mrs. Cohen in Queens. Something had come up with Jeremy, would it be possible for her to meet him in the city to discuss it?

She could, but she wondered if she should ask her husband to join them when he finished work. But, she said, on the second thought, that didn't seem too necessary; she knew Mr. Mothersill's time was valuable, and she, after all, could convey any message to her husband.

Mothersill glanced at his watch. She'd be in the city in an hour. He imagined her shutting off her television set, dashing around their small house and taking a quick wash and putting on makeup.

Mothersill calculatingly watched her enter the somewhat pretentious coffee house. She could have been extremely attractive rather than moderately so. The right clothes, the right hairdo, makeup and without that silly little afternoon tea hat and gloves. She might have been ten years older than she really was. But she walked quickly toward him, her heels clicking loudly on the floor of the almost deserted interior. She was smiling and instinctively Mothersill knew that being in Greenwich Village titillated her; he'd hoped this would be the case.

"Well," she said, glancing around, "so this is the Village."

"Yes, how are you, Mrs. Cohen?"

"Good, good. What do they serve here, just coffee?"

She glanced quickly around, saw there was no bar.

"Tea," Mothersill said. She hadn't asked anything about Jeremy yet.

"Oh, dear," she said, laughing, putting her gloved hand to her face, but her eyes behind them were not coy. "I thought—well. I don't want you to think. Parents do drink some don't they, Mr. Mothersill? I mean, they're allowed to?"

Mothersill laughed until the waitress noticed them and hurried over. "I think we've made a mistake," Mothersill told her. "We've just decided we wanted more than coffee or tea."

The waitress shrugged and left.

Mothersill stood up and guided Mrs. Cohen out of the shop by the elbow. "Do you have any preferences?"

"About restaurants? No. Don't you?"

"I live about four short blocks from here. We can drink and talk there if you like. I mean—"

"That will be just fine, Mr. Mothersill, if you don't mind."

"How is Mr. Cohen?" he asked as they walked, slowly, as if savoring something they both could detect in the air.

"Very good, thank you. Oh, I forgot. He just got a promotion, so that should be something in our favor for Jeremy. Shouldn't it?"

Mothersill nodded sagely. "The material things do count, yes. But there're other things that mean more."

She gave him a sidelong glance. "Mr. Mothersill, we're not really going to discuss Jeremy, are we?"

Mothersill walked a few paces before answering. "No. Everything's all right, so far." He heard her exhale loudly, and could not tell at first whether it was a sigh of relief, muffled laughter or outrage.

"Mr. Mothersill," she said, smiling and taking his arm. "How nice of you. Thoughtful, really."

In his apartment she removed her hat and shook out her hair while she removed her gloves, plucking carefully at each fingertip. She smiled again, a large, warm, knowing Negro smile. "Can I have a scotch on the rocks, please, Mr. Mothersill?" Her eyes dropped slowly from his face to take in his body, the warming bulge in his trousers, and then went back to his eyes. "Oh, my," she said.

Elisabeth Cohen without clothes was just the way Mothersill had pictured her. She came out of the bathroom, a large towel wrapped around her. She paused a moment to finish her second drink, took off the towel and threw it on the foot of the bed. "Let me look at you, Mr. Mothersill," she said in a soft voice. "Please get up and let me look at you."

Mothersill got out of bed and in silence they stood looking at each other. Then he kissed her while she took hold of his penis and rubbed herself with it, murmuring, "Ah, Mr. Mothersill, ahhh." They hurled themselves into the bed, which strained and creaked under the force, and Mothersill, clutching her breasts, trying to stuff first one and then the other into his mouth, was distracted by the frenzied way she kept trying to jam his penis into her. Mothersill turned her on her side and she twisted quickly to look questioningly at him, but her eyelids dropped and she sighed sweetly burrowing her head into the pillow when she felt it going into the right place. "Ah," she said. "Ooooo, Mr. Mothersill."

"Mrs. Cohen," he panted. "This is excellent."

"I'm so glad you like it, Mr. Mothersill. It *is* very good. Touch me here." She took his arms from around her waist and placed them over her breasts. "Yes, like that."

Mothersill closed his eyes and they found their rhythm, rocking slowly in the warmth and wetness, curving little sounds of pleasure into the air until in a somewhat louder voice she said, "Oh! Oh, my, Mr. Mothersill!" and began moving faster, her buttocks gyrating against his pelvis. And he, perceiving the movement of the comet also, from a dark distance, moving up fast, being massively overtaken by it, answered, "Oh! *Yes!* Mrs. Cohen, Oh yeahhhh!"

In the apartment below, Mrs. Brady, the seventy-year-old widow, paused over her hot popovers, butter, strawberry jam and tea. She liked to hear the muffled thumps and voices that came so often from Mothersill's apartment; they reminded her of her own younger, distant days.

Today the voices seemed unusually emotional; she'd always pictured Mr. Mothersill as being one of those calm, quiet lovers who elicited whispers. He was yelping today and so was the woman. Mrs. Brady bit into her popover and gazed up toward the ceiling, licking her lips nervously. The racket! she thought, picturing the wildest contortion of arms and legs. Mrs. Brady finished the popover and reached for another.

Upstairs, Mothersill and Mrs. Cohen bucked and heaved in the heat of their orgasms, moving back and forth across the bed, pulling sheets, crashing into the wall, knotting blankets and finally cracking a corner leg of the bed.

Mrs. Brady jumped to her feet as the falling bed resounded across her ceiling like thunder; her heart raced. Smiling and clutching the popover oozing with jam, she moved into her bedroom and stood quietly in the silence, picturing Mr. Mothersill and the woman.

Mrs. Cohen and Mothersill found themselves tilting downward when they opened their eyes and resumed normal breathing. "Ah, *Mr.* Mothersill." Mrs. Cohen turned so she could face him. He was thinking, Not bad for an old lady, not bad at all! Then, with a mixture of horror and admiration, he felt her coming at him again, fondling him slowly and tenderly, kissing and stroking, nibbling with the care and precision she perhaps employed preparing an important dinner party. She smothered his protests, which were in fact feeble. He had never known such exhaustion from one time around. At first he found himself responding out of politeness; a certain courtesy was due Mrs. Cohen after all. She was a guest in his house. Then he boldly accepted the challenge; his limpness began to fade and gristle rediscovered its purpose.

"Soon, Mr. Mothersill," Mrs. Cohen encouraged, hefting his penis, drumming her fingertips around its head softly, like the falling petals of a flower.

Now with a cup of tea held nervously above a saucer in her hands, Mrs. Brady heard whimpering sounds coming from upstairs and, sitting on her bed, crossed and uncrossed her legs at the sounds of stirrings, the scraping of the broken bed leg on the floor.

Mothersill was telling himself, *Yes!* He had seen himself stretched out on the bed, still trying to catch his breath as Mrs. Cohen left, hurrying to be home before her husband got there. But no. She was not going to leave him breathless; she just might leave him dead. *Yes!*

Just when she knew he was ready once more, Mrs. Cohen pulled back to look at him, a sure, mothering smile upon her face, and she rolled on her back, her legs furrowed up, her arms opened, and he entered once more, felt her legs creep up his back, her ankles locking them in place.

"Wooo! Mr. Mothersill!"

"Elisabeth!"

"Odell!"

Mrs. Brady started from her bed, walked nervously back to her living room, put down the cup and saucer, she thought, and took another popover and returned to the bedroom where she stood listening to the bumping and thumping. She took a bite. But her teeth closed around the warm saucer. Startled, she grinned at it and sat down on the bed again, her bottom lip clenched between her teeth.

C-raackk!

Another leg on the bed broke. The wall sounded as though a battalion of kettle drummers were pounding on it.

Mrs. Brady placed her ear to the wall.

"Baby!"

"Darling!"

Mrs. Brady hurried to her refrigerator and fumbled for the package of hot dogs she'd bought that morning.

Upstairs, kicking for more leverage, Mothersill put his foot through the sheet.

Clutching and gripping, Mrs. Cohen's hands ripped a pillow and feathers exploded upward and drifted down over them, as they loudly and savagely interrogated each other:

"*Now?*"

"*Now! Now!*"

"*Okay! Now! Right now! Okay, now?*"

"*Now! Now! Ready, baby? Now!*"

This time Mrs. Cohen lay panting, her arms outstretched, one leg up, her body making the feathers quiver. "You are quite something for a young man, Mr. Mothersill," she gasped. "Yes, indeed."

Hidden behind one of his arms that partially concealed his face, Mothersill peered at her. When she gave a great sigh, his heart leaped; she was leaving. She was going to get up, pull on her clothes and go home to Mr. Cohen. Then he would rest. Maybe even take some of the throbbing out of his penis in a hot bath. He smiled brightly, expectantly, when she sighed again and moved. "I guess I ought to think about going," she said.

And Mothersill knew by the tone of her voice that he was in trouble and knew it for sure when she threw off the sheet and smiled at him. A groan escaped him as she embraced him again. "Poor Mr. Mothersill," she mocked, sliding down on him.

Mrs. Cohen was a woman of purpose and infinite patience. She did not hurry, realizing that young people often overextended themselves brashly, and needed time to recuperate, to respond to stimuli; these, she knew, often hastened the recuperative powers. So she took her time, working in loving silence until at last her efforts began to take uncertain shape. She paused to offer encouragement: "You're doing nicely, Mr. Mothersill."

"Mrs. Cohen, thanks. I wouldn't want to disappoint you. Do you suppose we might take a raincheck on this one?"

"Make hay while the sun shines, Mr. Mothersill."

"Mrs. Cohen–"

"Shhh, Mr. Mothersill. Don't distract me."

They do nothing except watch television, Mr. and Mrs. Cohen, Mothersill thought, and he resigned himself; he was the victim of the priestess, a sacrifice to the gods, a tidbit to be nibbled on and at. Wearily the familiar sensation trudged up once again and he tried not to recognize it. Just before she leaped astride him, Mothersill glanced down and saw his erection. Then she was upon him, her legs wide, a firewoman hurtling down the pole. She threw back her head so that the cords in her neck were taut and shuddered. "*Yes! Mr. Mothersill!*"

Mrs. Brady, sprawled upon her bed, sat up dazed, listening to the sounds. Then she went to the refrigerator for another hot dog.

Mrs. Cohen gave another howl, then fainted upon Mothersill. When she came to, aided by an ice pack on her head, Mothersill gave her another scotch, watched her dress, roll her hair back into the bun, pull on her hat and gloves and walk out as briskly as she'd walked in. She was gone. Mothersill poured himself a stiff gin, no rocks, stared at himself in the mirror, then dragged himself into the bathroom, where he fell asleep in a tub full of hot water.

But it was still Potts to whom his thoughts turned as his sore, beaten body returned to normal days later. Everybody in the world was doing it but Potts. They were going to have to resolve this business, even if it was true that she'd opened his nose mainly because he couldn't get her into bed. He believed, really and truly believed, in trying before buying, or as they said in the social work conferences, "premarital sex."

That morning, when he was making a new resolve about the matter, he failed to see Hugh Mifflin, the agency director, approaching his office, and Mothersill stared at the soft knock Mifflin always gave before entering even an opened door. "Ah, hello, Odell."

Mifflin was a small, thin man with "womanish" ways. He sat down before Mothersill could answer him.

"Hugh. Morning."

"How's it going, Odell?"

What's that mean? Mothersill wondered. Then he said, "Okay. Why?"

"Oh, nothing. I think you're doing okay, too. Great asset to the agency."

Well, Mothersill thought. It wasn't every white social worker in this field who one day looked up and saw black kids without parents too, and decided that it might not be a bad idea to have a black supervisor around when things really became thick. "What's up? Or is this a social visit?"

"As a matter of fact," Mifflin said, "something is up. We've got something going in the Caribbean and I wondered if you'd be interested. If not"—and he grimaced—"I'll have to go to Lincoln. It's a leave of absence, but with full pay."

Mothersill quickly sat back in his chair mentally checking his performance at the agency. "I don't understand."

"We've worked out an exchange arrangement with the government of Grand Royale. Seems like a nice place. You'll see the brochures. There are a lot of what are called, to use loose terminology, 'illegitimate children' on the island. But up till now they haven't had to expend a lot of money on orphanages or work on any adoption techniques. Someone always took the children. Relatives, friends, even strangers. There was no such thing as a child not being cared for. And we, here, are supposed to be the civilized people."

"I never called the people here civilized," Mothersill said.

Mifflin flushed and managed a smile. "I know. But things are changing there. They're becoming like us. The relatives, friends and strangers are leaving the island to earn a living. They go to other islands, Canada, the States, South America. There's no one to take in the kids."

"So?"

"Our person will go down and try to get some adoption services techniques set up. That may mean showing them that they need an orphanage or two as a start. In a modified way, of course. Something that fits in with whatever existing practice they may have. They'll send a person here and when he goes back he can more easily implement the services you'll have planned out for them."

"You said full pay?"

Mifflin was grinning at him. "Yes."

"Passage?"

"They're paying that."

"Housing?"

"They'll see to all those things," Mifflin said with a wave of his hand.

Mothersill, musing, broke off and asked, "Why don't you take it, Hugh?"

"I wondered when you'd get around to that. They want a Negro. They're heading for independence."

"A forward-looking place," Mothersill said. "How soon?"

"April the first. You in?"

"Yeah," Mothersill said. "But I'm going to need passage for two. Can I have a week to kick it around, though?"

"Sure. Getting married? Anybody I know?"

"Yes. She's an actress."

The way he said it, Hugh Mifflin thought it better not to pursue the niceties that perhaps were not.

At the end of the week Mothersill accepted the assignment in Grand Royale, but waited to tell Potts about it. He didn't want it to appear that he was offering her the trip in exchange for marriage. December moved into short, dark days, and he thought he would tell her at Christmas, but didn't; the time never seemed right, and January seemed to slip right through his hands.

One Friday in February—the week had been rough, with Chesler being moved again and Mrs. Cohen, happy enough with Jeremy, calling to say that she thought, she really believed—guess what? She was pregnant. When he offered her congratulations and asked whether they'd keep Jeremy, she'd said, yes, they'd keep him. But she laughed at his congratulations, though she wasn't really sure, and whispered into the phone, "Oh, you sweet Mr. Mothersill," laughed again and hung up.

That Friday he glumly cleared his desk. The singles in the office were already gathering their oversized bags and in a few hours they'd be wined and dined and not long after putting out or getting got. He, on the other hand, would be with Potts, going through another of those evenings when she slipped from his touch or pressed her cheek hurriedly to his and withdrew. She'd avoid his eyes and again plead, although these days with unconcealed embarrassment, "*Time, I need more time.*" Then Mothersill would take her home, then start on the business of getting himself some leg. It wasn't right. She after all had brought gristle and life back into a member that seemed to have died after the murders of Marilyn and Marj. Why in the hell couldn't he turn her loose? Why couldn't she turn *herself* loose? Some decisions had to be made.

So, he was at first puzzled by the broadness of her smile, and then shocked by the warmth of her kiss. He noticed, shaken with this Eunice Potts, an oversized bag clutched perhaps just a little too tightly in her hand. Jellies, perfumes, plastic D-case, gown? Mothersill could not dwell on that possibility too long.

"Hey," he said. "You've got a part."

She laughed. "No such luck yet, but I'm not worried. Don't look so puzzled, Odell. Can we eat out and take champagne home and drink it with strawberries?"

He would have given her anything at that moment, ripped it barehanded out of the sky. "It's not strawberry season," he said huskily. "They've got to be frozen."

"I don't care. Let's have them, all right?"

Mothersill threw back his head and laughed. He wanted to skip and jump, do handsprings. Ahhh, he thought. No. Why was it that love and fuck were one syllable, with four letters each? "Sure, we can have the strawberries."

At dinner in a candle-lighted steakhouse, Mothersill half-listened to Potts chattering at him. He was relaxed, assured and happy. Of course he loved her. She was not the Potts he always knew she was. What's been wrong, what's right now?

"I need another drink," she said.

Mothersill waved at the waiter. This would be Potts's fourth *gin* martini. Suddenly he became wary. He could dig people getting half-crocked before making love; he'd seen a lot of that because people were afraid of sex and what it might mean. He looked at her. But you, Potts? However, what did he know about her, really? No man ever really knows a woman until he has touched her deeply, scraped the bottom of her stomach, the pinnacle of her psyche, heard the unguarded sighs, gasps, or felt the knuckle bones of the body straining for better grasp, slip; and who knows for sure then? Is passion to be trusted? Is it the only emotion to trust, slipping as it does out of convention, breaking the ropes of restraint? Mothersill imagined Mahalia Jackson and what her passion might have revealed; he had to work at it, but surely it was there. Cleopatra: had there been so much or was it merely that Caesar and Antony were not used to African ways?

He smiled then, when the waiter brought Potts's martini.

But after dinner, sensing her resolve slipping, Mothersill hurried Potts through the Village. High, she was talking bravely and much too rapidly. Mothersill, determined, grimly selected the champagne, then pulled her into a deli for the frozen strawberries.

In his apartment she said, "I'll have another drink while we're waiting for the wine to chill," and before he could say anything, before he could turn from the records he was putting on, he heard her in the kitchen, bottle against glass. Then she was in the bathroom. A long time it seemed to Mothersill. He fixed himself another drink and called, "Potts! You all right?"

Her response was a giggle. "Of course. I'll be right out."

Since artists have known to draw they've painted women's bodies. Titian, Rubens, Renoir, Gauguin, Picasso—countless painters, but few have been blessed with models whose bodies are made of the stuff of a billion wet dreams or a zillion fantasies that, like cobwebs, are spun in the mind every second of the day or night. Even those fortunate enough to have models with perfect bodies have failed the challenge of shadow and curve and angle, or missed that nameless special quality of inner lighting. There is no perfect artist, therefore it follows that none can capture the perfect body that simply is; one looks at it and knows; the impact of the senses, gathering as if at a traffic circle, only hint at what words, drawings, photographs can never capture. For most people nudes are at their ugliest. Naked beauty, naked perfection, is blinding and one must doubt what his first sense, sight, reveals.

Mothersill was sitting when she came out in a knee-length

gown, the bathroom light behind her starkly outlining her body in a golden, gauzy light. He tried to be nonchalant, stretching ever so slowly to place his glass on a table, and he missed it by a foot. Neither looked at the glass, which had bounced on the rug, clinking ice cubes; they looked at each other almost in fright until, finally, Potts drew in her breath. He heard it most audibly above the music. "Odell. Is it all right?"

Mothersill nodded and bent to pick up the glass, feeling for it like a blind man; he was still staring at her. "It's just fine," he murmured.

Moments later, drinking the champagne with the strawberries in it and listening to the music, Mothersill said, "Potts, goddamn, Potts."

She was trembling slightly when he went to her. He stroked her back under her gown down to her buttocks. She pressed against him and he felt her body spasming. "Re–*lax*, baby," he whispered.

"I'm all right," she whispered back, then took a long sip from her glass.

"But what is it?"

"Nothing. I'm sorry."

"That's okay, Potts."

"I mean for making you wait."

"It was a long wait," he said hoarsely.

She finished her glass and rested her head in his lap. His fingers traced her breasts. Never, never, had he held or touched any like these. He felt a gentle gnawing in his groin and moved his leg so his stiffening penis was close to where her mouth was slowly and seductively moving. He slid off his pants. She waited, then settled back in his lap. He peeled off his shirt and, as she shifted and closed about him with her special warmth, he pushed up her gown until her body, from her toes to her breasts, lay exposed, all of it feeling like silk. He bent into her, gently pushing apart her legs, breathing deeply of her, and marveled once again how clean black girls smelled there. The I'm-not-really-dirt syndrome.

Potts appeared to have gained more confidence as they moved to the bedroom, laughing over second glasses of champagne, the strawberries settling soggily to the bottom. In bed Mothersill stroked her body, awed by its sleekness, and he felt that here was a person wrapped in this body he would never grow tired of; he would only have to look at it to find himself, no matter how weary, back under desire. So eager was he to join with Potts, the body that was Potts, that he ignored the spasms that started to come again, and barely heard the sad moan that escaped her.

But Eunice Potts knew somehow that it was here, or rather there, where Mothersill now was with massive size, but gentle movements seeking entrance. There. She felt him stop a moment, then continue moving. He stopped again, then hastened back into motion, as if to conceal something from her. Potts fought a desire to reach down and see for herself; she, after all, was always content. She had orgasms easily. She gave herself to the motions of love-making, but continued to feel his bewilderment, a cue somewhere missed.

Strain though he did, Mothersill found himself halted, stopped cold, with most of his penis outside her vagina. He could not figure it, but he moved with her, since it seemed to be all right with her, shifting his weight guardedly lest too much on one side put such a bend in his penis that it'd break. But suddenly he gave up on the puzzle, jettisoned the restraint; his love had come rampaging down. He wanted in, right up to his testicles, to really join with her, to put himself among her inner places. Frantically he began pumping, the evening's drinking goading him on. He snorted, reared back to charge forward, and his penis popped out. He replaced it, grinding his teeth. He gave a mighty pump and Potts barely stifled a scream. Grunting, breathing heavily, Mothersill ranted, "Oh, baby, let me in. Open it up, let me lay it on in there." He sweated as he beseeched. He opened his eyes and saw that he had Potts angled between the wall and the bed, with its recently replaced legs.

"What is it, what's wrong?" she asked, humping backward, leaving him with all his heat and hardness stabbing the air. At the same time she snapped on the light and saw Mothersill's anguished, sweating face upon which was engraved rage mixed with desire. A sob-scream rose from her throat: "No, not again!" Somehow snaking and rolling over the bed, she eluded Mothersill's hands and fled to the bathroom. He was in hot pursuit and would have rammed his penis up anywhere, at racing speed, but he slammed into the locked door.

The impact brought him partially to his senses. He panted and pounded on the door. "Potts, Potts, come on out. What's the matter?"

"Were you in Odell? Did you get *in?*" Her voice was harsh through her sobs and moans. She snatched and tore at her dress, stuffed her bra and pants into her bag.

Mothersill knew she would burst out of the bathroom, rush past him out of the door and perhaps out of his life. He answered, "No, but–"

"Aw, shit!" she shouted. "Shit, shit, *shit!*"

He heard more crying, and he paused in his pounding. He didn't understand, really, but they could work it out, couldn't they? "Potts, it's all right."

"*No!* There's something *wrong* with me."

Frightened now, Mothersill rapped softly on the door. "C'mon, Potts. It'll be all right. You know, don't–" He'd placed both hands against the wall, a posture of weariness and resignation. He closed his eyes, trying to think back to things he'd heard or read about women who had conditions like Potts's where you couldn't get in. He was thinking hard when the door opened and she rushed out, her tears splashing. A second too late Mothersill looked up and moved to stop her, but she straight-armed him in the chest, toppling him off balance, and was gone.

Potts tore down the stairs, ignoring the elevator. She hadn't closed her bag, and her bra and pants, caught in the wind of her rush and flapping against the banister rails, tumbled out upon the carpeted stairs unnoticed.

In the morning, Mrs. Brady would find them and thinking herself discreet would place them in a bag and lean them against Mothersill's door. Outside, Potts screamed for a taxi, ran into the middle of the street unmindful of the squealing tires, the hint of death in the onrushing, blinding headlights. The cabbie took a look at her and knew that if she wanted to go to Lagos, he'd better take her, and without one suggestion of complaint. He listened to her sobs and gnashing teeth and, hurtling toward that part of the city where Puerto Rican, black, the Irish and Italian families lived huddled together in mutual fear, he forgot she was Negro. "It can't be all that bad, lady," he said. "Lady?"

Eunice Potts saw herself as a gross imperfection in a world where the appearance if not the fact of perfection was always being sought. She knew she was good to look at. But that was what acting was all about, looking good and drawing attention; going around things, seeming to be. She was a mess. Odell had been the last chance. She'd made herself believe all this time that with Steve and Philip it'd been something other than sex, cute Steve and handsome Philip who'd waited–she'd made them–until the papers were delivered. A hard thing to do, but she was an actress, after all. Maybe she suspected after Steve? No, before, she told herself. The boys who came and quickly left, never to be seen again except in the street: a brief nod, a twisted smile. . . . But Odell. No waiting for papers with him; what went in Hough didn't go in New York, and she had seen the restlessness growing in him, his peculiar loyalty thinning, fraying around the edges. New York frightened her; she could not bear being lonely, so what was she to do? At least now she *knew;* she couldn't fool herself any longer. She was a screwed-up specimen.

Oh, fuck it all, she thought, recognizing her block, finally, through her tears. She handed the driver the bills in her purse and leaped out of the car as soon as it stopped, leaving the door open. *Inside, you, off the street, out of sight. Get inside your hole and never come out.*

Reaching out of the cold shower for the scalding cup of coffee, Mothersill stopped. He had it, the terms he'd seen over the past four years in case histories, in the agency reports. Fibroids. Fusion of fibers, imperforate hymen. Bands of tissue. No vaginal tract. Anomaly. Big cherry. Still dripping, he rushed to the phone again, but once more, after several rings, it went unanswered. Mothersill ran to dry himself, glancing at the clock. Two-thirty. Where in the hell could she be? Somewhere safe, he told himself, having a cry, but she'd not mentioned the name of one friend in all these months. He dressed and brought his coffee to the phone and dialed again. Potts, he thought, listening to the ring, you cool, ain't you baby? He hung up, worried.

He tried to cheer himself up. It wasn't anything. Some broads rode horses. In other times, coming-of-age rituals for girls included sitting on the lap of a stone male figure with an erect penis, to make sure nothing grew up there. Hell, Potts, they just slit something open or, if they have to, make one, man, make a pussy.

He thought of her husbands as he dialed again. Got their hats and said nothing. Who said spooks weren't cool? Gentlemen. They could have said a lot of bad things. She would have known then. Again there was no answer.

He called Asa. "Hey, Asa, it's me, Odell. Sorry to get you out of bed, but I got a problem. If you can't get it in but so far—oh, an inch, two at the most—would that be because of fibroids, imperforate hymen or something like that? Yeah? *Yeah?*" Mothersill smiled into the phone. "It can be fixed, right? Okay. Thanks. I'm gonna cut you into somethin' good real soon."

As he was about to dial Potts again the phone rang under his hand making him jump. "Hello! Potts! Been trying to—"

She mumbled something.

"What? Baby, I can't *hear* you."

Her voice didn't alter a decibel.

"Potts, what's wrong, what's wrong?"

He slammed down the phone and with a bound was out the door, skidding quickly down the carpeted stairs, his sounds making Mrs. Brady raise up, startled, in her bed. Mothersill hit the street running and shouting for a taxi as he spun around and around in midstride. Luckily, a taxi skreed up and a black face peered at him carefully, then the driver unlocked the door.

"Man you better be careful runnin' down these streets holler ing at this time in the mornin'. You crazy or somethin'? These cops'll kill you first and ask questions later. Git in."

"Look my man, my ole lady's in trouble. Do me fast, will you?"

The cabbie left the front of Potts's building almost as fast as he'd arrived there. If there was going to be any trouble, he reasoned, it was going to have to catch him; damned if he was going to sit and wait for it.

Mothersill tried the downstairs door. Locked. He rang Potts's bell. No answer. He backed up and came at the door with his shoulder, movie images of a hundred heroes smashing doors with one charge alive in his mind. He should have been surprised when the door, fitted with a cheap lock, sprang open with only minimal pain and shock to his shoulder, but he wasn't. He took the stairs three at a time and reached her door panting. He tried the knob and it opened.

Someone's been in and—

His heart pounded loudly in his ears, each beat racing to overtake the previous one. "Potts?" he said, his voice searching out the darkness, his eyes unaccustomed to the dark. He fumbled for the light switch. "Potts?" The mercury switch moved silently under his fingers and abruptly the room was filled with light. He crossed the kitchen alcove, the living room and entered the bedroom, in which he'd never spent a night. "Potts?" His fingers, shaking, climbed over the wall, found still another mercury switch and pushed it.

On the bed, her head hung over its side. Her glazed eyes

slowly and painfully rolled up to the light. Spittle trickled down a corner of her mouth, which was covered with white powder. Mothersill moved toward her and felt things crunching under his feet. Pills, a thousand–sleeping pills?

Jesus, he whispered, and then heard himself saying aloud, "Potts, did you take these? How many? Potts? *Potts?* Can you hear me?" He reached over and slapped her, once, twice, three then four times, his mind racing. Mount Sinai, only a few blocks. He hoisted her to his shoulder and no sooner did he have her settled in one position, than, deadly, she slid into another. He grabbed her legs, angled her over his shoulder and struggled down the stairs. On the street, he bellowed, "Taxi, taxi, taxi," and, receiving no response, started to run.

After only a few paces, pains began stabbing his chest, his legs felt like wooden clubs. The half block to the corner seemed like a mile, but he reached it and, leaning against a lamppost, shouted for taxis again, and watched with growing alarm and anger as they passed him by, speeding up to do so.

Seen from the inside of a cab, Mothersill looked as if he were carrying a corpse or a soon-to-be-one on his shoulder; the drivers kept on going.

"I don't need you," he screamed, and hoisting the leaden Potts into a better position, he huffed, "We gonna make it, baby, you just hang on." He began running again, slue-footedly, angled over, down the street. At Park Avenue he screamed once again at the cabs, but without stopping this time.

Where're the fuckin cops?

Where's everybody?

He heard an occasional car horn, or car tires squealing in protest in a turn. He knew people were looking at him, pointing, from the few cars that rolled by, as if on missions of stealth, but he stumbled on to Madison Avenue, bathing in his own sweat and breathing loudly enough to be heard, he was sure, on Riker's Island. On Madison he turned north; this was slightly downhill. He settled into a pace where he listened only to the sound of his own feet slapping and scraping against the pavement. He was so bent now that he could watch them go down and then up, dragging and skidding on the filthy gray-black walk beneath him. Potts seemed to be pressing all her weight against him. Slap-a-scrape, scrape-slap, slap-a-scrape, scrape-slap, until up ahead in bold black letters, lighted by cold, white neon, he saw the sign: EMERGENCY ENTRANCE.

He started talking to Potts. "C'mone, baby, we got it made. Ole Odell made it. C'mone, honey, things gonna be cool now."

Scrape-a-slap, slap-a-scrape.

As he turned inside, Mothersill's knees went suddenly to water; bile rose to the back of his mouth, brackish, the dregs of steak, salad, liquor, wine a foul mix. He swallowed, forced it back. He had never fainted, but he knew he was close to it; a certain bothersome lightness was speeding toward his mind. The people on the bench he was rubber-legging to were becoming fuzzy, unfocused, but, somehow, they made room and he, clumsily trying to be gentle, dumped her hard nevertheless on the bench, sucking for air. He wobbled to a woman in a uniform sitting behind a desk. "Sleeping pills," he said. "Hurry."

"Name?"

"What?"

"Her name?"

"Eunice Potts." He was steadier now.

"Address?"

"Three seventeen East Eighty-fifth Street. Hurry up, willya?"

"Who're you?"

"A friend."

"Have a seat."

"But—"

"Have a seat, she'll be all right."

"Listen, woman, she took sleeping pills and—"

Her voice was gray and toneless, a recording, a tape, the sound of everyday reality, not spliced into a film sequence. "What's wrong, *qué pasa?*"

"I told you," Mothersill began, spinning about in blind fury and seeing only then the little Puerto Rican woman bleeding from the mouth, her handkerchief already soaked with blood, and also seeing a resignation, a meeting long ago set, being made. This was the person to whom the woman behind the desk was now speaking; he and his woman, the cells of her brain turned off by Nembutal, were already consigned to a numbered role.

He saw that Potts had drawn her legs up under her, as if afflicted by sudden chills. He pulled down her dress, from beneath which he saw the hem of the gown she'd worn. Glancing up, he caught the eyes of two men standing together admiring Potts's legs. They smiled at him.

Mothersill lit a cigarette and sank into the atmosphere of the place with its bawling babies, uniformed guards, silent and suffering adults, patient as the benches upon which they sat, and as immobile and dried. The terror-filled cries of a man with delirium tremens echoed from the back of the room, and in the seat in front of Mothersill, an addict, washed in his own sweat, was sending out a sweet-stale odor, pungent, inescapable.

The benches were emptying slowly; the guards repeated the names the woman behind the desk was calling out. It was almost four when Potts's name was called, another tree in the forest of Picos, Rodriguezs, Flahertys, Browns, Guillermos, Joneses. . . .

"Potts. Eunice Potts."

Chatting about movies: "—Alan Ladd's the baddest—"

"—Widmark, man. Thass a evil sumbitch, that Widmark—"

The two attendants lifted Potts and settled her on the rolling stretcher and pushed her soundlessly away, Mothersill following down the gray, scarred halls, the ass end of Sinai, having nothing to do, almost, with the awnings on the Fifth Avenue side. In the examining room, he gave the essential details to the intern.

"We'll pump her stomach," the intern said. "But in cases like these, you know, suicide attempts, the patient automatically goes to Bellevue for further examination. Psychiatric."

"Oh, that's not necessary—"

"It's the law. You can go with her, if you like."

Mothersill nodded, then settled down to wait. Outside, the darkness wavered; a silver-gray light labored upward. He turned from the window when the intern came back twenty minutes later. "She fought it, God she fought it, but we got it done." He slashed various papers with his signature. "Between you and me," he said, pausing to look at Mothersill, "it's a good thing we've got that law. She needs looking at."

"What do you mean?" Mothersill drew his feet up under him, getting set.

"They're usually different after a pumping than your girl is." He pressed a buzzer and a guard appeared at the door. "Mike, got an ambulance down there?"

"Bellevue?"

"Yes."

"One ready right now, Doc. What've you got?"

"Only onc. Female."

"Okay, I'll get 'em. They can make this run before the shift changes."

The guard, Mike, and the ambulance driver didn't bother to conceal the strait jacket Potts lay in, her eyes glazed, her hair in every direction. Nor had anyone bothered to wipe away the vomit which streamed down the side of the mouth to somewhere inside the jacket. Mothersill wiped it as they went by and threw his handkerchief away when he got inside the ambulance with her. He was too tired to look when the guard locked the door behind them.

Forward through the screened window, Mothersill saw a woman riding shotgun.

"Passed my exam, Joe," she said.

Joe started the engine and shifted gears; the ambulance moved from its place at the ramp into the street. Both Joe and the woman were silhouettes. "Haven't heard about mine, yet," Joe answered. "Hope I made it this time. Got to Tony to make sure there weren't any slip-ups. I need the dough."

"Who doesn't? I'd like to get off this detail," the woman said. "Ridin' up and down, down an up. I never once met a driver who was inclined to rape any of these dogs we usually get."

Joe sighed as he eased into FDR Drive. "That's the law, Martha. Gotta have a woman guard when you've got a woman patient." The vehicle picked up speed as Martha broke out in a harsh laugh. "You call these dogs women, Joe?"

Joe laughed.

Mothersill stroked Potts's hair, leaned forward and kissed her cheek. The odor of vomit was sharp. He didn't want to talk; they would overhear him. He rested his hand on her cheek. Now, over Queens, he could see the sky definitely lightening. The few cars on the drive shot by, headlights on. The early starters for the weekend.

"How about some coffee, we get to the nut house?"

Something in the man's voice made Mothersill turn forward and study both of them again. He could now see that she had a full, square face and gray hair; a big build, the kind he associated with female guards. A drinker, Mothersill guessed, envisioning her in a bar on Saturday nights, loud and raucous, a veritable giant of an Irishman beside her. Joe was small and slight and his features, Mothersill was sure, were bland, ordinary under the cap he was wearing; it was cocked at a purposefully casual angle. Saturday night suave.

"Wouldn't mind a cuppajoe," she said. "Just hit the spot."

Mothersill wondered if they fucked in the ambulances.

"Good deal," Joe said.

After another silence she said, "Wasn't so bad tonight, you know?"

"Naw, Martha, not bad. Every once in a while, even on weekends when you least expect it, things go nice and light. I don't know about you, but this is only my third run tonight."

"I had two others, one with Halpern and one with Palmer."

"Here we go."

Mothersill braced himself as the ambulance veered off the

highway, slowed, then swung up into a driveway. He squeezed Potts's hand and waited for the rear door to be unlocked.

Inside the building, he followed them through at a fast clip feeling the clutch of memories surrounding the Karloff Frankensteins and the Lugosi Draculas, for darkness pierced only by random bits and pieces of light surrounded them, and ancient machinery in hidden corners hissed, snapped and crackled at their passing. Inside a screened-off area, far from everything else it seemed to Mothersill, they stopped at a partition. Joe, Martha and their guide left, drifting back out through the shadows, talking of things real like coffee and raises and the weather.

"Potts," Mothersill whispered, intimidated by the dimness. He stroked her forehead and tried to see where they were.

"Steve? Philip?"

The tiniest chill began at the base of Mothersill's spine. He bent close to her. "*Odell!*" he whispered. "Odell," more gently.

"Who in the hell are you?" she was twisting in her strait jacket to get a better look at him. Her voice fairly smote him with its clear, rational tone; he could recall stories of a hundred black women, perhaps even a thousand, accosted on some corner, some bar, some church social, asking the same question in the same loud, indignant voice.

His brows were furrowing in the darkness, while his mind, sluggish now, reached wearily for the curve that would get to her, even when he knew it wouldn't; so it was with relief that he saw something white move out of the shadows, a jacket, then head, shoulders, skirt, muscular legs. A doctor, he guessed from the papers she held in her hand.

"This Miss Potts?"

"Yes," Mothersill said, suddenly aware of the presence of chairs.

"Yes, let's sit down," the doctor said, taking a chair herself. She crossed a heavy leg and lit a skinny cigar.

"You her boy friend?" she asked with a smile.

He nodded.

"I'll have to check her over thoroughly before I can tell you anything. If you want, you can wait."

"She doesn't know who I am," Mothersill said, looking at Potts accusingly.

"That sometimes happens," the doctor said softly, making Mothersill look up at her; she didn't appear to have much softness in her. "She really tried to do a job on herself. You want to tell me what happened? Were you with her?"

"You're the shrink?" he asked.

She smiled. "Yes, I'm the shrink."

When he was finished, Mothersill noticed for the first time the quiet Saturday morning rumblings of the city waking up. He wondered if married people had their crises during weeknights. One day he'd do a study on the weekend crises in the lives of singles. The psychiatrist looked up from her scribbling. "Okay, you'd better get to the waiting room. They'll call you as soon's she settled."

"How can I get her out?"

She said, "I don't think you can. You're not a legal relative, so you'll have to call someone to come down."

It was another two hours before he could see her. He followed an attendant through the women's ward where gray, disheveled hulks sat on benches humming or cursing, pausing only to glare at him. Others drifted about as if in waking dreams, bare feet skimming the floors.

Potts was in a tiny room all to herself. The one barred and screened window was twelve feet from the floor. She lay small and warped on the cot. The walls looked strange and Mothersill put his hand out to touch them. Padded. This was a padded cell. Inwardly he groaned.

"Hello, Potts," he said.

"Philip—" Tears filled her eyes. "You're back. Why'd you leave? Oh, I don't care why, you're back."

Mothersill moved automatically toward her opened arms, and

felt himself wrapped in them and pulled down to her mouth. "Potts," he said quickly, "it's me, Odell, Odell, baby—"

She opened her mouth and drew his to hers, and he felt her tongue jabbing, the grains of vomit slimy on her tongue. He broke away. "Eunice, it's me, *me*, Odell!"

"Philip, make love to me, love me, love me—" And she began humping on the cot, her arms open, her knees up.

It was cool outside. Taking a bus or a taxi never occurred to Mothersill. He started walking once he was outside the hospital and kept walking down Second Avenue, putting one rubbery leg in front of the other, left, right, as he would've been doing now in Korea had he not been declared 4-F. But his flat feet didn't bother him now.

"Hello, Odell."

He stopped and focused his gaze. He was at Second and Eleventh Street, and he had no idea how long it'd taken him to walk there. The girl looked familiar, the blue of the frames of her glasses almost matching perfectly the blue of her eyes. Ellie. From that party, Marilyn and Marj's. Another of those weekends.

"Ellie," he said. "C'mon, pretty, walk with me."

She seemed to be out for one of those Saturday morning walks, going no place special, inhaling the smell of fruits and vegetables just placed on the stands. Maybe just seeing stores opening up. He felt her at his side. They walked a full block without talking and then he said, "I need to make love. I want to make love. Ellie, I gotta make love." Mothersill turned to look at her and she, smiling small, glanced at him, the near-sighted eyes dilating slightly. She gave him no answer but continued to walk with him, and followed him as he turned into his apartment building.

Mothersill found the brown bag at his door. Puzzled for a moment, he opened it and stared. Potts's bra and panties. The evening rushed back at him and he crumpled the bag shut and opened his door.

Mrs. Brady paused while drinking her morning coffee; with

the second cup she'd read the *Herald Tribune,* having finished the *Times* with the first. She raised her head toward the ceiling as if the motion would help her to imagine better or to hear more clearly the muffled bumping, thumping noises that were coming from upstairs.

Upstairs, her breath returning to normal, the quiverings of her body stilling, Ellie thought she felt tears running slowly from Mothersill's already closed eyes; a deep intake of breath and the first of many soft rumblings to come told her that he was asleep already.

There are mills and odds-and-ends factories in some of the buildings in the Village. But the machines are not running this Saturday morning and the area is hushed, almost soundless as a vacuum empty and waiting to be filled, the silence broken only by great trailer trucks thundering over bricked roads where once John Jacob Astor walked with shifty eyes from his home in the Colonnades.

Mothersill sleeps, his tears drying, like one who wishes this sleep to be the access to a quiet death. But his snores are like the howls of one—the sower—gripped in terror as he strides off the edge of a gigantic cliff and finds himself falling, falling through a space filled with flying seed.

Ellie turns on her breasts and studies him, his color, and she marvels at the fullness of his lips; they are fuller than hers. She is pleased at the used, fully touched sensation that persists between her legs. Ellie turns on her back and tries to drift toward sleep. It does not seem so odd now.

Not odd any longer that she's made love with a man she's met only once before; not odd that he's black.

I need to make love. More than sex implied. She thinks now how he handled her in his embrace, as though he were making love to someone else, and Ellie envied her first, then assumed her place, moving as she imagined the other would have had she been there. The cause of his tears? Her eyes roll toward the brown bag.

It is very quiet in this apartment. Ordinarily she'd be with the children, but she came awake at the crack of dawn and rushed out, unable to go through with it. Their glazed eyes, rubbery necks and oversized heads; the froth on their mouths. She hears herself screaming inside and changes position in the bed. Next week, as usual. They cannot expect her to face them each and every week for the rest of their lives. They cannot expect her to accept the taint as being hers. What about him? Him, gone now, like one fleeing a whore with syphilis. Your genes are rotten, he said with departure, with your fat lips and that kinky hair and that skin. . . .

Voices out of childhood. Whispers. Giggles. Sniggles. What would it have been like if the Waffenbergs had not been filthy rich? They drove me to you, didn't they? she thinks, touching Mothersill. *Could* it be possible?

She seems to have needed people all her life, protection against the second stares of strangers who didn't know her. Parents, girl friends. Boy friends always wanted to do it with her right away; they never waited with her the way they did with other girls who didn't look the way she did. Then Lawrence. He wants you just for the money her father said, over and over. Still they married. Then came Theodore. Just one of those things, Dr. Korbin said. Try again. I'll guarantee . . . Then came Amy. I don't understand, Dr. Korbin said. Maybe you and Larry—maybe you'd better not have any more children.

Lawrence. Never sees the kids. Never sends them anything. For him they never happened and if they haven't happened neither has Ellie Waffenberg.

Her eyes glaze with sleep. Maybe I've happened, she thinks.

"I love you," Mothersill says. "Potts, I love you." He says it each time he visits her, says it over and over as a Catholic would repeat Hail Marys hoping that the universe in all its mystery, his words being quietly accepted by it, will make the great appeal to her wandering reason.

He spends hours consulting with his doctor friend, Asa, who sends him to the specialist who can perform the operation Potts needs.

But, Potts's father has moved to New York for the time being. He turns his back every time he meets Mothersill in the hospital and will not talk to him on the phone except to curse him and will not see him. Mothersill cannot explain the problem and even if he could, he doesn't dare. Mr. Potts, although a judge in some obscure court, looks like one of those black gentlemen good with a switchblade. Fathers are lovers of their daughters, he knows, and thus does not pursue the point of providing information, advice or assistance. Even the doctors cannot talk to Mr. Potts, and Mothersill understands. Mr. Potts has helped to make this vegetating creature, and he, a little god, like most parents, will not admit to imperfections in his own clay.

In the spring, the sun hovering over a greening Manhattan, Grand Royale canceled, Mothersill spends a final two hours with Potts saying nothing but, "I love you. I love you. I love you." Surely, he thinks, as his mouth goes dry, some beneficent African spirit will hear him, that *something* in his raging need of her in sound mind and body will come to his aid. "I love you, I love you, I love you."

This while she looks at him as if he were an object placed in her room for her to figure out: some psychologist's puzzle. Since that night she has not suffered his touch without screaming. He merely pleads with his eyes, wills her to be instantly well, to become the miracle of Havenhurst Clinic.

Yes, they can do the operation on her; it is nothing, they say. A flick of the knife. The channel's there. No need to graft one in. Just a flick of the knife. But they can't open her mind as easily. "I love you, Potts."

Then he hears them in the hall: Mr. Potts, the attendants, Asa. She will be driven to the airport and flown to Hough. Maybe the presence of familiar objects and people might help. "I don't want you to go. I love you."

Asa calling. Potts smiles politely and twists in her chair, and the two hours are gone, just as quietly as they'd come. The spirits, African or otherwise, have not responded. At night Mothersill dreams of the sower frozen in stride, some feet above the earth, his eyes buttons, and his nose, his mouth a down-curving line: a scarecrow, straw emerging from his fly; dreams of him sightless and motionless, whether day or night.

"I didn't know," Asa said, "until you called me." He looked across the table at Mothersill. The soft music—the wrong kind of music—Asa reflected, filled the restaurant. Mothersill framed a smile, the kind brave men in films do when overwhelmed by adversity.

"Yes, well," Mothersill said.

"She seemed like a fine woman," Asa said. This of course was not the time for street-hip synonyms like fine chick or groovy broad. They'd never talked about their affairs anyway.

Mothersill nodded. "Is there any chance of, you know, her getting better?"

Asa raised his drink, then set it down. "Sure. There's always that chance. Could be tomorrow, could be years. It'd be easier if—if—" Asa McDaniels raised his drink again and swallowed the whole glass. "Look, Odell. Sex is dirty business in this country. I mean, man, we *like* it, but too many people think it's special, think—"

"I know all that," Mothersill said with a wave of his hand.

Asa plunged on. "Okay, you know all that. But are your concerns still for Potts or are they for yourself? Man, you've had a rejection to end all rejections, if you want to break it down to a basic level. Whether because of a physical deformity or not, you have been rejected. How do you feel about that?"

"Oh, man, it wasn't her fault."

"I know it. So do you. But do your emotions understand that?"

Mothersill finished his drink and waved for another round. "You're trying to psych me, Asa. I'm not a client."

"Shit, ever since you joined the Good Shepherd you've been a half step away from being a patient, man. Everybody there. You think you can work in a setup like that without it affecting you? Sure, I'm trying to find out where your head is at. You love Potts. But Potts doesn't even know who you are. She's wrestling in her own private pit, thinking that maybe, because that thing's closed up tight anyway, she's not supposed to do it ever, with anybody. And she's drawn down the curtain. The act is over. Her father says no to the knife; he compounds nature's little joke. And who in the hell knows anyway, how she'd react to returning to her senses and finding that she could do it if she wanted to? Maybe she'd ask for a cell in the cellar of the nut house. If she had the operation. I'm lying to you, man. Potts has some long treatment in front of her. Every speck of dirt combined with sex has to be dredged out of her. She's got to start thinking one day that laying up is the healthiest goddamn thing that ever came down the pike. Then she'll have the operation; then she'll be okay."

"I thought I could get out there and see her from time to time—"

"From time to time," Asa repeated, picking up his second drink. "How can I say no? I'm not her doctor. You remember this, Odell: as far as she's concerned, you were the catalyst for her incarceration, for the discovery. And she is not going to like you, man. Not today, not next week and maybe not next year. She's going to have to do it alone; there's no other way.

"But what about you? Yeah, love and guilt all mixed up in the hopper. You drove her to the asylum, penance for the rest of your life—these things *happen*, Odell. I've known guys who had labor pains when their wives were about to deliver. The mind is a powerful thing, man. But in the final analysis, the wives had to deliver alone. You can have labor-guilt feelings—you're having them now. But Potts has got to come back alone. And you've got your work to do, these kids that have to be looked after, and Mifflin wants you to take some time off from the agency to get yourself together."

"I thought that's what this was all about," Mothersill said.

"Okay?"

"Hell, yes. But, about seeing Potts."

"Why don't you let her get in touch with you when she's ready? You can always check with your sister to see how she's getting on."

"How's the practice going?" Mothersill asked. It was time to change the subject; he'd got the message.

"A little slow, but growing. I look forward to the time when I can cut the Good Shepherd loose altogether. I'm not complaining." He looked steadily at Mothersill. "You're not going to spend the rest of your life there, are you, man?"

Mothersill glanced away. "I—well—you know, Potts, I guess we were going to make some plans."

"Not good for the head, that place," Asa said. "Those two chicks that got sliced up; that kid who burned up his folks in Nassau County—there's always something. Not good. Think about it." Asa rose.

"Let's have a drink sometime, or lunch," he said.

Mothersill smiled. "Want to check me out again, huh?"

"Naw, nothing like that. Take it easy, hear? And think about getting your hat. These kids'll break your heart."

Part Three

MOTHERSILL HAD LIKED it earlier, the way she snuggled up to him, plucking at his elbow and smiling toward the dance floor. But now, in their fifth club, he was beginning to tire of her, of what she was, of the way the night was becoming filled with those unctuous, dark, Caribbean smiles, a fine mix of envy and the sardonic; smiles that measured him against the smilers; smirks, they were, and they assured him beyond a doubt that he was about to become one more black penis stuck up the empire.

He smiled at her. "I'm a little tired, Minerva."

She pouted and picked up her daiquiri with a grandiose motion. Maybe it was a planter's punch. The drinks were beginning to sound and taste the same. Still he could pause from his own drinking to marvel at the soft blackness of the night, the wafting scents of the rich island earth, the smell of the sea, the distant, hilltop lights in the homes of the wealthy, the cruise ships in the harbor, their masts strung with lights.

So this was Grand Royale.

"See that laddie over there?" Minerva pointed, her finger a small splinter of white in the club's darkness. She spoke over the music of the steel-drum band. "He's bucking for premier when and if independence ever gets here."

"Good evening, Lady Minerva."

Her hand flashed in greeting. Mothersill glanced up, but the man had sidled off into the darkness toward the bar.

"You know everybody, Minerva."

She smiled and brought her long face with its thin nose and wide mouth close to him. He'd found her attractive with these British features and graying hair. Nude he'd imagined she would be lumpy, skinny on top and have one of those sad, dropped, pear-shaped British behinds.

"Why, Dr. Mothersill. You *are* noticing."

"Why, yes. It's kind of hard not to." The "doctor" sounded like stale mush coming out of her mouth. It was as if she was secretly laughing at it, and therefore dismissing those hours of classroom work and the study, the exhaustion that suffused his entire being at the weeks' ends. Between the Good Shepherd and shuffling over the Washington Square Park campus, the myriad lectures and projects, and, finally, the dissertation, he had earned it, having grown thinner in the process and positive that the society cared only for children when it was forced to. The more he came to know, the greater were society's failures. The Ph.D. had led him away from the Good Shepherd.

But before, he had been deeply into it, sure that Aichorn and Healy and Anna Freud and Lasker, certain that Aldrich and Ames and Gesell and Piaget, would show him the way, the true light. He had hoped and worked. And this woman—

He saw that she was studying him. They'd only met four hours earlier, at the Blue Whelk, and he'd been on the island only four days.

"You Americans," Minerva said resignedly, gesturing. Out of the milling people glided the waiter.

"The same, Lady Minerva?"

"Yes, Todd and Dr. Mothersill, too, I believe. No, Odell?"

"Yeh, sure. The one for the road."

"And your nightcap?"

The waiter was one of those young, clean-cut men processed every year into the Caribbean tourist trade; not too black, not too brown; somewhere in between. "Nightcap?" Mothersill said. "I guess I won't have one tonight."

Minerva took her fresh glass. "Perhaps you'll change your mind."

"Can I drop you off after this drink?" he asked. Lady Minerva Wadsworth-Price made hints like the collapse of a building. Black eyes, Mothersill thought. She'd quit her mist-girded islands to move to one of the hearts of darkness. No more student soirées or dinners for the Africans or West Indians studying at the London School of Economics; no more teas for the lower-level diplomats from those same overexploited countries.

"But of course you can drop me home, Odell. I just may have some of that Barbancourt you haven't been able to find. A hundred years ago when this island was French you'd have no trouble. But this, dear boy, is now a British island."

"Is that the problem?"

"It's not really," she said. "Some of us have Barbancourt."

"Well, I don't mind the Cockspur."

She said with a smile, "Interesting name though, isn't it, Cockspur?"

Mothersill glanced across the bar and said, "Yeh. It does have a certain ring to it." He caught the waiter's eye. "Look," he said. "If you'd rather stay, Minerva, I'll just get along to my cottage."

"Oh, I'm finished." She swallowed her drink in a gulp. "See?"

She took his arm as they passed to the outer patio and, as smoothly as the breezes that came and went through the open club, he felt the eyes of the men in the club slipping over them.

"Taxi?"

"Taxi, sir?"

"Hello, Lady Minerva."

As stolid as the night the drivers and their cars hung to the edges of the dim club lights. Here and there the presences of the drivers were betrayed by their glowing cigarettes.

"Hello, Isaac. Walter. Clifford. How are you?"

One led them to a car and opened the door. Mothersill saw that he was grinning thinly. When the driver got in himself he said, "Well, Lady Minerva, where to, the Regatta Club, Pink Lobster, Fire Tower—"

"Just home, Walter. Wouldn't you say, Odell?"

Before Mothersill could answer, the car was started, put into gear and was in motion. "Walter, this is Dr. Mothersill from the Mainland."

"Very happy to meet you, Dr. Mothersill. First time down?"

"Yes," Mothersill said.

"Fine, fine place, sir. They'll tell you about Barbados and Jamaica and Grenada and all those places, but Grand Royale, it is the very best."

"It is a lovely place." Minerva took his hand and placed it on her thigh.

"Down for long, if I might ask?"

"Two or three weeks. Haven't decided." He glanced at Minerva, then back to the mirror.

"You'll come back, man. I'm tellin' you. Lady Minerva, now. She came all the way from England to make Grand Royale her home. Yessir, and has not regretted it one moment, right, Lady Minerva?"

Mothersill wondered just how often Walter had carried his Lady Minerva home drunk from a round of the clubs.

"We mustn't rush him, Walter. He's a quiet one."

Walter chuckled. "Oh, he's an all right fellow though, Lady Minerva. Walter can tell."

They sped over the narrow roads, passing in a sudden flash of headlights people walking along the edges. The city dropped farther down behind them as they climbed and curved around hills.

"All the drivers know where I live," Minerva offered, as if reading Mothersill's mind. "I just get in and away we go."

Mothersill patted her hand. "That's obviously one of the advantages of being so well known."

When they arrived at her home, which sat squat and forbidding, an anomaly here where patios, sliding glass doors and picture windows were ordinary, she said, "Thank you, Walter," and started to get out still holding Mothersill by the hand.

"Wait, Walter," Mothersill said, looking past Minerva's startled expression.

She pulled him away from the cab. "Oh, pay him, do, and send him on off, Odell."

"I think I'll ride home with him, Minerva."

Her hand tightened on his wrist. "One more rum at least."

"No, thanks," he said.

She smiled through clenched teeth and came close to him. "You'll spoil my record, Odell. Everybody on the island knows that the man I drink with is the man I make love with."

Mothersill listened to Walter's engine running tinnily in the night.

Minerva tossed her head and jutted her chin. "Of course they know. D'ya think I care?"

Wearily he said, "I just don't feel like it, Minerva."

"You mean not with me."

He tried to loosen her grip on his wrist.

"Okay then."

"I'll go with you," she said, and he began to catch the leading edge of her panic.

"Oh, Minerva," he said more gently than he could have ten years before, "it's not *where*. I don't want to make love with you."

She said in a rush, "I can do all sorts of things Odell, and I'm good at them."

Walter's engine ran on, little flicking noises in it making it sound like a time bomb.

A lifting wind played with Minerva's hair. She should be on a moor, he thought, or a heath, and I should be the gardener or the groundskeeper.

"Then tell me why," she said, the urgency and pleading in her voice hardening to resignation.

"Oh, it's too long a story."

"The others?"

Mothersill shrugged. The others. Hell you could use it but it'd never wear out. But he said, "I guess so."

She seemed strangely calmed now. "Suppose they'd all been white?" She smiled at his hesitation.

"But they weren't. And it would have made about the same difference."

He walked her to the door. "Night."

She seemed not to have heard him. "I need someone," she said absently. "I *need* someone."

On the way to his cottage Mothersill parried Walter's intrusions with grunts and single words until finally, parked by Mothersill's driveway, he said, "I tell you something, man. I glad to see you, a black man, turn that woman down. She may be high class and a lady and all that right from England, but she is a whore. Naw, she don't sell it, she gives it away, left and right, the way a black woman would never do, man, never."

Mothersill paid Walter and went through his gate to his cottage. He could feel the winds blowing strongly in from the sea and hear the waves shattering against the foot of the bluff upon which his house sat.

Walter turned around and, whistling, removed a bottle of Glenfiddich from under the front seat, and drove rapidly back to Lady Minerva's.

"Ah," she said, smiling at him as he held the bottle up before him. "I thought it was Dr. Mothersill returning. But do come in, Walter, and hand over that lovely bottle."

WWwwwwyaww! EEEeeeYaww! The sound of the mule rode on the morning breeze parenthesized by the slapping of the palm leaves and the now muted roar of waves pounding against the cliffside. Down where his driveway joined the main road, Mothersill could hear traffic—lorries and motor bikes rushing by. And he heard the voices calling out, the words rapid, the pitches falling or rising rapidly; they reminded him of Africa. And, indeed, were not these islands the remnants of peaks of old mountains, a halfway house to Africa? Had not the slave ships, their sails billowing full of the south and northeast tradewinds, heaved to in these bright blue harbors? Halfway houses from the ports of the Bight of Benin, Biafra, Guinea to those of New Orleans, Charleston and Savannah?

Looking from the patio he saw a catamaran, a three-master and a few tiny fishing boats already moving into open sea. The wind blew softly against his face as he drank his coffee. From such a hilltop as this, he thought, surely two hundred years ago men stared eastward, awaiting the arrival of slave ships that moved in the path of the sun.

He poured another cup of coffee and grimaced as his thoughts moved back over last night. He had not told Walter nor Minerva quite the truth; he did not know them and felt he owed them nothing. This was not his first trip to the islands. He had come to Grand Royale directly from St. Thomas, where he had been in charge of training PeeCeeVees. The last group had been trained for service in Ethiopia, one of the places he'd most enjoyed. His assignment being completed on St. Thomas, he'd come to Grand Royale on whim. It would be the Washington office for a while, and then he'd see. But this place, he mused. Perhaps something remained of it that would've been there a dozen years ago, the time when he and Potts were to have come.

The children.

He would have been concerned with the children then. But, perhaps, his having joined the Peace Corps as a director of specialized recruiting placed him back with the kids, except that they were older and so was he. It had been a natural step after nearly a decade with the Good Shepherd and the doctoral studies, a kind of growth, a harmony with the world. For, winging on the crest of the words of Kennedy, words coupled with an action no President before him had been able to mount, the Peace Corps became fact, and thousands of youngsters, passing through the PeeCeeVee training center on St. Thomas, had been sent overseas, their enthusiasm, skills and hopes, however (and this was a later assessment) unable to make a dent in the premises set down by Western colonialism. But, before that assessment was set down there was the fire, the image come true of kids swelling over African and South American mountaintops, of the young pushing through the valleys to help strangers. And the black young were among them, and Mothersill himself had been fired up. "We belong over there," he told the young audiences. "Maybe we have a future there, but you'll never know until you go and help the brothers and sisters." He left the razzle-dazzle to the ex-football players the Kennedy administration had a penchant for. Their pitch was going to play ball; a challenge, can you score, not only the touchdown, but the extra point, and the young blacks got up and went. Specialized recruiting: hustling the young blacks for the PeeCeeVees. There were his own trips, there, of course, the wading through the hot blasts of Africa, witnessing the birth of the term "culture shock," and more understanding it and helping the kids to get past it, *into* its past. The world had blunted itself against Africa for five thousand years, he'd told them, sweating in their tents. It had taken for five thousand years, and they, the black PeeCeeVees—he was not always sure about the white ones—were making the first step to put something back into the continent. The Hyksos (he did not tell them that they might have been black; no one knew for sure) the Assyrians, Greeks, Romans, the Arabs, the Europeans from Iberia and north and then the Europeans again, all had taken and were taking still. Maybe he did too good a job recruiting, for, finally, they sent him to St. Thomas, in charge of training.

Mothersill now closed his eyes and put his feet up on another chair; it was good to slow down, to have outdistanced most of the ghosts in his life. Ghosts and foxes, sometimes one and the same. Potts would have looked good sitting across the table from him, he thought.

He got up and carried his dishes into the kitchen. Maybe he should have stayed at a hotel where all the services were taken care of. Mothersill washed his dishes and made his bed, wondering if this was a good day to search for old slave cemeteries. He'd found none in the U.S. or British Virgin islands; yet, in many of the older graveyards some of the markers were over 150 years old. In the white graveyards.

There had been slaves in those places, and some of them had been "broken" and sent north to the States. Nearly every island's tourist material mentioned sites where rum had been made from cane sugar, but few mentioned slavery. The material did not possess a sense of anger or even outrage at the past; no warning that whites owed this and other islands' blood. In fact, the four-colored brochures were written as if that past had not even existed.

Yes, search for slave cemeteries. It was possible none existed; people did not advertise crimes.

Yes. Forsake the beaches, which would start to fill in another hour or so. Just crossing the horizon Mothersill saw another brightly painted cruise ship heading for Grand Royale. By midday her passengers and others from the ships already in and those tourists who'd flown in for a longer stay would be crawling through town or over the beaches. Groups of calypso singers would weave in and out among people lying on the sand, serenading them and bowing low in thanks for the gift of each American dollar; women selling spices and straw hats would prowl up and down the sand, their huge behinds and larger breasts intimidating the visiting women, they being a profusion of Saat Jees; the visiting women would flash their American smiles, flex their slow-browning legs, legs and bodies that never would become as solid and black as the flesh they sought to some safe degree to imitate, and buy the spices and straw hats. Little black boys would scurry up into the coconut palms for their fruit, and middle-ancient black men, frizzles of gray curling on their heads, would take the coconuts, rend them from their layers of fibers and shells with their razor-sharp machetes. The white milk would first be offered up by their black, hard-gnarled hands, then the meat of the fruit. Some tourists would walk away thinking how kind the natives were; others, hesitating for seconds, would deposit finally some money into the hands, sculptured pieces in their own right, held as they were limply, but with a reserve of strength, cunning and guile somehow present. . . .

The scenes would be repeated and repeated across one beach and down another, each group playing a role so old that new ones could hardly be devised.

He would go to the beach later, when the cruise ships were steaming out and the sun passed over the mountains and began to settle into the sea.

Mothersill does not know what to do with time that does not have to be occupied. Seldom in the past twelve years have his date books not been filled to overflowing: things to do, people to see, trips to make. So he is now, with a plan for the day in mind, content. He moves swiftly about the small cottage, fringed with palms, pea plants and flamboyants and hibiscus, seizing swim trunks, in case he finds a private beach or lake, a map. Then he fills a thermos with ice and water, removes bread, beer and cheese from the small refrigerator and goes out to the car.

He does not drive the rented Ford Cortina at night. On Grand Royale there is left-side drive and the roads are bad and the drivers far surer of their skills than they have a right to be. He has driven in many countries and was always sure of himself. That confidence was swiftly eroded one night on the Ibadan-Lagos road when he was run off the highway and into a stream that was, luckily, mostly dried up. He knows now that Spanish, Italian and most African and Caribbean drivers are more related than they ever could imagine. But it is morning now and his fears rest.

He wonders, as he tools out of his driveway and pauses at the main road, how Minerva is. Not hearing the crescendoing buzz of a motor bike or the clattering of a bus or a car or truck, Mothersill roars onto the highway, heading toward Tutubonga. Minerva. No good shacking up with women you might happen to feel sorry for. One of the important things he'd learned in past years. Because all that sympathy became swollen gristle and blood and then was past. And every woman had her thing. The attractive ones never tried to awaken your sympathies; they didn't have to. For the lonely ones, making you feel sorry for them was just as much their way of getting you into bed as it was the foxes' way to have you chase them into it. Sorry for their loneliness, their problems, their looks. Ellie, finally, had made him understand. He wondered where she was now. Gone with those years that saw him tearing his doctorate out of time, filling every second of it with work and study and some of it with her. Had to keep busy then. Important not to think, but to fill that wound in the mind with matter, that emptiness in the body with the warmth of still another body.

About a mile away Mothersill slows and picks up a young girl.

"I'm going to Tutubonga," he says. "That okay?"

"Yes, sir," she says, not looking at him. Ah, my people, he thinks.

Wherever he'd been in Africa, too many Africans called him "master." It first shocked, then infuriated him. Then the fact that it simply was, "master," historically, linguistically but mainly economically, settled about him, like an old suit he could not remove. Africans of one class themselves, allowed the term to be addressed to them, by members of a lesser class.

Oh, fuck! Mothersill thinks. Maybe she's just being polite to an elder. He recalls that he went through a period as a child when every man was "sir" and every woman "ma'am." Relax. That's what you're here for.

"Nice day," he says, and glances at her.

"Yes, sir. Every day is nice here."

"I guess so."

They sweep along a narrow asphalt road between rows of banana trees; up ahead Mothersill sees a mass of royal palms, standing up to forty or fifty feet.

"Go to school?" he asks.

"No. No more."

Mothersill nods. Yes, she is about that age, straddling girl and young womanhood.

He has not seen too many kids her age in school uniforms; they tend to be younger. What do they do here when they leave school? What's here for them to do? Mothersill sees himself, a little black boy, a native of Grand Royale or half a hundred other islands, growing up, the rain pelting the corrugated tin roof of his home; his mother protects his school uniform not only from the rain, but from mildew. His father's on the beach trying to milk the tourists without losing dignity; Mothersill sees himself growing into larger and larger school uniforms until one day there is neither school nor suit. Where then does he go? Into the kitchens or dining rooms of the hotels where the mainlainders pay outlandish sums of money to soak up the sun, gobble up the rum and, if they wish, rub black flesh? Or maybe he goes to the bars where he can be seen and therefore chosen, quite possibly by one of those women with varicose veins whose eyes can never be seen behind blue-black sunglasses. A taxi driver? Cane or banana farmer? Fisherman?

Mothersill glances again at the girl beside him. It would be worse for her. Baby-sitting for the tourists, if she's lucky, or cleaning and attending to their vacation cottages. More than likely the babies, the washtub, the scrubboard; the long bus rides to the central market. An entire life of mountains, bush and water, filled with others who come and go by silver plane or white cruise ship, passing like water through her fingers, leaving them empty but totally aware that they'd been touched.

"This is Tutubonga," the girl says as they crest a mountain and find themselves on a main street. The street contains a bus stop, a gas station, a two-by-four post office and a store. People turn to stare boldly at them, the men's eyes wry with the humor of their kind, the women's insinuating.

Mothersill drives off, a despair he has known since Africa settling within him like heartburn. The world seemed better from the office of the agency, was indeed better until Potts sent him reeling out into it. He swings too wide into a curve half-concealed by the wide banana leaves, but is not concerned;

he has seen or heard nothing coming. But, suddenly it *is* there, a truck, a rushing Mercedes-Benz loaded with bananas, comes hurtling from behind the leaves and Mothersill sees in slow motion, almost, the yellow-green fruit upon the stalks, the light gray, battered mass of metal, the dented grill, the expressions of horror on the faces of the driver and his rider, and he swings the wheel over, tromping the accelerator and bursts off the road, threading with great noise through the banana trees closest to the road; then he swings back and is bumped to the road again. He is untouched by the truck; the truck is untouched by him and both continue without stopping.

Mothersill found himself chuckling even though his hands trembled on the steering wheel. He drove slowly for a time, not believing he had escaped the kind of death he had seen in other parts of the world, deaths so brutally meted out and so casually witnessed. The games we play with these killing toys of white men, he thought, remembering the Sudan.

He had been riding to the museum in Khartoum where the relics of the Mahadi wars against the British were displayed. Some instinct made him look up. The driver, teeth bared, was driving head-on toward a car which was trying to pass another. For seconds hypnotized and unbelieving, Mothersill watched as the two vehicles sped toward each other.

"No," he said aloud to the driver. The driver was in a trance. "No!" Mothersill shouted, and his pent-up fear, converted into energy, raced into the arm with which he reached over and smacked the driver on the side of the head. The driver slowed instantly and gave the oncoming car a chance to pass safely.

Mothersill slowed to enter and pass through the town of Petit Nantes, bouncing over the sleeping sentries, a series of bumps built up in the road to make speeding hazardous, and with the approach of noon he came to Plantation St. Anne, marked on the maps as a tourist attraction. As he entered the rubble-strewn driveway, a small group of young women passed him. He waved;

their smiles were shy and retreating. Where's that bold black look? he thought.

One of them had reminded him of Phyllis, Malone Lincoln's wife. What's become of Lincoln? he wondered as he braked to a stop and turned off the ignition. Africa always did that to him, too. He'd see a face and it would remind him of someone at home, someone he'd grown up with or knew later. Strange. With the laughter of the young women drifting off in the distance and silence starting to settle over the smoke-blackened remnants of walls, Mothersill heard Lincoln's voice: ". . . they glow in the dark, man, like fine silver." He had paused then said, "Now you take Phyllis. She's so black you can't even *see* her in the dark."

Mothersill hoped Phyllis, if she was still married to Lincoln, never found out that her husband preferred the Lady Minervas of the world to her.

He took the food and beer and prowled around the walls, trying to ascertain the layout of the plantation and where a cemetery most likely would have been placed. The tourist material said: "*One of the oldest plantations of the island, St. Anne's was built in 1750. Thousands of barrels of molasses and rum were produced here every year. These were carried to the American colonies and to England.*"

After dropping off the slaves. Or with the slaves. People still believed in magic. Don't talk or write about things and they will cease to exist and perhaps never did. If you don't talk about Moses being born in Africa, he wasn't an African. A reedian? Found floating in reeds?

Mothersill had passed cemeteries along the road, but they were for the whites, with stones bearing old Scotch, English and French names, and they all seemed to be on hillsides overlooking the ocean, as if the bones, once the word was given, could break out and fly away, to heaven presumably, their launching positions being better located than others buried at sea level.

Plantation St. Anne was completely grown over and he could

not begin to guess where the slaves had been buried. He cursed while he ate and stumbled through the underbrush. Not even the blacks kept records, yet hundreds, most likely thousands, of slaves had worked here. Now they were gone without a trace, as if they'd conspired with the writers of the tourist brochures to produce a void.

Standing hip-deep in the brush sipping and munching, he heard the warm winds sifting through the rain forests and the distant breathing of the sea; he heard birds singing and mongooses chittering. Gone, all of it, if there'd ever been a cemetery. Of course there'd been a cemetery. The whites gave them that, and when the blacks were finally laid in their graves at least the plantation owners no longer worried about the uprisings that came and went on these islands as regularly as the seasons.

There were white slaves, too.

Yeah. Well, if they didn't care about them, and they surely didn't, you couldn't expect them to care about us. Besides, of a hundred million, they were a drop in the bucket. Everyone knows minorities don't count, never did.

Mothersill's was to have been a journey of personal discovery, a coming-upon in a secret place of African burial items, carvings, sculptures, strange signs, stranger words. He flung his beer can, his second, into the undergrowth and listened to it tinkling against the limbs and leaves. A tinkling and then silence. Maybe that was the way it all is.

Forty-five minutes later, between the walls of a ranging green valley, the car engine gave a bark, shuddered and stopped. Mothersill cut the ignition and got out. The vast silence was like being under water; it surrounded and seemed to impede him. The view beneath the car hood was unenlightening; he touched what was touchable, twisted what he could reach, then tried to start the car again. When it kicked over and died again he returned to his seat, opened another can of beer and studied his map. First he frowned at it, then scowled, then spat, "*Shit!*" He'd taken a wrong turn and was now halfway between St.

Anne's, where there'd been no service station, and Pont Noir; he could not be sure there was a station there either, and besides, it was twenty miles away. Looking up he saw no telephone or power wires over the road; in fact, he'd not seen a house since leaving St. Anne's.

But, he reasoned, this was a road and sooner or later someone would be driving on it. At first he got out and paced up and down some distance from the car, trying to hear the sound of an oncoming car engine through the silence. Giving up, he returned to the car and fell asleep.

Terrence and Melanie Holdenfield rode without speaking, their Mercedes-Benz sedan gently blowing conditioned air upon them. They appeared to have been stamped from the same mold except for color. Both were tall for islanders, and tending toward thinness, and both were extraordinarily handsome, with their carefully shaped heads, nose bridges, lips and cheekbones. She was jet black; he was café-au-lait colored.

The Holdenfields were natives of the island, had studied in England, and traveled on the Continent and in the United States. Like the car in which they rode, they appeared to locals on the roads to be sleek, purring with an almost noiseless power. Dressed with studied casualness, they nevertheless exuded a wealth unusual for natives of Grand Royale. Others of their class were most careful that their dress and style did not excite any undue jealousy on the part of those beneath them. There were already too many groups forming, splinters of those in America, vowing to break free from England; the Caribbean for the Caribbeans, they said. Melanie and Terrence Holdenfield agreed. But the *proper* Caribbeans, like themselves . . .

They waited, as their forebears had done, for the proper time, the proper deal. They were the people who held the land and sold it to the onrushing hordes of mainlanders; they were the people who were warmly greeted in the secret clubs, set in coves, for whites; they were the people who pushed forward the candidates for the offices that would come with independence.

While they waited for the confluence of events, they grew bored, and today their boredom had reached unbearable points. They were between guests—they were always coming—from New York, London, Paris and a dozen other places in the world. Otherwise they would have rushed past Mothersill's car without a second glance. On Grand Royale stalled cars were the norm, junk as they were from Britain's network of crooked used-car dealers. Besides, the car was rented, Holdenfield could tell by the tag, and the driver might be a visitor from another country, one who could be properly impressed with them, their home and their fun-and-games.

Mothersill's sleep had not been deep. He came awake instantly when the sound of the Holdenfields' car reached him. He was awake when it stopped and sitting up, staring at Melanie Holdenfield when her husband's door opened on the other side. In the background Mothersill noticed that the shadows had shifted, but mainly he gazed at the smiling woman in the car. She moved slightly and her window slid down. "Hello," she said. Almost at the same time he saw the slender, light-skinned man, adjusting a Gucci scarf at his neck, leaning into his car window. "I say there, old boy. You seem to be having a spot of bad luck. What is it?"

Mothersill moved his eyes from the woman to the man. "I don't know. The engine just quit." His eyes rolled past the man back to the woman, whose smile, though she was not looking at him, indicated that she knew she was the focal point of his gaze.

The man's long, tapered hand came down on the window with a soft bang. "Well, fellow, that's Grand Royale for you; mostly nothing works. Tell you what we'll do: we can take you to our home and call a service lorry. I can tell you now that it won't be out until tomorrow morning, but it will *be* here then. I'll see to that." The man smiled at Mothersill.

"So you be our guest tonight." He thrust his hand inside. "I'm Terry Holdenfield. That lovely creature there is my wife, Melanie."

Mothersill thought quickly. There was nothing else to do. And the man hadn't offered to drive him back to Cité Grand Royale. In any case, what was back there? He might profit from spending the night as a guest of the Holdenfields; come to know a little bit more about the island than was otherwise possible. He smiled up at Holdenfield and extended his hand.

"Dr. Mothersill," he said. "Odell Mothersill." The man's accent had put Mothersill on the defensive.

"Good show, old man," Holdenfield was saying, gripping Mothersill's hand. "Let's get your things. There. Just driving around?"

"Yes."

"Oh, you won't have to lock it up, Doctor. If anyone comes down this road, they won't bother it."

"How do you do?" the woman said, turning in her seat as Mothersill climbed into the back of their car.

"Dr. Mothersill, dear," Holdenfield said. "You're an American," he went on, starting the car. "New York?"

"That's right."

"Did you hear that, Melanie? New York. We love New York, London, too, of course, and Paris. Do you know the dancer Carlyle Swanson?"

"I've seen him perform. I don't know him."

They were moving easily through the green valley.

"He's a very dear friend of ours," Melanie put in. "He visits us here once or twice a year."

Asa had told Mothersill that Swanson was homosexual. "You live here, then," Mothersill asked.

Holdenfield laughed. "Yes, we're what you might call natives, old man."

Mothersill said, "Listen. I can't thank you enough. This is not the most well-traveled road on the island."

"You probably noticed that there are no homes around here," Holdenfield said. Mothersill saw him glance at his wife. "It's all private land."

Melanie turned around. "He's too modest to say it's ours." Her glance was direct, calculating, the look of the very rich who can afford everything.

"Is that right?" Mothersill murmured.

Melanie had half-turned, her arm over the seat back.

"You live pretty far off the beaten path," Mothersill said as the car was driven onto another, narrower, dirt road.

"Yes, a bit," Holdenfield said, glancing at him through the rearview mirror. "We don't like to feel hemmed in."

They were going uphill now, at about a fifty-degree angle, the main road already out of sight.

"We like it like this, old boy. We have to hold onto spots like this, Doctor, because if we don't the white man'll have it all. Some we must give him in exchange for what he can bring to us. But not all. The world moves on compromise."

Suddenly the road was smoother; they were on a wide band of asphalt and it sliced neatly in two the rain forest around them. They broke into a semicleared area and up ahead, seeming to rest on the horizon itself out where the sun and sea met, was a monstrous, flat, white stucco house, its orange roof tiles blazoning in the lowering sunlight. As the car crested a slight rise, Mothersill felt that he'd been flown to the top of the world.

"Marvelous," he breathed, noticing Holdenfield and his wife exchanging pleased glances.

"It took a bit of doing, damned if it didn't, but there it is, Estate Holdenfield."

It's like, Mothersill thought, where God might build a house. The land fell away abruptly and down on the sea Mothersill saw two boats tied up and a red wind sock funneling in the wind. He wondered what Holdenfield did for a living. They were approaching the house now, on a long, curving driveway, and he could see on the sunny side of it a large swimming pool.

A wind sock, Mothersill thought. What, he asked himself while smiling in the mirror to Holdenfield, does this cat *do?*

As the car slowed, majestically, Mothersill thought, and stopped, a strapping old man in a white jacket materialized out of the growing dusk to open the doors.

Holdenfield said, "Stuyvesant, this is Dr. Mothersill. His car broke down between St. Anne's and Pont Noir. Be a good fellow and call the garage and ask them to come out first thing in the morning to tow it in." The man nodded, his face impassive. "Then bring us drinks by the pool, and after, prepare a bed for the doctor. In our wing would be nice, I think. The blue room."

Arm in arm, with Mothersill following, the Holdenfields walked leisurely to the pool, already lighted. Beyond, the sea was turning a gray-blue except where touched by the rays of the setting sun. Beautiful, Mothersill thought. Twelve years ago it would have been beautiful.

"Like it old boy?"

"Yes, I do. Very much," Mothersill said.

"Are you a medical doctor?" Melanie's smile was warm, curious.

I was hoping they wouldn't ask that, Mothersill thought. "No, social work's my field, or was. I've been doing some work for the government that's sort of related. Twelve years ago I was supposed to come down here and help set up some adoption agencies. Didn't make it then."

He knew they didn't have children; they would have spoken about them. Or the kids would've come out of the house to greet them, but he asked, "Have you children?"

"No," Melanie said briefly. Holdenfield said nothing. "Do you?" Melanie asked.

Mothersill laughed. "Me, no. I'm not married."

"That would be no impediment around here, old fellow. We pride ourselves on our high rate of illegitimacy."

Mothersill laughed again, softly. "Well, there's really no such thing as an illegitimate child."

"Well put—" Holdenfield started. "Let's dispense with formalities. Can we call you Odell?"

"Sure."

"I'd like a swim with the drinks," Melanie said.

"Capital, capital. How about it, Odell?"

"Okay." He wanted to see what Melanie looked like in a swim suit.

They turned at the rattle of bottles. "Here's Justine," Holdenfield said. "Justine! Hello! Meet Dr. Mothersill." The woman, whose face showed as little as Stuyvesant's, nodded a greeting. "I'll set up the drinks. Melanie, show Odell to his room. See you back in five."

Following Melanie through the house, Mothersill was so busy watching the movement of her buttocks that he almost ran over her when she stopped in a corridor, turned and kissed him. She smiled at his alarm, then took his arms and placed them around her and kissed him again, pushing her pelvis hard against his.

"I'll see you later?" she whispered.

"Ah, I—"

"It'll be all right. Don't worry." Then she was gone and Mothersill, inside his room, which was on the weather side, heard the wind gently blowing against the walls. He pulled on his trunks and rushed back to the pool; he needed a drink.

"Good show," Holdenfield said. In his swim suit he was as slender as a girl. "What'll you have, Odell?"

Mothersill glanced quickly at the array of bottles and said, "Gin. On the rocks." He dived into the pool after taking a big top off the drink. I'm going to need all the gin I can get, he thought as he came up from his dive and saw Melanie startling in a white bikini, pulling on a cap. Oh, he thought again.

"How is it?" Holdenfield called.

"Perfect. Just right."

"It's heated," Melanie called, sipping from a stemmed glass. She set it down and in two quick steps was at the edge of the pool, gathering herself into a dive, and then she was in the air over Mothersill's head. She hit the water cleanly, rose in a trail of froth, and laughed. "Marvelous!" She began to swim with dainty strokes, all elbow.

Holdenfield jumped in feet first, came up and began to swim with the seriousness of a man training for the Olympics. But he had no style and moved clumsily through the water, kicking and splashing excessively.

"God this is great, Melanie," he called out. "The most sensible thing we ever did, putting in this pool."

"Race to the bar," Melanie called out, and they sprinted through the water, bumping and splashing to the other end of the pool. Mothersill climbed out first. "Help me," Melanie said, and he turned and extended his arm, felt her body flowing up out of the water toward him, moving so surely, so smoothly, that he thought she was going to rise to his lips and kiss him again. He glanced behind her at Holdenfield, to see if he was watching, and just caught, he thought, the snapping off of an amused smile, the light dancing in the man's eyes. But Mothersill was not sure. He finished off his drink and accepted another and went back in. By the time dinner was ready the gin was screaming inside his head and he knew he was ready for Melanie Holdenfield, whatever the situation was.

As Mothersill drifts wearily to bed, the house stilled now, the kitchen-cleaning sounds of Stuyvesant and Justine ended, Holdenfield gives him a last soft slap on the back and Melanie offers a bright good night. A full moon hangs in the sky like a hole through which a brilliant circle of daylight pours down upon the world, lulling the ocean gently back and forth. A caressing wind puffs at the house and the curtains in Mothersill's room lift and drop, swaying from side to side. It is at night when he becomes most conscious of the water and its endless movement, and it is hard for him to recall when he has not heard it.

His head is abuzz with the gin, the Barbancourt on the rocks, the Laffite Rothschild, the Napoleon cognac. He undresses himself, nearly losing his balance a few times. Nude, he hefts his penis and shakes it in the general direction of the Holdenfields' room and he climbs into bed, waiting, the sheet drawn up to his neck. Moonlight does not enter his room; instead, it floods the rooftop and slides off past his windows. He falls asleep, but wakes when the bed sags slightly and she is upon him, kissing him, forcing her tongue deep into his mouth. He tries to force her tongue out so he can give her his; there is a struggle: tongues, thick and eager, roll up and try to dart past each other. Mothersill wins and his tongue is inside her mouth, sliding on a partial. Melanie intensifies her efforts, as if to distract him from his discovery.

Mothersill does not fear Holdenfield, even though he is the type who would have a gun in the house. But something nags, and Mothersill reaches over, snaps on the light and is startled to see that there is nothing and no one sitting in the chair across the room, which directly faces the bed. He snaps the light back out.

"Silly," Melanie says between kisses. Then her hands are on his head, the pressure of them insisting that he move down her body, down and as he goes she comes up and they are playing the numbers in silence. Then they part.

He is trying to bring her shudderingly down, and in the darkness, with the moonlight slanting off his window, he thinks of the English, French, Italian, Swedish, American, Brazilian, Spanish, German and Danish lovers this woman has had. For the conversation earlier detailed their travels and he gathered that she, like him, like most people, he imagines, had come to know nations by their lovers. She makes a small, high-pitched sound, which seems to measure the spasms of her galloping orgasm. Mothersill, having brought her there, wishes to end it quickly, for something still nags, and he forces himself around the corner to the start of his own orgasm, while she is still thrashing through hers, and he feels it rising quickly to overwhelm him.

"O,O,O,o,o."

The light comes on without a sound, as if controlled remotely, and Mothersill tries to start in its glare but his orgasm has frozen him to Melanie and she to him, and in the chair, quite naked, his right fist a blur on an incredibly long and unbelievably thin penis, sits Holdenfield, his eyes half-closed, the pupils tiny bits of glass; even as Mothersill watches out of his warm, paralyzing prison, Holdenfield comes, snapping down in his chair, groaning, and Melanie stiffens again and gasps with yet another climax.

The room is quiet save for the sounds of their heavy breathing and the wind outside softly punching the walls.

The light goes out.

Mothersill feels himself going limp rapidly. Melanie slides away from him, the bed heaving under her movements. He hears no doors opening or closing, but he knows they are gone.

Breakfast on the patio was stunning in the sun. Mothersill began the meal, after extremely cheery greetings from Holdenfield and Melanie, with a certain uneasiness, not unmixed with apprehension. They did not mention the evening before.

As if on a schedule of which he was not aware, the tow truck came just as Mothersill finished breakfast. "Perhaps if you return to our island, you'll visit us again," Holdenfield said. Melanie, too, shook his hand.

His car replaced, Mothersill drove to his cottage, put on trunks and a sun hat and sat on his patio, looking toward the sea. Although he'd also taken a book, he couldn't get past the opening line.

Well. It was one thing to read about such things as had happened at the Holdenfields'; and it was even funny to hear people tell stories about incidents like that. But being a part of it. Thinking even that he might be—otherwise, why would he have turned on the light? What if they'd had another game in mind, a *ménage à trois* in which each participated fully? What would his response have been? He thought he knew, now, away from it, his head nearly clear.

Was it possible, as he'd heard, that pussy after a while became quite ordinary to some men, and they moved on to whips, to doing it on top of caskets, to tying women in the positions they dreamed up in adolescence, and, finally, gave up on women altogether, to try something else, like other men, or men and women.

No, not me, he thought. Not ever. Not at thirty-seven. It was too late for him to change his habits. He liked women. Mothersill sighed in relief; he had convinced himself by looking back over his life, from Etta Mae forward. Last night had been just one of those things. A helluva way to remember Grand Royale. It would be some story to tell one of these days.

He started to read his book again and this time, with great difficulty, finished the first paragraph. He closed it with a snap. Fuck it. The beach. Defeated, he stood. The beach was where people were, women, life, action, happenings. Mothersill found himself always torn between his need for people and his fear that being with them would make something untoward happen. Afraid of the closeness, but wanting it, too. He created elaborate retreats, then was driven from them to touch others.

He put the book, a towel and a thermos of iced rum in the car and drove to the beach and bumped his way down to one end of it where he was sure none of the tourists would come. His eyes shaded by sunglasses, his hat pulled low, Mothersill leaned against a palm tree. Still he made little progress with the book. He'd read a line, glance up at the anchored yachts rolling in the swells, or take in the skimming sailfish, bright sails snapping as they pitched and heaved beyond the swimming areas. On the horizon he saw a graceful sloop heeling into the wind, dipping momentarily out of sight, then, like an idea, he thought, heaving back up, its sails taut and white in the gleaming sun. Sipping slowly from the thermos, he looked up the beach where most of the people were, and he caught the sounds of women's voices and thought of them, how they would be later, after lunch and a few more hours at the beach; thought of them lying in their hotel beds nude, bronzed by the sun, and under-rock-white where they'd been covered. The brown ones would be made like old gold and their covered parts would be striped, too, and less brown. He thought of them, their bodies although washed free of sea salt, somehow salty still, making love and then sleeping, after which they would emerge ready for dinner in one of the cove restaurants, and dancing and more drinking and more loving.

And he wished one of them were with him.

A pleasure of the moment, he thought, of the time and the place. Rarely had his relationships gone beyond that neat, psychological arena. If the woman tried to build beyond, pushed for more, the magic went, the pleasure curdled, the faking began and he eased out. If he wanted it all, the woman didn't, and one way or another, they too eased away.

"You should want who wants you," his mother had said.

A good, safe rule. And that woman would probably give you all the kids you ever wanted, Mothersill thought. *Want who wants you.*

He stared down the beach, his eyes quickly licking over the forms of women by themselves lying or reading or sitting, knees pulled up.

Thirteen years, he thought, drowsily, thinking of the feel of women. Some too dry, some too wet; some placed way down, it seemed, and some placed way up. Nearly all with magnificent cradles, the carrying space for children. Thirteen years and alone; thirteen years of tight and loose and just right. Hotel rooms, his apartment, their apartments; three continents. And still alone. A hundred kids washed down a hundred different toilets.

Maybe he'd really stopped wanting after Potts. Or maybe because he wanted so much, the fix on some still incomplete ideal, that he could never have it. And maybe he'd carried that air with him into every affair, like a flag, and it was perceived. Maybe he was just supposed to be alone.

Margo Purchase was a loner, too. She sat ten yards behind Mothersill behind another tree. A magazine she'd finished an hour ago lay beside her. She was full of the island although she'd arrived on it only the evening before. But she didn't know where to start, knew only that it was approaching lunchtime. She could have it on the enclosed patio of her room, which she was inclined to do, or she could saunter down the beach to a restaurant. She was trying to make a decision when Mothersill came and sat down.

She could not believe it. It seemed eerie, yet it was he, Odell, one and the same. She studied the part of his back that was not obscured by the tree and his profile whenever he turned to look up the beach. She smiled at that. Looking for leg, as usual. There was something lonely, almost pathetic, about his movements, the desultory waving at flies, the futile attempts to read his book, the hungering looks he cast toward the sound of women's voices. Odell. The last she'd heard he was in Africa. Something with the Peace Corps. Margo watched him drink from his thermos. She could ask for a drink. Knock him out. She wondered if he'd changed as much as she thought she had.

But, maybe it wasn't Odell at all. Just someone who looked very much like him. Margo Purchase stood and brushed the sand away.

The fourth paragraph was going easier; Mothersill was starting to hook into the book. Still looking down, but past the page, he saw the feet, toenails painted a dainty pink, the right ankle braceleted. He looked up, startled, not having heard anything more than the waves beating into shore, the wind through the palm trees and children screaming. He pushed back his hat and whipped off his glasses.

"Odell, is that you?"

"Margo," he breathed, squinting into the sun.

"I don't believe it," she said. "I've been sitting back there watching you for twenty minutes, trying to make sure."

Mothersill did not like to think that he'd been watched for that long. "Strange things happen on this island," he said.

"Can I have a drink?" she said, crouching beside him.

Mothersill leaned over and kissed her cheek. "Yes."

She sat down beside him, still shaking her head. Her brown skin was still flecked with the white sand. Her muscles, rounded and firm, slid beneath her skin at every movement. He passed the thermos to her and watched while she drank, studied her from her sun hat to the edge of the bottom of her bikini. Had he willed her to him? The way they said Joshua's soldiers willed down the walls of Jericho? The way they said so many people chanting the same word could will a five-hundred-ton rock from the ground to one hundred feet in the air?

Finished, Margo capped the jug and said, "Odell, what're you doing here?"

"Resting." He took a long pull on the thermos.

"They say the world's small."

"You look good, Margo."

"You mean not like a student any more."

"Maybe," he said.

"So do you. More settled."

Mothersill laughed. "How long've you been here?"

"I got in last night." She took off her sunglasses, replaced them and took them off again. Her eyes moved quickly over his face, pausing here, and then, as if embarrassed, shifting somewhere there, seeking new lines, wrinkles. "You?"

"Almost a week. Where are you staying?"

"The Palm Tree. Where are you?"

"I've got a cottage near Lobster Bay." He added, "Great view."

"Well," she said and fell silent, staring out to sea.

Then they looked at each other without speaking until Mothersill asked, "Are you with anyone, Margo?"

"No," she said softly. She removed her hat and ran her hand through her hair. "How about you, Odell? You're the original Mr. Hotnuts. Who's with you?"

"Oh, I'm not with anyone."

"That's right. You said you were resting." She put her hand on his arm. "I'm not being snide or nasty or anything, Odell. Besides, it's been a long time."

"Yeah."

Margo looked at him with a certain tenderness before saying, "There was a picture of Ellie in the paper a few days ago. She'd jumped out of her apartment."

Mothersill felt a sudden coldness rushing through his groin, as if he were, with Ellie, plunging down the New York night to the sidewalk below. He did not know that it had been night; didn't even know she'd returned from Paris. But he remembered the look in her eyes the nights when they used to stand looking down from her balcony. "Dead?" he asked, knowing it could not be otherwise. Her kids, then, would be institutionalized forever.

"Yes."

After a while Mothersill said, "Then you're still in New York. That's what I'd heard. I could never picture you anywhere else. Finished law school, too."

She smiled, touched that there were some things about her that he'd followed. "There's one thing I bet you didn't know. I've been married."

"You've been? You're not now?" He watched her slip her glasses back on.

Margo laughed. "You're missing things, Odell. No."

"Yeah, I got you. Sorry about that."

"I don't suppose you—"

"No," Mothersill said, passing her the thermos again.

When she finished sipping she said, "Look, I'm sorry about Ellie."

"That was over a long time ago."

"I'm still sorry."

"How about some lunch, Margo? Walk down the beach somewhere." He held out his hand to help her up as he straightened himself. He took her magazine, his book and thermos and they began walking close to the water where the sand was wet and cool.

"Dr. Mothersill," she said and smiled.

"Makes the paycheck just a little longer, that's all. Weren't you in politics, running for councilwoman or something, in Washington Heights?"

"I lost, but I've got a small practice, and I'll run again for something else."

"Yes, you were always a little tough."

The beach was filling now and, rounding a curve which gave a fuller view of the sea, Mothersill counted four cruise ships, painted white and yellow and orange, at anchor. The spice women were already moving up and down the hot sands.

Margo looked at Mothersill. "I didn't know you thought that of me, Odell. Was I, really?"

"Sometimes you were very tough, Margo. Lovely, but tough, too."

She walked deliberately, looking down at the sand. "You were with the Peace Corps in Africa?"

"Yes. Back home."

"What's it like? I want to go next year."

"I'll carry your bags," Mothersill said, staring back at her startled look at him. He went on: "Interesting. Throw away your conceptions. It's a massive place with hundreds of different peoples. You probably wouldn't like it too much the first time around."

"I've heard that."

"On the other hand," Mothersill said, "being a woman and

traveling alone could make it very different. . . ."

Margo caught the indecision in his voice and said, "But on the third hand?"

"Third hand. It might not make any difference at all."

"But I should go?"

"You should go, yes."

"Are you still with the Peace Corps, Odell?"

"Yes, but thinking of quitting. On to bigger and better things. Hey, here's a place for lobster. The lobster around here is not to be believed. Let's go in, okay?"

"Shall I let you be my guide?"

They'd stopped a few yards from the restaurant and were standing close together. "You could do worse, Margo."

Grimly she said, "Odell, man, do I know it. Let's have the lobster."

"Before we go in there," he said, taking her hand, "I want to tell you that I'm glad you're here. I hope you're glad I'm here. We had a thing that didn't work. Nobody's fault. I am dying of loneliness here and until you showed up, I was beginning to feel that I'd made a big mistake. I don't know what fortunes brought you here, but I'm glad. Now, let's eat."

"Wait." She pulled his hand. "I'm glad you said that. At least right now I am."

They took a table with a view of the beach and ordered rum drinks. They clinked their glasses together, their eyes meeting, his serious, hers amused.

She's older now, Mothersill thought. What was wrong before was that she was too young, younger in spirit than she looked. What's she like now? Having been married, what did that do for her?

"Odell, you look just the same. Exactly the same."

And in truth he did. Inside he felt himself aging, weathering, slowing down. If he dreamed of "The Sower," he moved in slow motion among the furrows, his arm going back and forth, jerkily, and sometimes when he released the hand to let the grain fly, there was nothing at all in it.

"What do you do to stay in shape?" Margo asked.

"Nothing," he said. "You, you look rounder, softer."

They ordered the lobster salad and Margo said, "Yes, I've put on a little weight. Is it in the right places?" She smiled, knowing it was.

"It's pretty okay where it is, yes," he said.

"Have you been close to getting married or anything?"

"No, afraid not."

"Afraid, is it?"

"You know what I mean."

She said, "Have you been with anyone?"

"You mean, living with anyone?"

"Yes."

"Not since you."

Margo looked at him, then slid her glance past to the other patrons. "That was a long time ago. Was the experience with me so bad?"

Mothersill laughed. "I should be asking you that question."

"No. I've had time to think."

"So have I."

The restaurant was becoming crowded now with tourists from the ships. Their stay on the beach would be brief, Mothersill knew, like the passing of a hurricane. The passengers and crew therefore did not consider themselves bound by the unspoken, unwritten laws of the Grand Royale beach: that one ate quietly enjoying the view; that one did not become drunk and raucous—as so many did—and that one paid his taxi fare and generally did not try to cheat or demean the locals. The rules were in fact ones that could be applied the world over. A hurricane? No. The tourists were more like locusts. They swept in in bunches, devouring everything in sight, food (especially the hamburgers prepared by the new Holiday Inn down the beach), a variety of rum drinks, beer, coconut milk; they rented all the sailfish, paddle boats and snorkeling and scuba-diving gear; they bought out the spice and palm goods vendors and rode the donkeys until the animals dropped. They hired boys to climb trees to bring down coconuts and their fathers to open them. They littered, shouted, danced and fornicated, then swam and walked, then danced and fornicated again.

All of which was pretty okay, as far as Mothersill was concerned, except that he had observed over the past few years of traveling that whites always seemed far less reserved among darker people than when with other whites. "Going native." "Jungle fever." Conrad. Kafka.

"Social working?" Margo asked.

"Yeah, I guess. What'd you think of the salad?"

"Fann-tas-tic!" She wiped her mouth with the napkin and drank her water. "The water's pretty crappy, though."

"Drink beer. But that's more expensive than rum. Want to swim?" Then he realized that he didn't know if she could swim or not. How could he not have known? "*Do* you swim?"

They had left the restaurant and were walking toward the water's edge. The swells moved toward them, changing in color from a cobalt blue to green, and then, transparent, smashed against the beach.

"I swim," she said. "I didn't know you did." Living in New York you could not know who did what because the city gave you only the frequent chances to drink or make love. The clubs where there were pools or tennis courts were hidden in the forests of concrete; the serfs did not belong in them. And in the summers the club members retreated to the Hamptons.

Almost with a sigh of pleasure, Mothersill slid forward into the water. For a moment he exulted in the feel of his body moving, then he slowed, rolled on one side and came up with his first stroke and kick, moving easily, sensuously, taking in the air and blowing it out in silvery bubbles under the water. Beside him, matching him stroke for stroke, was Margo. They swam briskly to the floating dock, climbed aboard and lay belly-down looking toward the shore.

"Where'd you learn to swim?" he asked.

"At the Y. After."

"After we broke up?"

"Yes. Something to do. That and other things."

"I didn't think then that you could swim."

She chided, "You thought you knew all about me. Does my swimming upset you? That you didn't possess me completely? Men! Christ." She turned away from him.

"It's no big thing, Margo." He wanted to call her baby. "I think it's great. I somehow have the impression that black people don't dig swimming too much."

Now she turned back to him. "You, too?"

"Yeah. Wonder why."

"It's probably not true," she said. "Maybe we like it as much as other people."

"Anyway, it doesn't matter."

Then lay face to face in the warm sun, their feet sticking into the water.

"Did you love me when we lived together, Odell?"

"Yes."

He had. How could she not have known? Otherwise, why would she have been with him in his apartment? Mothersill almost smiled with the remembrances. Margo, young, hesitant, lovely, filling the apartment with beauty and intelligence, her laughter. He wanted what he did not talk about, and he did not talk about his need because he had to wait; had to give her time, a little more time. Which is what you do when you love someone. As before, however, more time did not work.

"I think you were in love with Ellie, too."

"No, I wasn't. We met each other at bad times in our lives. Both drowning. Hasn't that ever happened to you?" Why now, Mothersill wondered? Margo seemed to have understood it then, had smiled before she moved in with him, like a mother watching the antics of irrational children.

He and Ellie never mentioned love, the way he had with Margo. Too modern, or too knowing? Neither tried to extend the bounds of that neat, psychological arena; neither really wanted to.

"Yes," Margo said. "It has happened to me."

Mothersill felt that he was winning her back. They listened to the water lapping against the dock and to the sounds from the beach. "That was all," he said, finally. "We were together for a while, healing hurts, but she must've had one I never knew about. She was a fine woman."

"I don't know much about it, but I think she was a good sculptor. Was she, Odell?"

"Yeah, she was good. It was almost as if not seeing any real life in those kids of hers, she had to create life out of stone. She was good. Remember that Hell's Angels piece she did?"

"She hung out with them for a while, didn't she?"

And had taken a lover while with them, Mothersill remembered. Ellie had told him. Even now, remembering the fine detail of the rider's genitals within the cloth of his pants, spread out on motorcycle seat, cut with a certain lovingness, Mothersill recalled his lack of jealousy.

"Why did she do it?" Margo asked wonderingly.

"No idea. I hadn't spoken to her in years."

Two swimmers were approaching, but veered off, then headed back to the beach.

"You know something," she said. "I had the feeling back then that you loved every woman you could get your penis into. You radiated that somehow; that was a part of your charm."

"I loved you," he said. His chin now rested on the backs of his crossed hands. "It felt good to love you."

"Was that why you called me Jennifer sometimes, because you loved me so much? Because I reminded you of your first love?"

Mothersill inclined his head toward her. "Then you never believed me about Jennifer, did you? Not once, even when you said you did."

Her eyes stilled; she became attentive. "I guess I didn't."

"Jennifer Randolph," Mothersill said. "You look just like her. I mean you did then and for all I know, maybe now. I told you about Etta Mae. I mean there was almost nothing I didn't tell you." He hadn't, though, told her about Potts.

"It goes this way, baby." He paused to see if she would say anything. She didn't.

"When I got to be fifteen I had a crisis. Social working a little now, okay?"

Margo smiled.

"There was the kind of love they put out in Hollywood, clean, pure, so goddamn sure of itself. Well, I dug it. But there were the dirty books, the Petty girls who, every time you opened *Esquire*, pleaded with you to rape them. Every minute of the day and maybe the night too—I know I woke up often slick with wet dreams or with my Jones as hard as the Rock of Gibraltar. You'd never met such a slick, cunning, pussy-hungry boy in your life. All my time went into thinking about it, how to get it, in planning the precise moment at which I could meet girls in the clothes closets in school to feel them up."

Margo smiled again.

"I started to lose weight. I was nervous. My old man didn't know what was the matter with me. I sneaked around the house and peeked through bathroom keyholes when we had women visitors. I woke up some mornings exhausted, having beat my meat all night. I mean all night, and it would be swollen like an army had walked on it. I was in rough shape. Then a new girl came to town—"

"Jennifer Randolph."

"Right. She was something, maybe a dusky Diana Lynn, a June Allyson; saucy like Ann Sheridan. I mean, you couldn't compare her to Hattie McDaniels or Butterfly McQueen. Not even Lena Horne, who didn't have that many speaking roles. Jennifer was mine. I knew it as soon as I saw her. I kicked ass and got my ass kicked. I carried her books. I groveled in front of her mother and father, and even went to church with her because we knew her folks would like me better. Cunning. Scheming. We did our homework together. We held hands, we kissed and we petted, they called it then."

Mothersill felt Margo's hand on his.

"Well, you know my folks had a copy of this book, *Eugenics and Sex Harmony* by a cat named Havelock Ellis. Ellis was great on foreplay, on tenderness and patience; it was like that part of the book was written just for me and Jennifer. I mean, she responded."

"How old was she?"

"Same age."

"It was on a Columbus Day. Jennifer's folks were at work. We had no school."

Margo said, "You made a discovery."

Mothersill broke off to laugh. They used to banter this way.

"Yeh. It wasn't that I hadn't *done* it before. In cellars, looking over my shoulder. In parks behind bushes, sliding my thing in around drawers that girls didn't want to take off. That was the big thing, not taking off your drawers. That left you—unviolated in some way, at least that's what I think the girls thought. In short, I had gotten laid. But I'd never made love. You know the difference?"

"I've learned the difference."

"I'd never looked at an entire female body without clothes before," he said, gazing at the beach. "Never."

Their clothes, Mothersill remembered, had been barriers, perhaps of asbestos, preventing one body from searing the other. Her eyes had been closed against all commonplace visions and she had undressed with a luxury—yes, a luxury of motion—while he, frantic, ripped and tore at his own clothing, his eyes overflowing with the view of young, full breasts, brown, rippling curves, but he came anyway, spewing, riddling her with sperm as he groaned and cursed. But, desperately he had seized his hunk of lank penis and tried to stuff it into her, and, failing, brought her head down, dialogues of dirty books peppering his tongue, and then he felt her, and it did not take long before he was erect again, his chest heaving with relief.

He recalled the smell that had risen between them, brackish, like pond water, touched with the scent of water lilies and the odor of cedars blown in. She surmounted orgasm after orgasm, until they had lain in stupor, the world impinging upon them.

Ah, the first one.

"I liked that," Jennifer had said. Mothersill remembered the words clearly, even the lay of shadows in the room, the radio: Wendy Warren with Douglas Edwards. "All of it."

Mothersill had smiled, thinking of the poolroom, sewing-group, tonk-night gossip: "That's filthy, man, people doin' that to each other. Woman suck your youth away like that. Somethin' wrong with a man git down on a woman the way I hears white folks does all the time." Or overhearing adults saying:

"Now the Lindy Hop is one bar I do not go into because ole Corley Atkins goes there an I understand he likes to put his mouth in women. Ole nasty thing! I might get a glass he done drunk from!"

On the dock Mothersill broke out into loud laughter.

Margo, watching him, laughed softly to herself. She must've been something special, she thought. "Are you going on?" she asked.

Mothersill nodded, still convulsed with laughter, but his thoughts were already returning to Jennifer and that day.

"Would you do it to me?" she had asked.

Ah, Mothersill reflected. How many orgasms does the good Lord grant fifteen-year-olds on any given Columbus Day? Many, but youth can sustain them without danger of the heart ripping from the sockets. The Lord, also in his infinite goodness, provides the young with great recuperative powers, measured not in the half hours or hours of older people, or even days or weeks, but in brief minutes. He also provides constant blood to the pump, and gristle with the staying power of the plastic in a Mattel toy.

"I knew," Mothersill said to Margo, "that some of the times we made love, the way we made it, you didn't like it. Do you remember the time you said–"

"Don't say it," Margo said. "Please don't."

"Jennifer did for me when I was fifteen what you wouldn't let me do for you when you were twenty-one. There weren't the two peaks, one dirty, the other purity; there was absent that concept that loving like that was what freakish white folks did. Ellis said a woman should be a saint in the street and a demon in bed. I called you Jennifer because I thought sometimes you were, or because I wanted you to be."

"I was twenty-one," Margo said, "and you were–what–twenty-seven or twenty-eight? I was such a clod. You *were* very tender. You had the experience. Now I thank you. I couldn't then. I didn't know anything. God, I thank you. I still remember that first time, when I turned my behind to you. I thought that's where it was done. I thought a peehole was *just* a peehole. In college. Boy that scene's changed. You knew I had a lot of guilt about sex, what you did and what you wanted us to do. Sex. Like gold to be bartered for the good life, the fine man; argh. Nothing more puritanical than a half-smart black woman.

"I invested Ellie with all kinds of sexuality. *She* was the one who'd taught you all those–*dirty* things. I hated the way I was. But how can you walk up to a man and say 'I know nothing of making love. Will you teach me and be tender, kind and sweet?' "

"But you got over your hang-ups."

He expected her to answer right away, and when she didn't he looked at her.

"Well, yes. I guess. Are you completely free of them? Isn't being something like a satyr a hang-up, Odell?"

"Is that what you thought of me?" He scooped a handful of water at her.

She rolled away and stood up. "You see? What other people may consider bad isn't necessarily bad to yourself." She took a shallow dive, came up and called, "Race you to shore."

"Now what do we do?" Mothersill asked when they were standing near the thermos, hat, glasses, book and magazine.

"Well, I'd like to nap—alone," Margo said. "Shower and all that, and you could take me out. Okay?"

Mothersill thought there was a small anxiety in her tone. "Great. I hear it's noisy right on the beach at night."

"Yes, but that didn't keep me from sleeping last night. Tired, I guess."

Mothersill kissed her on the cheek. "See you about seven. Meet you in the bar there."

Margo smiled. "You don't even want my room number?"

"You didn't seem to want to give it to me, Margo. You know me."

Alone in his cottage, nursing a tall rum and soda, Mothersill reflected on his meeting with Margo. Strange. If it had not been for Marilyn and Marj's party, he would not have met Ellie; and had it not been for Ellie, he would not have met Margo. Had it not been for Potts, he probably would not have come to Grand Royale, and he would not then have met Margo again.

But another violent death. How they seemed to trail in his wake. What in the hell had propelled Ellie Waffenberg Mannheim to her death? Again, with her, he opened the windows, steel-framed they were with the paint peeling and chipping, showing rust. Which windows, the studio ones, the bedroom, or the first floor of her duplex? And did the giant-sized mahogany sculpture, a replica of her smaller but voluptuous body, full of motion, hinting at shyness, much like Lachaise's "Walking Woman," but nude—did that piece which filled her lobby, the radiating point for the Chagall, Appel, Shahn and Kline—

finally move, turn and stare, mutely, perhaps even blink as the cold air of the twenty-fifth floor struck its face? Facing east, the reservoir a great piece of glass thrown into the park, Mothersill accompanied Ellie, leaned against the railing of the tile-floored little balcony with its single lounge upon which they sometimes made love. She would not have vaulted over; that was not her style. A dainty step over, hands shaking on the railing, then another step, then letting go, rushing down.

From the distance of an affair long ended, Ellie seemed to have done well. She'd shown at MOMA, Paris, Berne, Amsterdam, Madrid, Washington. Her sculptures, admittedly grotesque, were accepted and praised as that part of life, often sordid or strange, that other sculptors avoided.

Now it seemed to Mothersill that he'd never touched her; that she never sat demurely on his bed bravely sipping whiskey, just for him, because she'd never liked it. But she wanted to become as light-hearted as he, as much fun, when he was high. "I don't know how to get away from myself," she'd said.

Yet he had known her, held that body which hinted of browns in back generations; had kissed the mouth with its tauntingly full lips. He used to tease her about them and her steatopygia, while stroking it. It was the most sensitive part of her body, which may have explained her penchant for being on the receiving end of the "German vice."

The Swedish *au pair* who lived with Ellie, to care for the children if they spent a weekend with Ellie, had a friend, another *au pair* in the building. Her name was Margo Purchase. Margo was a student at NYU.

Ellie liked to sit and watch children in one of the Central Park playgrounds. Invariably, Margo would be there with her wards. There was much to be observed in the playgrounds. Some cocksmen stalked the museums to make out, and others were very good at bars or parties, but children's playgrounds, Mothersill realized one afternoon, were virtually gold mines of leg. They were filled with young, bored mothers who eyed each others' attire over the tops of books or magazines or from behind oversized sunglasses. Brought to that sandboxed, slide-specked cul-de-sac of screaming children who were victims one moment and oppressors the next, the mothers seemed to be biding their time. Margo, too.

"Don't think you're going to start climbing all over me after you've been laying up with that white woman," Margo said.

Mothersill had met her in Washington Square Park late one afternoon when he'd finished class. He'd been working on his doctorate then and invited her to his apartment. Margo spoke without looking at him; the Charles White prints on the walls drew all her attention. "No sir, Mr. Odell Mothersill."

She had had to set her defenses for being there, but she was there nevertheless. And shortly after she enjoyed being the mistress as it were, the little witch who had copped the white woman's paramour. She could enter Ellie's apartment ostensibly to visit the Swedish girl, but really to laugh secretly at Ellie. When Ellie moved to Paris, assured that Mothersill would visit her, Margo moved in with him.

Mothersill had been nervous about the arrangement. Margo looked like Jennifer, was Jennifer as far as he was concerned, *but* he was not going into any marriage without practice. She was extremely unpredictable in bed and a little afraid of him, he felt. Nevertheless he had planned to do it.

He'd envisioned himself growing old with Margo, a prospect that excited him at odd times and in tingling small ways. He saw himself tending to a fullness everywhere in his body and farting all over the place at night, and his stomach rumbling at the most embarrassing times, his penis not always obeying the urgent commands from his brain. Until then Mothersill had taken marriage or coupling for granted: two people sharing the same place, time and, often, things. Two people waking every morning, breaths foul, eyes encrusted, racing each other for the bathroom. *Every* morning, not just one or two; not for a couple of weeks, but maybe for as long as they lived!

He had not thought of living anywhere else so he and Margo would grow old together in the flat where he then alternately stood and paced, waiting for her to arrive with her bags. The years would gather upon them, perhaps sweetly, as dust settling from an explosion of talcum. That space that had been his alone would be disturbed by another presence it would have to get used to. Mothersill would enter rooms and find her there instead of an emptiness that itself had become a living organism. The floors would creak nervously with her unfamiliar tread. Entering at night, Mothersill had known that he would find lights on and maybe music instead of soft, empty darkness and silence, which, once he was away, filled the apartment, to come alive again, not unlike a curtained stage, at the movement of his finger on the light switch. The place would be alive with Margo in it.

The years of weekend or day-long trysts had not conditioned him to living with women. He had wondered if Margo's veneer would rub off and leave her like so many others? Would she, too, dash for the bathroom, her period having caught her unaware, leaving bright, scarlet droplets on the floor? Of course she might leave a few dark turds swirling in the toilet bowl if the pressure was down; not her fault. There would be bad meals and dripping washcloths and toothpaste glop all over the bathroom sink. And maybe her douche bag would slap him in the face often enough to make him angry.

Would the underwear that was so stimulating on her become quite natural and about as exciting as the bedspread? At what point would he stop marveling at her body, stop touching it, stop *wanting* to touch it? When would he begin to feel that it was not at all necessary to make love every moment he thought of it, or they, together, thought of it, and put it off and off until it became a duty, a routine, a thing they did together once in a while, like walking to the park on summer Sunday mornings to read the papers?

But other people had done it, lived together, and the women, at least those Mothersill met who were married or coupling, still looked good, still excited. And their men looked pleased with themselves, proud even. They couldn't have had good meals *all* the time or limitless delight in making love with their wives or girls *every* night.

Then Margo had walked off the elevator with her bags, the door keys he'd given her in her hand. The arrangement had lasted seven months, with Mothersill leaving her in the flat while he moved out.

And here she was again, ten years later.

It would be nice to make love to Margo again, Mothersill began to think after five days of swimming, dancing, driving, sailing, shell hunting and picnicking. It would have to come down to that, in spite of the ways she put him off. Not that he'd been forward; he merely took it for granted, and assumed she did too, that one night they'd get into bed and make love. Given their situation and past, it would be natural.

Margo talked around them: politics, like Bob Wagner was old blood and New York City needed new blood; like the way the courts dealt with her clients, nearly all of them poor and black; like Castro and Cuba and Jack Kennedy and Harry Belafonte. But she did not talk about *them*. And finally he came to know that this was just a vacation. You went away somewhere, met someone you liked, perhaps made love and returned home to do what you were doing before. All right, Mothersill agreed, silently. But there's one thing left to do, only one.

They were at the Blue Whelk, high even before the swordfish steak came, and holding hands and sitting close together, murmuring to each other. After dinner they went out on the patio, which overlooked the sea. "Lovely," Margo kept murmuring. "Lovely." Her fingers wrapped around his.

"Ah, now I see why I haven't been able to find you, Odell."

Lady Minerva, already in her cups, a small island intellectual Mothersill had met standing impassively beside her. "Enjoying your stay it looks like. How do you do? I'm Minerva, and this is Hubert Webster."

Reluctantly, Mothersill introduced Margo, but did not ask them to sit. He watched Margo watch Minerva's hand rest familiarly on his shoulder. When they'd gone Margo said, "So that's what you were up to before I got here."

"No. Just met her."

"That's all it used to take for you."

"Jealous?"

"Of that white bitch? Hell, no."

Like daylight oozing out before the darkness, the pleasure went. There was no explaining to Margo. Why did he owe her an explanation? She walked back into his life. "Well, it's late," he said. "I'll drop you off."

"Like hell you are," Margo said.

Mothersill paused.

"I mean we're going to your place." Her eyes challenged him, then softened. "Okay?"

Guiding her out and ignoring the flamboyant wave by Minerva, he said, "If you think I'm going to say no, you're crazy."

"Shouldn't we?" she asked in the taxi. "For old times' sake? Or something like that?"

Mothersill squeezed her hand. He wondered how many black women gave trim to black men just because they got leg from white women. Maybe they wanted to prove they were better, sexier, more sensual, more of everything the clichés said they were. What would happened if Minerva hadn't shown up?

"I'm sorry I didn't come before," Margo said. "It's a real cute place. Lots of room. Expensive?"

"Cheaper than your hotel room."

There was a curious mechanical quality about Margo's movements in bed, and Mothersill sensed that she responded to his touches perhaps a second too late, and then with the haste that did not quite conceal her lack of timing. Her sounds, too, seemed forced, unnecessary, theatrical. When he was ready, she whispered, "Wait, wait a minute, baby," biting off her words as though about to undertake something that required more than ordinary effort. "Okay."

He went in and commenced his motions and she said, "Oh, baby, don't wait for me. Don't work to make me. I'm not going to come. You go ahead." A little pump. A little sucked spittle. A tightening of the arms around his back.

"What's the matter?" he asked.

"Nothing. Come on, darling. Please. That's it. I want you to have it."

Mothersill pulled away.

"Don't, Odell."

"What is this shit, Margo?" He felt her turning away from him.

"Nothing. I guess I'm not even as good as I used to be."

"Tell you the truth," he said, "no."

"If I tell you something don't be angry, please don't be."

"I don't know. Try me. Let's get this talking and funny acting over and get down to business, baby."

Margo said plaintively, "I guess I prefer women to men, Odell."

Oh, shit, Mothersill thought.

"I'm sorry," she said. "I thought I could. I haven't since my marriage."

Tiredly, Mothersill said, "Even back then you were on your way. That business of being upset about Jennifer was just an excuse. Your calling me all kinds of freaks was because in the back of your mind you thought you might be even dirtier than you believed me to be."

"Yes, yes, I guess so," she said abruptly.

Mothersill pressed. "But there was a certain thing you came to like to do."

Margo turned her head.

"In fact, you preferred to do that more than anything else. Ah, yes, I remember—"

It had not been like *making* love in that fashion; it'd been more like *taking*, ingesting, and then wishing it would grow so it could be used as he used it. He sat up suddenly. "It was really Minerva you wanted tonight, like maybe you really wanted Ellie?" Can't get Cheyenne, get his ole lady, can't get Cheyenne, get his ole lady, he thought.

Margo exploded on the bed. "Can't it just be? Do we have to talk about it? I like women. I *love* a woman. I wanted us to make love because once we had something, however little."

From across the island Mothersill heard a faint hissing. Rain, he thought. The sound grew louder and the drops pelted the cottage, heavier and heavier, then slackened off as the rain moved on across the mountains. He poured a drink and handed it to her. "She's white, the woman you love." The words sounded clumsy in his mouth.

Margo accepted the drink, looked at it carefully. She drew the sheets up above her breasts. "You're really putting it to me, aren't you?"

Mothersill laughed bitterly. "No, baby. Not really."

Margo smiled at that, sipped her drink and said, "Draw your own conclusions, smartass. You've been doing it all night."

He drew on a pair of briefs and said, "Cheers." He tossed down his half glass of rum and snapped on the radio, hoping to catch some Jim Rudin jazz from Radio Grenada: jazz to wing him on back home, away from this. He was sick of steel drums.

"Yes," Margo said.

"What?"

"Yes, she's white."

"Gee whiz," Mothersill said mockingly. "I thought black guys were the only ones into that." He poured another drink and stood looking out at the ocean.

"What about kids, Margo?" he asked when he turned to her again. "Don't you want any?"

"I don't know. I really don't. But I don't have to get them that way in any case. You ought to know that."

Mothersill pulled up a chair beside the bed and put his feet up on it, breathing deeply of the freshly wet earth. That brief rainstorm might be approaching Martinique by now, he thought. He wondered what the adoption rules were like these days. "You know," he said to Margo. "I forgot. Seems like a thousand years since I left the agency. You're right, you don't have to get them that way."

"Or don't they let lesbians adopt?"

"I don't know. It probably wouldn't be wise to announce that you are."

Except for the small bedlight and the kitchen light which angled into the bedroom, they were in darkness.

"Tell me something, Odell. How's it you're not married? I mean, when a man gets into his late thirties without having been married—"

"Yeah, I get it. Maybe he's a fagot, huh?"

"Latent, maybe?"

"Could be." Mothersill stood up and removed his briefs.

Margo watched him in shock. "Hey, wait—" He slipped her glass from her hand, spilling the drink in the bed. "Odell, I thought—"

"You bastard!" she yelled, feeling him gouging, retreating, driving in again. "You think this makes you a man," she panted. "C'mon, Odell. Stop. I hate it! I hate it!" Her anger made her cry. "You sonofabitch, you black sonofabitch."

That big Swedish girl who was her buddy, Mothersill thought. I wonder what's happened to her?

When they both had dressed in silence, Mothersill broke his rule and drove Margo to the Palm Tree.

Later, he was startled by his dream. Peering under the sower's hat, where most times he saw himself in Millet's suggested lines, he now saw a face in pure Corot lines, a face starkly drawn, heavily lashed and rouged. There were flowers in the hat and ribbons on the sower's pants, and he minced saucily over the field. And for the first time a voice merged with the image in his dream, a woman's voice, and it said:

> "I am not merry, but I do beguile
> The thing I am by seeming otherwise.
> Come, how wouldst thou praise me?"

Desdemona, Mothersill groaned, assuring himself in the dream that it was real, and not a dream at all.

The next morning he packed, caught a rare no-show and flew to New York.

Part Four

IT IS MIDSUMMER, July 1967, and dusk is about to merge with the humidity that is silvering New York City, softening the harsh outlines of its towering buildings. Mothersill sees this from his office window on the sixtieth floor of the Empire State Building. His view is of the East River and Queens beyond. The temperature is in the nineties and the heat seems to be generating not only from nature in collision with metal, glass and concrete, but from the raging fires that sweep over the country from the west and the south, and, in fact, north a few blocks in Manhattan itself. Mothersill is sure that if his view was of the west, across the Hudson, he would see Newark smoldering; the smoke, ugly, twisted, bearing the sadness too of futility, mixed with the fires raging or dying in Boston; Wadesboro, North Carolina; Minneapolis; Birmingham; San Francisco; Waterloo, Iowa; Witchita, Kansas; Tampa, Florida; Cincinnati; Buffalo; Dayton and Atlanta.

Like most black people distant from the scenes where their brothers and sisters are being contained, murdered, beaten and humiliated by the police and the U. S. Army, he is stretched between sadness and rage. The sadness is a private thing, the rage public; he feels himself being tempered, like steel, shaped in the fire and cooled quickly in the water. This month, he knows, will pass. All months pass. The black victims will be buried and prayed over. But every black person who reads or watches television will no longer be the same when this July passes. They, too, will have been tempered by what they have seen, read, heard or participated in.

Mothersill, in shirt sleeves, has been in the office two days, sleeping on the couch. His every belch brings up aftertastes of low-grade hamburgers and french fries and coffee and scotch. There must be something he can do to help stop this madness.

Why, goddamnit, the young boys who flash across television on the news shows or bulletins were practically babies when he worked in the Good Shepherd. How many years ago was that? Seventeen, eighteen years. Add on two centuries. But, he knows, people do not kill the way black people are being killed unless they have great and secretive fear.

Mothersill's office is one that has been proliferating throughout the nation; it is an OEO office, a Poverty Office. These were seeded at the time of Kennedy's death and are now beginning to sprout like wild alfalfa. When this month has passed, he expects there will be even more of them.

Working just loudly enough to let him know he is not alone is Dorothy Nigro in the outer office. She is Mothersill's assistant. Usually in these offices it is the other way around; the black is the chief's aide. Dorothy doesn't mind working late. She has not spent the past two days and nights in the office with Mothersill only because it wouldn't look right. This is something she does not have to discuss with him; they both know it, and know if he'd asked, she would have stayed. The vibes between them are clear and sharp. They've gotten along well for two years, and know as much about each other as each has deemed to be enough. In another time they would be lovers, but not now. The office is filled with too many "right-on" people, black and white, and black nationalism has sprung to the ramparts of the blazing ghettos with clenched fist and starch-sharp overalls. This, too, Dorothy and Mothersill understand, and so share a sweet, unspoken longing which is all the sweeter being unfulfilled.

There are times when Mothersill wonders just what has brought Dorothy to this work, and thinks perhaps her name. He pictures kids in her parochial school calling her Dorothy Nigger, or the students at Fordham. No matter. He is glad she is there, just outside his door, her sleek, mini-skirted thirty-five-year-old body erect in her chair. Dorothy has good legs, and like most women who know it, that their legs are good, rarely wears anything but mini-skirt outfits. Mothersill saw his first mini skirt on Broadway, outside Birdland, seven years ago. The women wearing them stopped traffic. Now, 1967, they are commonplace, and Mothersill wonders why skirts are up at the same time the black rebellions are going down. What happened to the chastity belts, both literal and psychological? They used to be snapped on and locked in a flash when the "insane" black shook up the town by cold-cocking Charlie. No more. Would the next series of rebellions bring absolute nakedness?

Even if Dorothy is not inside with him, she is near her phone at home, picking up before the first ring has stopped.

"Odell," she calls softly, her voice modulated just above the laboring air conditioners.

"What?" he looks up from his paper, which he has just finished reading for the third time. The mayhem in Detroit, the police murders, the invasion by the paratroopers and the retreat of responsible civilian authority from active participation in smoothing out the rebellion, have sent Mothersill to work with an urgency. He has been working on *Instantstart.*

"You've got a seat on the noon plane, LaGuardia, American. Tomorrow. And you're booked into the Statler. I think you ought to quit for tonight."

"Okay. Can I read it to you?"

She comes in and sits across from him, all legs and thighs. He says, "You need to get some sun."

"I know, but—" She shrugs and smiles, pleased by his concern.

"This place won't fall apart if you take a couple of days off while I'm gone."

"Maybe," she says.

"If anything comes up in Rochester, I can reach you on the Island, okay?"

"I'll see, Odell."

She would want to hold down the office. Mothersill starts to read.

When he finishes Dorothy sighs and says quietly, "That's wastebasket material, Odell. They're not ready to do that. But you ought to include the information that the Homestead Act went into effect January 1, 1863, the same date as the Emancipation Proclamation, thereby effectively eliminating almost four million people from participating in the land rush."

"Good," Mothersill says, frowning as he scribbles in the margin. He says, "Maybe it *is* for the wastebasket, but I had to say something drastic. Hell, I sent a memo down to Washington this afternoon on seeding the clouds over Detroit to make it rain. Maybe rain would drive people out of the streets or send the cops and the Army into shelter."

Finished writing, he shoves the paper away and they both look across the river to Queens. "Shit," Mothersill says softly, with an excess of sibilancy.

He is reluctant to go home. The apartment would only underline the emptiness he now feels. Once an empty apartment was like a silent, smiling co-conspirator witnessing without utterance or movement the comings and goings of Mothersill and the foxes, sharing with him their scents and sounds. Over the years he has moved from the Village to Chelsea to Washington Heights and now lives on the West Side, a neighborhood that is being demolished and rebuilt at the same time; often it reminds him of Ellie. He knows he will enter his apartment and turn on as many lights as he will pass; he will turn to WLIB or WWRL to get the other side of the news of Detroit and the other towns. He hardly notices any more the objects he has collected from his travels. Dogon sculptures bear a thin coating of dust; a Felix Edubo head stands out from the wall, somber; calabashes rest without pattern on shelves. The prints from Kröller-Müller have not had their glass coverings cleaned in months. The small Jacob Lawrence, a Hausa setting in bright near-desert colors, nearly always draws his eye. It embodies a quintessence of loneliness.

Odell Mothersill is forty-two. For three years running he has been cited in *Ebony* as one of the one hundred most eligible bachelors. True, he is lonely, but he is not unhappy. He is not happy either. Lately, he has been dreaming of the sower, and he is curious and pleased both; he has not dreamed of him regularly. Perhaps working with young people, older to be sure than the kids at the adoption agency, but kids nevertheless. PeeCeeVees, a mixed bag, mostly white, and civil rights workers, mostly black for the past year. None were pure and none certainly filled the valleys and covered the hilltops behind him, their innocence as atmosphere. The kids were losing; they were not going to overwhelm the world and he only rarely thought of leading them.

Maybe Candace Cone was a new breed.

"You're right," Mothersill says to Dorothy. "Maybe I better get going. But let's go over this Candace Cone thing again."

"She's seventeen or eighteen. A little sister," Dorothy says with that tolerant smile she can give. "She's marched in Selma, did the COFO summer thing in Mississippi, and so on. She was hired as a part of a riot study team for Rochester. Stokely spoke there last year and things came unstuck, and Stokely may be returning."

"Yeah," Mothersill grunts. "Was this team put together by Sociomatics?"

"Right. We fund them but their reports go to Washington. We're supposed to get copies."

"And?"

"No copies. We do have copies of her reports, though."

"There are six members on the team?"

"No, five. Three black and two white. Two black males, one black female, and one white male and female."

"And this girl says . . . ?"

"The white members rarely go to the black areas, but they

sit in their hotel rooms and file reports which she considers to be incendiary and completely untrue. Like the black militants are planning to put LSD in the city's water supply."

"That sounds white," Mothersill says.

"They use a lot of grass, too, according to her."

"The white team members?"

"Yes."

"No big thing. Unless they get caught." So many of the young whites Mothersill knows saw life as a lark as long as they were not starving Gallahs or Fulani or American blacks. For them the crunch was always the fare to get back home, safe. He and Dorothy talk about this all the time. "Who's in charge of the team?"

"The white guy, Ploski."

"Has Cone seen any other of this guy's reports?"

"Yes, but hasn't been able to obtain any copies. The team members turn their reports in to Ploski. He sees them all, but they don't see his and—"

"Then how did she get that LSD in the water supply bit?"

"She was in his room when the project director for Sociomatics called, and he fed it to him over the phone."

Mothersill and Dorothy stare at each other for a moment, then Mothersill shifts his eyes. He knows something about this Sociomatics outfit. They are also into the Pacification Program in Vietnam. It would be to their enormous advantage, financially and politically both, to ensure the aura of trouble in Rochester.

He glances now at the crossed spears on his wall: one a Masai, the other a Hausa. Mothersill believes them to be beautiful, works of art. There was a story that the Masai lance was adopted from the Roman broadsword. There was not any evidence that Roman soldiers penetrated east Africa south of Meroe. It could have worked the other way around; the Romans, but first the Greeks, adopted their swords from the Africans. As for the Hausa spear, it was two weapons, or became so with a twist of the hand. It was also a riding lance. No one seemed to see not only the art shaped in the metal, but the utilitarianism embodied therein.

Mothersill sighs. "This Cone is—"

"The whole team is in the Statler," Dorothy says. "I'll give you her report. Read it on the plane. Get some rest tonight."

Mothersill stands. Dorothy stands. He sees exactly where he would place his hands on her hips. "Okay?" she says lightly, turning away from him.

"You going to be on the Island?"

"Try here first."

The poverty programs were making a lot of corporations and individuals, if not rich, pretty well off, Mothersill mused on the plane. The young Miss Cone obviously was not one to be jived around. As far as she was concerned everyone was going to toe the mark. Mothersill opened her papers to her first report:

> Rochester has less public housing than any other city in New York State—just over five hundred units. The Negro population is around 45,000. The housing situation here is comparable to Newark. There is very little middle-income housing even for people who earn, husband and wife together, $200 weekly. They have absolutely no place to rent with their money. They must buy or forget it. There is one "Open Key" project in the middle-income range. Private builders can come in and build housing which may then, at some later time, be turned back to the public housing authority. Two hundred families per year, that is black families, may be displaced within the next six to seven years under planned urban renewal. Medically, the county hospital reports rickets and tuberculosis carried by patients who have arrived from the southern states; these diseases have not been observed in Rochester in black or white patients for at least ten to fifteen years. It is said that blacks from the South have been given one-way tickets to New York State because it is easy to obtain public assistance. Negroes are underemployed here, mainly because they do not have the skills to work in a high-pressure industrial center like Rochester—and Rochester

> is Kodak. Three to 6,000 jobs reportedly are available. Most of the plants, however, are located in sections of the city that do not have public transportation, so it would be difficult for even black janitors to accept employment in those factories. Instead the labor market pool tends to be filled, at least in the fall and winter, by farmers from the outlying regions. They have cars or trucks.

A smudge of red on the periphery of his vision caused Mothersill to look up.

"Drink, sir?" the stewardess said, reaching to let his tray down, her smile saying, I know you're going to have one, aren't you, baby?

She was black and Mothersill smiled back at her. "Scotch, please."

"Scotch it is. Rochester? Chicago?"

"Rochester," Mothersill said.

"Ah, well," she said, and was gone.

> Approximately 1,000 West Indian workers are said to now be employed at the main Kodak plant. They are from the U. S. Virgin Islands. Since wages in those islands tend to be low and costs high these workers may feel they have found a good thing. In terms of Kodak, low wages, compared to what white workers get, would seem high to the islanders. It seems likely therefore that in addition to everything else, intra-racial problems can be expected to arise. The Reverend Davis Hudson says that his studies reveal that no more than one hundred Negroes own property in Rochester. They also show that 82 per cent of the families he has contacted have both parents in the home.
>
> Candace Cone

Black stewardesses, Mothersill noted, were not wearing their hair natural. Company rules, maybe. Pity he wasn't going on to Chicago. She looked interesting, like fun, too. Was it his imagination, he wondered, or were females maturing earlier, ripening sooner, or was it that psychic going over the hill of a man over forty? Could that be what made so many women look so good all the time? But women were freer too; skirts on the way up, more and more subtle makeup. You saw a woman in her fifties in short skirt and all done up, you knew she hadn't given up the ghost. The same for women far older. Masters and Johnson. They took the dirty from old men and women—who never believed they were anyway.

"Another?"

"Sure."

She was as old as, certainly not much older than, a couple of his nieces. Marvelous how the range expanded as one got older. From sixty to eighteen and why not?

The man across the aisle from him smiled. Mothersill nodded. The man got up, stretched and looked out Mothersill's window. "Nice day, isn't it?"

Mothersill wondered why white people bothered at times like this. It was as if they hadn't heard or read anything about Newark or Detroit. "Yes, it's all right," he said.

"I'll bet you've got a big one," the man said in a lowered voice.

Mothersill jerked up. He couldn't have been hearing right, but looking at the man, he knew he had. "Get the fuck out of here," Mothersill snarled. The man backed up a step as the stewardesses squeezed by, still smiling. "Get away from me or I'll kill you," Mothersill said evenly. The man's face went flat, then red. Nice day, Mothersill thought. You cock-sucker.

Do I look like that? Mothersill wondered, turning to stare out his window. What did *he* see that *I* never see in my mirror or feel? Could he have seen something no other person I've ever met saw? Oh, the hell with it. A guy like that'd suck off a cobra and enjoy it.

> Crime involves to a large extent elements of the Negro and Italian communities, with blacks holding the lesser roles, such as pimps, pushers and ostensible bar ownerships. The prostitutes are said to be women from Florida who came north with their families to do migrant farm work and then moved into the 3rd and 7th wards. Their present price is "Ten plus two," or $12 per trick. The "vice lord" of the 7th ward is a

man named Mangione. Heavy police patrols of the two wards apparently have had no effect on cutting down on crime and vice. In fact, while on Clarissa Street, twice police car No. 14 passed by an open crap game without stopping. It is most ironic, or perhaps not, that while crime is heavily controlled by the Italians, the vigilante groups and the police force are also composed of many Italians. There is no Negro newspaper in the city, but *The Challenger*, a photo-offset job is brought in weekly from Buffalo. Black groups from Buffalo and Rochester exchange visits frequently.

In the course of this investigation I met Mrs. X, the widow of a Baptist minister. The minister, white, like his wife, was found dead last December, hanging by his neck in his church study. He had tried over a long period to integrate his church whose congregation was made up of some of the most powerful men in Rochester. There was strong opposition to integration. The family of the minister was subjected to unbelievable harassment: nightly telephone calls, scurrilous letters being circulated saying the minister had a drinking problem and was having some kind of relationship with his associate minister. The X's secured an unlisted number which was given to but a trusted few of the church membership, but within a few days the obscene calls began again. The FBI was called in, but nothing happened. On two occasions, the family car had the lugs on its wheels loosened, once with nearly fatal results. The threats against the minister and his family continued. The younger daughter had to be placed under psychiatric treatment. Then the minister took his life—so the official verdict went. But there were two people in the church at the time of his death. The widow has never seen the body and the minister's parents were advised not to look at it because "he had gone through torture." The widow has never received a notice of death from the coroner or a police report. She had spoken to her husband only an hour before his death and he had asked her to come and pick him up, since he had no car. The widow still gets threats. On Thursday evening on the way to her home to tape more about this matter, we were followed to within a block of her home by a sheriff's deputy. Mrs. X gave me the names of the people on the board of deacons who had the minister's

> unlisted number, and who knew of his death at just about the same time she did. There are a number of people in Rochester who do not believe Reverend X took his own life. That the community has reacted so nonchalantly in this matter is a measure of the racial situation. It feels like stomp-down Mississippi.
>
> Candace Cone

It feels like stomp-down Mississippi. They had been his kids, Mothersill thought, prowling the backwoods and back cities of the South, frightened but going on nevertheless, the ancient convict amorality of the Scotch-Irish something to blot out, as one had to blot out human life among dinosaurs. From civil rights to the PeeCeeVees and back again, not filling any valleys, no, not covering hilltops, but dying horribly and being so frightened that the might of the frightener/inquisitor came to be right. Some slunk home. Who could begrudge what they called "Movement Leg" under such circumstances? Somewhere there had to be love measured in minutes at least.

And now Miss Candace Cone had discovered that she was not in Mississippi, but she was still fighting.

> At 6:15 this morning I received a call and then a visit from a young woman I had talked with in the 3rd ward. Her name is Henrietta and she works as a domestic, although she went to Johnson C. Smith college for two years. She told me that the Negro domestics—maids, cooks and baby-sitters—had been organized by the Red Ball. (She explained that the Red Ball Express was a black army outfit during World War II. They drove trucks, carrying fuel for General Patton.) The Red Ball would use some of the cars involved in the drag races. Each car will hold three men in case of a racial outbreak. They will be the driver, a bomber, or someone with firebombs and a gunner. The cars will move in squads of threes. While the Red Ball is operating in the business sections, the domestics will be preparing meals that will result in the sickness of nearly everyone along Ambassador Drive and other wealthy sections, and kidnapping the children who are their wards. These will be exchanged for the

members of the Red Ball who may be caught or detained by the police. Henrietta did not know when these events would take place, but indicated certainly not before any trouble.

Candace Cone

Mothersill was still smiling at Cone's last report when he checked into the hotel. The halls were dark, depressing and, like his room, had seen other if not better days. It was the kind of place where a house detective, last publicized in Marx Brothers movies, could be expected to pounce out of the shadows. He had been in many better hotels in Africa. Kodak, Mothersill thought, was capable of doing better; Rochester was Kodak.

He read the local papers until five, then turned on for the various newscasts on television, local and national. Then he called Candace Cone. Yes, she could come for a drink, and if she could get away, dinner. Mothersill tried to match the voice with a face even though it never worked out. The years had not taught him to avoid this game. Maybe because he enjoyed playing it, in having his expectations miss their mark, sometimes for the better, sometimes for worse.

Candace Cone looked vaguely familiar, a disquieting contradiction of ideologies. Her skirt came midway up her thighs, and her natural hair was extremely well-groomed. But that was not all. The face, the movements of her body, her quietly smiling eyes which barely concealed a wariness—he'd seen these before in a thousand pictures of a half a hundred different marches, at rallys, at community discussions, on the front covers of national magazines, on television forums.

"How many days have you left here?" Mothersill asked when the drinks had been brought.

"Just three. Wow. I can't believe you're here. I mean, I know the government doesn't give a damn what happens to its money, and so many of these programs are jive. Like this study."

"Tell me about Ploski."

"He's scared shitless. He only goes out to eat downstairs, or to get a paper. We took him to a Black Muslim place the other night. I thought he was going to fall out. The white chick is his girl. They have the same room. I mean, they aren't even cool."

"He's been with Sociomatics for a while?"

Cone shrugged. "Don't know. He seems to have some connections there. The rest of us are just pickups. Need the bread, have the interest."

She acted older than seventeen or eighteen, Mothersill concluded. But black kids usually were like that, and if you had a summer in Mississippi behind you, you certainly were mentally, at least, closer to forty. "What about the Red Ball you mentioned in your report? That's not true."

"How did you know?" she asked, smiling.

Her smile told him they were sharing the details of a plot.

"Just a guess." He returned her smile hoping it wasn't fatherly. He didn't feel like a parent with her. She smoked a lot and drank with an ease that told him she'd belted many down before. "You were hoping it'd shake them up at Sociomatics and Washington, right?"

"Right," she said. "Oh, I just got tired of Ploski and Hatha—that's his chick—sitting around piping all those lies back to New York and Washington. And if they aren't lying, they're copping our reports. Just shake them up a little. The big lie with a bigger lie. They aren't going to do anything anyway. Just a little snot in the stew."

Yes, she could have been one of his kids and he was torn between behaving like it and acting like any normal man would with a fine young thing in his hotel room. "How about dinner?"

"I can make it," she said. "I told the others I wanted to check something out alone. But it won't be too cool if we leave here together."

"Oh?" A little razzle-dazzle, Mothersill thought, pleased that she had mentioned it before he had. "Where shall we rendezvous?" he asked.

"We've done it. Room service. Can I have a steak? Get one for yourself. Nobody can mess up a steak too much."

"Wine?"

"Can you dig it? I'd love to—"

The young were very much into wine, Mothersill knew, and because they were nobody else could be. "I like wine," he said. "And another drink." He picked up the menu and dialed room service. When he finished he said, "Do you think you can let me see the reports of the others, excluding Ploski and Hatha tomorrow morning?"

"I can get them later and slip them under your door, if you want?"

"That'll be okay." Well, that was that; she'd blocked out the evening. They'd have dinner and talk and she'd leave. He felt an unusual mixture of relief and a fleeting sadness. He'd not made love with a seventeen- or eighteen-year-old girl since he was that age himself. The relief had as much to do with his peace of mind as anything else. Like every man his age, he'd heard about and seen fast little tricks of fourteen or fifteen. But they were unusual; he preferred to think that young girls came to their sexploitations more slowly. Damn! They all seemed now to be as Jennifer was then. He did not like to think of his girls like that, yet he knew that, like the earth, he was not the center of things, although he might have thought so once, and this thought contributed to his sadness. Also, it would soon be too late for him to approach any teen-ager except those to be found hustling around Times Square or some schoolyards. There were instances, of course, where men older than he bedded girls in puberty, and cultures where a twelve-year-old female was much sought after by men past the mid-century mark. Not Mothersill. Yet—

Cone was looking at him, rather tenderly he thought, as if reading his mind. "I figured I was wasting my time writing to your agency. You're the boss? You run it?"

"That so unusual?"

"You know it is, don't you, Mr. Mothersill?"

"I guess so."

"These are jive times, jive times. Newark, Detroit. Ploski and Hatha. Jive times. But, big brother, I sure am glad to see that some of it's real. Are you married? Have you children?"

She was genuinely surprised that he wasn't and had none. "I would have thought you'd have a lovely wife, one daughter and two sons. Didn't mean to be nosy."

"It's all right. How about you? Where do you go to school?"

"Bryn Mawr. I'm a junior there. Started early. Smart. Mother, Father, brother. Brooklyn. We get along fine because we like, really love each other, believe in each other." Her expression gently gave off pity when she said, "I don't know how people get along without family. When I was working in the South it seemed to me that as hard as it was for the brothers and sisters there, it was easier because of family. You know, children, cousins, parents, grandparents."

Mothersill laughed as the dinner was rolled in. "Listen, I've a sister who's got enough family for herself and for me."

"I bet you go out a lot," Cone said in her quiet voice.

"Not too much."

After a while he said, "You with Sociomatics just for the summer?"

"Yes. The bread is outa sight, but I guess these poverty things pay some people pretty good. Mostly I feel guilty about taking the money, but if I don't some other people like Ploski and Hatha will get it and just continue fucking things up for us. So I might as well take it."

"That makes sense."

"Is that why you're in it?"

Mothersill looked at her. There didn't seem to be anything cute about the question. "No. I'm basically a social worker. I was working with the Peace Corps before I got into this."

"Out of the country?"

"Sometimes."

"Africa?"

"Some parts of it, yes."

She clapped her hands and crossed her legs, shoving her feet up beneath her, and Mothersill got a disturbing glimpse of young strong thighs. He sighed. Everyone wanted to know about Africa. What did you tell them?

"Are you going?"

"Oh, yes, *yes.*"

Well, the kids were off to a great start. People his age had had to overcome African missionary collections and Tarzan and the textbooks. Yes, a new breed. "Interesting place," he said.

"Did you like it?" she asked intently, her eyes following his.

"Yes and no. I can see that you're determined to like it, so what can I say?"

"Tell me it's fabulous."

"I can tell you it isn't. Not always."

"Did you see Kenyatta?"

"No."

"Selassie?"

"No."

"Nkrumah?"

"No."

"Nyere?"

"No."

"Were you in West or East Africa?"

"Both." Mothersill smiled at her. "It's a great big place. Lots to see and do and learn. Go."

On her coffee now, Cone pushed back. "Still have contacts with the Peace Corps?"

A real little hustler, Mothersill thought. Maybe they could make a deal? Is she old enough for that? "Yes, I still know some people there," he said. "When you're ready, come and see me." He fished out a card. "I think it'd be best for you to finish school. Have that behind you. You may not want to later."

"What I plan to do is go on my own for a short trip. Then check out the Peace Corps for a longer stay."

"When you finish this study," Mothersill said, changing the subject, "will you still be working for Sociomatics?"

"Well, there are teams going out all the time. I may be assigned to another city. Usually the teams spend a week in each one."

Mothersill knew that the teams were to gather material which would tell government officials just how close a city was to having a race rebellion. All the predictions of such rebellions had been way off. But, Sociomatics had developed the team study system so that at least the grievances of the blacks were on some record. He imagined that the technique had been developed in Vietnam—"Pacification Teams."

Copies of Sociomatic's reports had not been sent to Mothersill's office, he had concluded, because Sociomatics' top white people wished to deal with other top white people in Washington. They spoke the same language. A black man in the middle would fuck it up, criticize, make suggestions which might be too emotional, too black, and not as objective about matters as the whites would be.

Cone said, "Maybe Chicago. Somebody mentioned Syracuse. I just don't know."

"Just what does it look like here?" Mothersill asked.

Cone recrossed her legs and smiled as Mothersill's eyes followed her thighs. "Kodak could make the whole thing cool, if they wanted to. I've got a couple of kids working in the shipping department. For the past few days they said there've been photographers all over the place taking pictures in case they get burned out, so they can get their insurance."

"I wonder how many of those boxes photographed are empty," Mothersill mused aloud.

"Hey! I never thought of that," Cone said.

Mothersill leaned away from the table. "A guy whose business is marginal or running at a loss and who's covered by pretty good insurance can start his own fire during one of these things and blame it on rioters. That's getting harder and harder to do, though."

"Do you want to look around the city tonight?"

"Sure. I've got a car. Why don't I meet you in the Plaza, say near the rent-a-car place in half an hour?"

Cone got up. "Okay. I've got to go to my room for a hot minute. I'll see you there."

When she was gone, Mothersill, peering out into the night that had settled down, telephoned Dorothy at home. She picked up on the first ring.

"I think I can get back by tomorrow night. But I want you to call Sociomatics the first thing in the morning and have them hand-deliver copies of the reports of their Rochester riot team. No excuses, or we'll recommend suspension of their contract to Washington. How come you didn't take off?"

She thought he might need something. No, she wouldn't take off tomorrow; she wanted to make sure those reports came in. Would he call her tomorrow evening when he got in? Was everything all right? Was Candace Cone helpful? Oh, dinner together. Seems like a bright young woman.

"This is North Clinton Street," Cone was saying as they cruised through the city. "There was some rock-throwing action here a couple of days ago. The Xerox people got pretty uptight about it, though. Too close for comfort."

Mothersill liked the way she sat, fully at ease, as though she rode with him every day of her life. She said later, "This is Nassau Street. Drag racing. Really explosive. You get thirteen to fourteen hundred people who come and watch some nights or weekends, and although the streets are cleared, the cops still try to break it up. The Fight group asked chief Lombard to keep his men the hell outa here unless he really wants a riot on his hands."

"Where do you live in New York?" Mothersill asked.

"I share a place with two other girls on West Seventy-fourth

Street. My father thought I was too young, but my mother didn't. You know, I'd been down south and all that. My mother's great, so's my father, but I think he worries a lot. I don't know why. They say I'm just like my mother, so I can take care of myself."

She touched his arm. "Clarissa Street. The main drag, as you can see." People were sitting on porches or standing on corners following the approach and passing of the car. "Pete's barbershop, and there's Big Jeff talking to a couple of the girls. Have you ever been to a prostitute, Mr. Mothersill?"

"No," he said, startled.

"Oh, there's Mamma Smack," Cone said, rolling down the window and calling out, "Hi, Mamma, what's happening?"

The woman's voice drifted after them: "Your world, baby."

"She supposed to have a two-hundred-dollar-a-day habit—Donnafrido that's one cop hates bloods, Mr. Mothersill. That's his car, number fourteen. That pink house there," she said, pointing. "A whore house owned by the Italians." The black neighborhood slipped by, the voices and music from the bars fading behind them. "It's too late now," Cone said. "We should have stopped in Shabazz for some bean pie." She turned in her seat toward him and Mothersill knew without looking that her dress had ridden way up. For just an instant he thought of reaching over and touching her thighs, then the instant was past. "And they've got great all-beef sausage that tastes better than pork pan sausage. I mean they really burn over there."

"Which way back?"

"You're heading right, but let me out here. I'll bring the reports to you in about fifteen minutes, okay?"

"Thanks, Mr. Mothersill," she said when she got out. "I'm sure glad you're on the case."

In his room Mothersill spun the television dial for news. He always found it strange being out of New York where one was bombarded by news nearly every minute of the day. Outside New York, the news came with less urgency and with far fewer portents of imminent disaster. There was a roundup on Detroit. Sure. Every city was potentially a Detroit.

He started at the knock on the door, then crossed the room with three steps and opened the door. Candace Cone stood holding the papers, dressed in a full-length night gown. "Hi," she said softly, making no move to enter. Her eyes searched his and while he was sure he was returning her gaze, he was more certain that he was limiting his perception of it. "Hi," he said, noticing the swell and fall of her breasts, now free of the bra. *Come in, come in* raged in his brain, commanding his mouth to speak. But he remained silent, conscious of a strange hurting that slowly spread through his body. "Thanks, Candace. I enjoyed the evening."

Only then did she move the papers slowly toward him. Mothersill felt them in his fingers, his eyes still locked with hers. "G'night," she said, lowering her eyelids and raising them, as if in pain. "Night." A second passed, then she stepped back. Mothersill fought the desire to watch her walk down the hall. He closed the door and returned to the set where, with that air of finality that marks the oral paragraph of both television and radio, the former moving on to a new scene, he heard the last remarks concerning the Algiers Motel.

Shaker Heights, Cleveland.

Mothersill has finished up in Rochester and on whim has decided to visit his sister. Dorothy sounded disappointed on the phone, but she has the reports in hand, and Mothersill, posing as the house inspector, has seen Ploski in his room with his girl. They had been smoking and Mothersill asked matter-of-factly, "Grass?" and Ploski put a twenty in his hand. If he didn't succeed in sinking Sociomatics altogether Ploski was gone and they'd think twice before hiring anyone else like him.

He sits now in the living room, watching the evening news, which is filled with Detroit. Mason and Lispernard and the two teen-agers who live home are also watching. One boy is in Vietnam, one in college; both girls are away at Clark College. Mothersill wonders if every black family in the nation is watching the news, boosting the ratings of Cronkite. The only sound comes from the set except once in a while Lispernard "tsks." Mothersill sees her hands clutching the necks and shoulders of Darcy and Dan. Mason and Lisp, he sees, exchange glances that mean more than words; they have been together a long time, struggling up and away from Hough to this mostly Jewish neighborhood.

Mothersill remembers, in 1942, the stillness that had come to Hough during that first riot in Detroit, and how poolhall groups (strange how the militants moved from the poolhalls to the schools) talked about caravans to Detroit to help the cats out.

"Look! *Look* at that goddamn cop!" Mason shouts, crouching and pointing toward the set, his face lumped with a rage that cannot be released. Lisp has covered her face with her hands; the black man goes down under the club, one hand outstretched to ward off the next blow. There are tears in Darcy's eyes; she's the sensitive one. Dan, her twin, is biting his lips, his eyes loosed from the diddy-bopper's cool, have gone wide.

"I can't watch any more," Mason announces and thunders down to his den.

As he goes the television film slides to Cronkite, then to the Pope's visit to Turkey, De Gaulle in Canada, Sandburg at death's door. Mothersill joins his brother-in-law downstairs in the paneled den, leaving Lispernard to clean up the kitchen with the help of the twins. Mason motions toward the bar and Mothersill pours himself a scotch.

"I just don't know how this motherfuckin' country can keep goin' the way it is," Mason says in a voice shading from disgust to sadness. He is as old as Mothersill. When he sits, the flab around his middle, not so obvious when he stands, collapses down around his belt like a parachute settling to the ground.

"It'll keep going," Mothersill says. "It's too big. Television only moves along what happens in one or two places. By the time the shock waves travel across the country, man, the events that caused them are already fading out. Like Detroit is fading out. If this sumbitch was the size of France or Germany or Spain or England—any other country except Russia or China—there'd be collapse."

He takes a long pull at his drink while Mason studies him. "They brought both Russia and China down, man, what the hell're you talkin' about?"

"Other times," Mothersill says. "Russia, 1917. China, finally, 1949 officially. Just under the wire, before Sam got his shit together, and even so the Chinese ran them the hell away from the Yalu only a year later. Russia, China today—" Mothersill shakes his head. "Like the States, man, all the new technology, the power, the control."

"Well, this motherfucker got to go," Mason says with finality.

"Yeah, one day," Mothersill says. He has never seen Mason like this. Usually he's full of stories of his customers; he sells cars. He's full of fun and sport. The challenge of life is as nothing to him. A husky man, now graying in the head and mustache (as is Mothersill, who only recently has discovered a few white pubic hairs) Mason reminds Mothersill of a bear: easy to get along with when his mood is right, a lumbering, growling terror when it isn't. Mason has never spoken of Potts; that is a very private area, and he knows in any case that his wife has.

"So, how you gettin' on, Odell?"

"The top."

Mason bats his knee and laughs. The explosion of laughter lightens the room. Detroit has been sitting too heavily upon it. "I bet you are. Man—" the word is drawn out, curved. "Ole Lisp really frets about you not being married. She figures you're out here ripping off leg left and right, doin' chicks *in.* Women are like that, they *trained* to think like that. Way I see it, it's all jive. *They* been rippin' cats off. Half the cats I sell cars to, their ole ladies made them buy, or they doin' it for their ole ladies.

Shit, man, they *know* they can look up longer than a man can look down. I tell Lisp to leave you alone, it's—"

"Odell?"

Mason shakes his head. "See there? She won't listen. You know she's sent the kids out of the kitchen so she can talk. You're leavin' tomorrow, right? She will talk tonight."

Mothersill gets up and climbs the stairs. Lisp is sitting in the kitchen, which is all cleaned up. There is a pot of coffee on the stove and she has a cup before her. She squints her eyes from the smoke of the cigarette she has just lit, and points to a cup. Mothersill nods, and he sits, observing her pleasure at his acceptance. A refusal would have signified a truculence on his part, a raising of barriers. Mothersill has never refused. They have shared coffee like this often, at the deaths of their parents, during those visits he once made soon after Potts was sent back here, after his first trip to Africa—so many times and in about five different kitchens.

Lispernard places the coffee on the table and sits down. Her study of him is brief but thorough. "You look tired, baby. And preoccupied. Work or the chicks?"

"The times, I guess," he says. He doesn't wish to talk in pedantic riddles when with her, but her questions are so flanged that he can best ward off all innuendo by supplying answers just a bit outside her scope of things. Not that the times are outside her range, but she certainly doesn't know *exactly* how he feels about them.

"Barbara's dead," she says simply. "Barbara Smith."

Strange, Mothersill thinks, to remember someone back to life in your memory when they're dead. Lispernard's playmate upstairs, Etta Mae, ah, of course a special memory. Barbara, later, was for feelies in the park. And Popa and Momma, too, gone, all gone, their presences closed over, as with the surface of quicksand. He feels these things when he visits Lispernard; they do not reach him through the concrete screens of New York City, at least not as much.

He knows that those who condemn the rebellions are bereft of a sense of the past. Perhaps that is why he visits his sister, to recall it: recall, though he didn't know then, his father earning $15.62 a week not including tips, and sometimes these were small and grudgingly given by the passengers; his father sleeping only four hours a night, while on the road covering ten thousand miles a month, making up berths, cleaning bathrooms, "yessiring" his ass off and browbeating the Toms to join the Brotherhood of Sleeping Car Porters; that, and like black musicians, bringing the news to black communities, spreading it around the barbershops and poolhalls and bars; it was from his father that Mothersill first heard about A. Philip Randolph. ("Well, his last name and my first name was the same, so I had to go along with him. He was right all the way. He told them peckerwoods what it was all about.")

His father died in his sleep, and when Mothersill went back for the funeral that little "new" house they'd dreamed of when Belle came seemed a mockery of their dreams. His mother went just as quickly and quietly, in the same house, attended by the same people, or so it seemed. She had earned four dollars a week in the old days, when he was a boy. Nineteen dollars and change a week, altogether. But they had been yoked to a future, to "gittin' up in the world," even as they cleaned someone else's toilet or sanded.

Mothersill does not recall when he got it altogether, put all those random statements, looks and circumstances into perspective, but he did. And he recalls his shock. It was not so much that they'd worked hard, but that they'd taken pride in that work, too much pride, perhaps. Because there was little else, he finally concluded. If the best you can do is to plow a straight furrow, then you try to plow the straightest—

"Her old man's been runnin' like a chicken without a head after young girls. Been doin' it for years, but the girls seem to be gittin' younger. One not much older than Darcy. Barbara took the little one, went into the garage and started the car. Found them there. That no good"—she struggled and won—"Negro."

"What do you hear from Ronnie?" he asked. Barbara, what the hell for? Why?

"He's counting the days. Talk about Detroit. He says they've had some riots in Saigon and the jungles where black and white just stand and shoot it out. Mason is sick about it, but he won't let it show. Ronnie ought to be back here, in Detroit or Cleveland."

"Kim and Kate?" Kim and Kate. God. They were as old as Cone.

"They're fine. Working down there this summer, and Brother, he's working with a friend in Los Angeles. Can't get any of them to go to New York. Afraid of the big city, I guess. How's it treating you these days?" Eyebrows arching, a smile playing around her lips, and he wonders what she would say if he introduced her to someone like Candace Cone and says, "This is it." Or Dorothy Nigro. Or, or, or.

"Same old thing. What's with Potts?"

"Oh, she's the same. Goes about her business, goes home, goes to the doctor. Never see her. And her father's been sick a lot lately."

Mothersill sees the thought forming. Perhaps Lisp senses that his defenses are down. She wants to know, has always wanted to know what happened to Potts. She's never asked, though she may feel she has a right to; she warned him.

"Too bad about that," she says instead, and in the silence Mothersill hears an electric clock whirring. "Anything about to happen?"

Mothersill stretches, fakes a yawn, and Lispernard, quick to catch signals, hurries on. "I know. You'll never get married. You're settled in your ways now. Be hard to change them." She starts to say something about kids, but changes her mind. His usual retort is that she has enough for both of them, but she knows he calls her kids regularly, slips them checks, and that in a tight, they know they can call on him.

"I worry about you Odell, being there all alone. I mean alone. No family. Suppose you get real sick in the middle of the night? Who can you call? Suppose you get a stroke and can't move?"

There are tears in her eyes. He's never seen this before. Maybe it's Detroit, the kids flung all over hell. Maybe it's something showing on his face that he doesn't see. Maybe she sees him the way he sees other people sometimes. He reaches over and takes her hand, surprised at its warmth.

"Hey," he says. "What's all this? If you're so worried about me, why don't you come visit sometime. Never been able to get *you* to New York, forget about the kids."

"Oh, Odell. That's not what I'm talking about."

He pats her hand. "I know," he says, and pauses on the verge of entering a kind of confessional. He grins and lowers his head. What could he say to her? How could he say things to her? She has lived, after all, a preciously sheltered life, and she has apparently enjoyed sex with great pleasure—it shows in her slightly plump form, the care she takes of herself, the little glints and glazings of her eyes; she thinks her brother has not seen her sliding her hand around Mason's buttocks or up between his legs during all these visits. Mothersill finds these motions loving, and they are, the way she does them. And Mason, for all his talk and sly looks and tales of conquests that strain his brother-in-law's credulity, has grown fat on Lisp's loving and loving care. They are one and the same, Mothersill knows. Smothered pork chops, the meat just barely resting to the bone, the seasoning calculated to challenge the most obdurate taste bud—yeah, there was an old saying about that kind of love.

So what could Lispernard know that she would or could share with him, this woman, his second sex experience, to be blunt. Still he wished he could talk to her, but says simply, "I guess I'm not the marrying kind, Lisp, for the millionth time, and there are people I can call, don't worry. I mean, you might not *like* them, but I get along with them—"

"You mean they're white."

Mothersill looks at his sister. "Not all of them. Not even most of them. I thought you were worried about me. You mean to tell me that, if I were dying and the only person I could reach was a white girl friend, you'd rather I die? Is that what you're saying?"

She does not like where the question puts her. "You said I might not like them—"

"That didn't necessarily mean white—"

"I guess Detroit—"

"We're going way past Detroit. There may be a thousand other Detroits but black people will go on—"

"I'm sorry," she says.

"No you're not, but it's all right."

"It might be hard for me, though, to get used to someone white. I have to say that, Odell."

"Then that'd be your problem to work out, wouldn't it?"

They have never talked like this before. Mothersill is defending no one, but perhaps a position, one of which he has not been aware of holding. As he speaks again he hears Mason coming heavily up the stairs. He will go into the living room and turn television on again. "When I said you might not like them," Mothersill says, "true, they could be white, they could be young, almost as young as Darcy; they might be fast and slick, superfoxes; they might have one leg or one tiddie—" He pauses. "And they might be more inclined to suck than fuck—"

Lispernard places a palm over her mouth, a ladylike gesture, but her eyes remain intense, interested. Her brother, as she always suspected, once he started talking, had things to say.

And in the living room, Mason has tuned out the show he's watching. A man with as many children as he has must often do this and he's become an expert; watching television at times like these is like watching it without the volume turned on. He thinks: I haven't had any good head in *years* and this cat is talking about—wheee! Once, once a year, if he is lucky, and Lisp is high enough, she will give him some head, but it takes days before she gets over it. Maybe, thinks Mason, *I* ought to visit Odell.

"—and all you can think of," Mothersill is saying, "is that it matters to *you* what the color of the woman is."

He's into white women, Lispernard thinks, and places her forehead into her hand, a gesture of their mother's, remembered and now automatic. "More coffee or more booze?"

No, it won't work, Mothersill thinks, talking with Lisp; her view is fixed, squared, completely determined. She believes (and he, too, would rather believe) that his life has been and is now filled with sexual triumphs. He knows better, although he thinks of the triumphs with a tingle in his penis.

But there are things that pass between a man and a woman that can never truly be shaped or set by the spoken words, yet, for just a second, Mothersill thought he could tell his sister. Drawing back from the edge, he grimaces, stares at the light on in the oven. Those things that pass between a man and a woman, sights, sounds, smells; attitudes, the roll and curl of the eyes, the feel of skin, of lips and bodies opening—describe those things or the incline and decline of tone, the deciphering of their meanings; or battles that are fought with armies of eye movements, harsh octaves or shrill and sudden dangerous motions that threaten even greater danger.

Lispernard does not understand that he has lost more than she could ever imagine him winning. Mothersill smiles. "I don't want anything. Thanks."

"C'mon, Odell. Let's go down to the bar for a taste." Mason is stuffing his wallet into his pocket. Get this man outa this shit, he thinks, watching Odell rise. "Be back in a while, baby," Mason says. In his car, a demo Tempest, Mason whips on the air conditioning and chuckles. "I know you glad to be outa there." He kicks the car in and they lurch away. Mason wants to get to the nearest air-conditioned bar to hear more about those head-jobs in New York, whether sisters or grays. It doesn't matter to him. Wheeee!

Candace Cone felt empty and abused; Jesse's coming had changed nothing. Now she was gaily waving her fingers at him and smiling from behind the latch-chain. Yeah, bye-bye.

"Be talkin' to you, Momma," Jesse stage-whispered as he went down the steps.

She did not really hold it against Jesse, his inability to make her feel anything solid; he was just doing the natural thing. Call up. If she hadn't said, Yes, come on over, someone else would have. But she had hoped—one always had the hope—that his coming this time would have meaning. Hungry, she opened a can of sprats and poured some of the cheap vodka Jesse had brought over ice. She turned on television and expertly rolled a cigarette and lit up.

Her roommates were away, Marie at Sag and Jan at Bar Harbor. Jan would come back broke, cadging bits of money from her. She never paid back unless nearly begged or threatened. Marie was okay. Bad luck with men. She'd just had an abortion in Puerto Rico. Men used her badly, but maybe now she'd get her head together. Both had invited her to spend time with their families, but Jan, whose father was a doctor, hadn't meant it. Candace, as much as she liked Marie, whose father was a dentist, didn't want to play nursemaid to her. Besides, she had to work. Lately, Candace had the impression from Jan that she, Candace, should have been happy to room with them at school as well, they being daughters of professional men. It hadn't been that way at first. They'd been a little intimidated by her exploits in the South at such a tender age, and a little shaken by her "brightness." Both wore great 'fros; Marie to conceal her shyness and Jan to appear to be what she could never really be, a black militant. Candace was a beard for both their innermost feelings and was tired of it. Maybe it was about time she moved into her own room at school in the fall. New York, too. But she liked them, just as she liked Jesse; she could understand them. It was only at times like these, becoming more frequent, however, that she became sad, cynical and fed up with the way people used her, her goods, her body. It was terrible and it left her with a sinking feeling that all the marching, killing and hell-raising, all the cries for Black Power and Freedom Now, were just catchwords of the day and that day was past. Didn't anybody else see that?

Candace laughed softly, thinking of the first registration drive she'd gone on with Jesse. Talk about a man being scared! But he had bulled on through. Ah, Jesse. Sweetly she thought of him then, and the others, hooting down all the jive preachers and standing toe to toe with cracker deputies. Even now she didn't dare tell her parents all that'd happened. Maybe her mother would be okay; she was tough behind that sweet, housewifely routine, gloves and hat on in church and all. But her father. He couldn't be as old as he seemed. The white people who worked on Wall Street photographed young even though they'd been there since Year One. Daddy, she thought, the vodka making soft, warm tears come to her eyes. My people. Down there picking up ticker tapes, seeing all that money going and coming and then back home to Brooklyn, the brownstone a tiny shelter from the storms that attacked it from all directions. And her brother, Jerr. A family rebel from the git-go. She supposed he was in Vietnam or Thailand or Cambodia, one of those evil places over there. Strange, how different he seemed from everyone else, turned in on himself looking for God only knew what. Maybe the Army was the best place for him.

Her cigarette had gone out and she lit up again, glancing at the television screen, which she was sure she'd been looking at all the time anyway, only she'd not been paying attention to what was going on. The stuff was good; she felt it curling through her stomach.

She did not know when she first thought of Mothersill. Silly name, she thought, Odell. She giggled. They sure went in for some strange names, those old folks. Why was it that Mothersill, who couldn't have been more than a few years younger than her father, seemed to be of another age, more in hers, than in any other? That night standing in the door of his room in Rochester had been something. She hadn't realized until she knocked how she might have looked to him in a nightgown. The team visited each other nights dressed in bedclothes; no big thing. But Mothersill couldn't have known that. It was all right, though, once he opened the door. She was glad she'd had it on. It was all there in his eyes; she'd seen it, and perhaps—she was sure of it—he'd seen what was in hers. In another two days she'd be off for a study of Chicago. She would—

Yes, call him. He'd never call her. The age thing. She'd seen it that night.

"It's that Miss Cone," Dorothy Nigro said, her face impassive. She closed the door of Mothersill's office when she went out.

"Hi, Candace."

Mothersill leaned back until the springs caught, easing him back even farther. He was pleased. But what—how did you talk to a seventeen- or eighteen-year-old woman? "How are you? Wondered what you were up to."

"I'm getting ready to go to Chicago for Sociomatics. I understand Ploski's gone."

"That's a relief," Mothersill said. "Something worth celebrating. When do you leave?"

"Tomorrow."

"Tomorrow," Mothersill echoed, wondering why that upset him. "I'd like—how about some dinner tonight?" He tried to make his voice brisk, atonal, so he would sound offhanded.

"Sure. Will you pick me up or shall I meet you? Pick me up. Have a drink." She laughed and Mothersill could tell she was pleased they had the date. "What do you drink? Vodka, I hope."

"Vodka's fine." He pictured her rushing out to the nearest liquor store and with her last ten dollars buying a bottle of vodka.

"Oh, anything," he said. "About six-thirty?"

"That'll be fine."

Mothersill sat motionless after he hung up, watching an occasional barge move up or down the East River and listening to the noises of the people in the outer and adjoining offices. Well, he thought, it's not every post forty-year-old man who can attract a fine chippie like Candace.

But, he continued, she's under twenty, under *eighteen—eighteen*, jailbait. He hadn't heard, thought of or used that term in a long time. Could it be that now the world thought that people who looked and acted eighteen or older were considered to *be* eighteen or older? Did this mean when he was ninety he'd be trying to make it with seven-year-olds? Or did it mean nothing at all, just a deal, his name as a reference for the Peace Corps for a little of her youngish leg?

At six-thirty promptly he rang the bell that had three names inked in the space at the top: Bowman, Cone, Hilliard. He paused a moment in the brown-painted lobby, sniffing the odors of the dinners being prepared in the building, one of those singles' quarters on the West Side. He knew them, their scuffed carpeting, the odor of coffee mornings (bacon on Saturdays and Sundays), the boeuf bourguignon or coq au vin with their winey smells for those special dinner dates; he couldn't tell what he was smelling, but it was good and his hunger started to come down. He knocked softly at the door, wondering what the neighbors would say should they happen to look out and see him, graying everywhere. They probably wouldn't know that Candace was younger than they thought she was, he considered with some relief.

Oh, shit, Mothersill thought when she opened the door. The simple black mini, with her in it, was perfect. She smiled at the expression on his face and he walked in and said, "Wow," quietly.

"Glad you like it," she said. "It's one of three dresses I own."

"Yeah, well the other two can't look that good."

"How'd you know? Gee, it's good to see you, Odell. I mean, New York, not Rochester, is the place, yes?"

Pleased that she'd called him by his first name, he accepted the vodka martini. "Sure is. How'd you know this was one of my drinks?"

"Just a guess. You don't strike me as being a gin man. The other's scotch, right?"

"Right again."

She sat down in a chair directly across from him, her legs pressed together, the skirt slipping soundlessly to within inches of her hips. "Smoke?"

Mothersill nodded as she passed him the cigarette. For him the sessions with grass were few and far between. He glanced at her glass. White wine. It really was a thing with this generation, grass and wine. Well, no worse and probably better than the hard stuff that went with his generation; they didn't call it rotgut for nothing, no matter how expensive it was. He hoped she didn't smoke on the job. "Hey," he said. "What would your folks think of you going out with someone their age?"

Her expression became exaggeratedly innocent. "You mean this isn't just a harmless dinner date?" Through her smile she cut her eyes at him.

"Sure is," Mothersill said. "But even so?"

"I dig my folks but I don't tell them everything I do. You know people do reach that age. I'll bet you did the same when you were eighteen." They had passed the cigarette back and forth several times and now Candace carefully crushed it out. She bent over him to get his glass, stopped, looked at him, then took it and went to the kitchen nook where she refilled it. "Maybe I shouldn't say this," she said, standing over him. "But I wanted to see you again regardless of your influence in the Peace Corps." Mothersill's hand closed around her hand on the glass and pulled her toward him and kissed her on the forehead. "Oh, Jesus," she said. "That's the best I can get?" She pretended to pout. She sat down. "Where do we go for dinner?" she asked.

"Where would you *like* to go?" he countered.

She looked at him coyly. "I imagine you like to eat in all those downtown places." She had emphasized "down."

"Sometimes. Some of the food is good."

"I guess, but—"

"—you want some soul food," he said, and then teasingly, "Jewish soul food? Italian soul? Greek soul? Chinese soul—"

"Okay, okay I got the message. How about some 'cullud' soul food?"

"That can be arranged," he said reaching over for another toke of the new cigarette she had lit up. "My favorite joint. The Red Rooster. Know it?"

"Mmmm," she said. "Crab cakes."

"Tender, juicy hocks."

"Butterfly shrimp."

"Fried chicken," he said.

"Hot fried fish." Their dishes were being named faster now.

"Yams."

"Collards."

"Blackeyed peas."

"Roast duck."

"Chitlins."

They lay back in their chairs and Mothersill said, "We'd better get started or I'm going to pass out from hunger."

"Odell, I *been* ready."

In the cab, rushing through the barely cooling air, Mothersill took her hand. She opened it and clutched his a little tighter. "You know something," he said, and without waiting for her answer said, "I am feeling *good.*" He glanced at her smile. "Not from that. Being with you. When do you get back from Chicago?"

"Oh, you don't have any business in Chicago while I'm there?"

Mothersill scowled at the cab driver's neck. "No."

"Could you have?"

He hesitated. "Yes."

"*Will* you have?"

He sighed and turned away from her as they left Central Park West and entered Eighth Avenue. She can't mean it. All these young men out here, he thought. Fool, don't let yourself go, now. Finally he said, "I have to say maybe and hope you'll understand." Christ! I was twenty-five when she was *born!*

She looked at him thoughtfully and said, "We look a little alike, you know that?"

He turned quickly. "I did notice." Wryly: "We could pass for father and daughter."

She laughed. "Brother and sister, but really maybe like two people who feel the same way?"

"What way is that, Candace?"

"That sounds so much better than Candy. Well, you know."

"You move fast, young lady."

"Only when I'm sure of myself. I'm a Sagittarian with houses in the right place." Offhandedly, looking out her side, she said, "And I know enough to know."

Her manner made him hesitate on the verge of saying, You think you know, and then the cab was peeling around the Seventh Avenue center strip and braking before the Rooster. The papers and magazines on the newsstand were heavy with the name "Detroit." They stopped to scan them. "Know anybody there?" Mothersill asked.

"Everybody black," she answered, and then, starting down the steps to the restaurant, softly, but hard, like iron gleaming in the sun, "goddamn them."

They found their way to the rear of the restaurant and sat down. Candace's mood became light again. "Now you can have your scotch," she said.

"No, I'll carry on with what I had. You? Wine?"

"White."

He said, "I know." Mothersill glanced at his watch; it was much earlier than he thought. The night had a lot of life left in it.

When the drinks came and they toasted, she said, "Do you like me?"

Mothersill said, "Yes."

She smiled and looked down into her drink. "Thanks."

"No thanks. That's very easy to do, and I think you know it."

"Yes, but I don't want you to like me the way other people do. I want to be special."

He picked up the menu and shoved her one. Deep stuff, he thought soberly. "Hey, chicken fricassee. I'm for that."

"Can I taste? I'm having the crab cakes, stewed tomatoes and collards. Why don't you have the lucky peas and potato salad and we can taste each other's?"

The waitress was hovering over them, pencil poised. "Y'll look like you're into somethin'," she said, smiling. She took the orders and whipped into the kitchen.

"Does that mean we look like lovers?" Candace asked in a voice that teased.

Mothersill grinned. What it really meant was that the waitress was flattering him, an old man with this chippie, in the hopes that his gratitude would show up in the tip. "Something like that," he said, taking Candace's hand, which she'd slipped under the table. He took it with mixed emotions: embarrassment, gratitude, pleasure, pride.

"Would you tell me something, Odell?"

"Sure." There could be nothing, he knew, he could not answer for her.

"How come you've never married?"

Mothersill shrugged.

"Been close?"

"A few times."

"You don't like to talk about it?"

"There's really nothing to talk about," he said. He felt a tremendously sudden sense of displacement of time. This girl, he told himself, is only three years older than Jennifer was. *Three years.* He shook his head. Her hand tightened on his.

"What's the matter? You got this stricken look on your face—"

"Look," he said, hunching forward. "I'm sitting here holding your hand and feeling just fine to be with you. I don't want tomorrow to come and have you go off to Chicago—"

"—but I'm coming back and maybe you'll—"

"—no. What I mean is, where are your *young* men? Why are you with *me* on a night in the middle of summer when quick, good-looking black young men are being ground out every hour . . ." His voice trailed off when he saw her eyes misting over. And she was nodding her head vigorously, and tightening her fingers in his.

"I love them and I loved them. Tell them I wasn't eighteen? No, sir. Don't I look twenty in the right places, Odell? You know it!" She winked as a tear fell from one eye. "You're right. Where are they? Detroit. Lowndes County. Wichita. Rochester. East Harlem. Newark. Out in the street. The others are in Europe. Summer school. New jobs downtown. They are hooked, drunk, crazy; they are scheming, conniving, jive and dead and dying and some of them don't even know it. A lot of 'em have turned the symbols of the rebellion into high fashion; they're super'froed, superdressed; getting like the women they see preening at home? High-fashioning the rebellion to death. White folks'll be caricaturing 'fros for the next three hundred years the way they caricatured nappy hair. Gotdamn!"

She lowered her voice to sound beneath the music now playing on the record player. "My brothers and my brothers. But I know I can't run around for the rest of my life giving up pussy just because I know what's happening to them. I've done a lot of that. They seem to expect it," she said quietly, yet defiantly. "I need shelter, and I want to shelter—"

"This is a new time, Candace, and they will—"

"I can't wait, I can't wait."

Her whisper hit him like a scream. "I was one of those young men," he said, his thumb moving frantically back and forth over her hand. "We don't often get it together like the white boys—"

"Odell," and her voice curved down in recrimination. "What're you trying to tell me?"

They sat back and let the waitress set down the plates.

"I just don't want to be a father," Mothersill said weakly.

"I've got a father," she said, mockingly.

Mothersill wanted to reach over and take her face in his hands and kiss her, but instead pursed his lips toward her and she did the same. They bent to eat.

Mothersill was smiling to himself. Now it was grass, sounds and wine. In his younger days it'd been booze and sounds. Grass was tea and the people who smoked it, vipers. Then you listened to the instrumental solos, learning all the improvisations by heart; you whistled them nonchalantly—piano, sax, trumpet, trombone, it didn't matter. Now the young people listened to the words of the vocalists, nearly all of whom sang messages. A hundred meaningful messages an hour. How come the world was still so fucked up? They didn't have fun any more, like with "Mr. Five-by-Five" or "Be-Bop-She-Bam" or "Flat-foot Floogie."

They sat silently on her couch listening to Gloria Lynne and Nina Simone ballads-messages-blues. They sipped wine and passed the grass back and forth, smiling at each other, and Mothersill heard faintly the air conditioners humming hard, and jets in flight patterns hurtling down over the city.

"Do you ever cry?" she asked. She did not look at him.

He answered, "Not in a while. Would that make me a more tender man if I did more often?"

"Oh, just asking. So you won't be coming to Chicago?"

"No." They'd discussed it again on the way home, and he'd said probably not.

"All right."

"I'll see you when you get back?" This to take the edge off. He expected her to say something about his calling, but she didn't. She merely nodded thoughtfully. "Hey, that's all right, isn't it?" Of course, there was nothing she could do about it, if he didn't want to go, but his question softened things. He felt that responsibility and it bothered him. He took her face and turned it toward him and kissed her tentatively. They parted and drew back, looking at each other. "Odell–" She broke off and he thought, Chicago again. They did not hear the noise behind them.

"Oh! I'm sorry, I–"

Startled, Mothersill and Candace turned, and he took in with a glance the tall, statuesque girl, all the taller for her Afro and the shortness of her dress. Her stricken face begged their forgiveness. Mothersill dropped his eyes as the girl's focused on his, surveying, questioning. Then she moved across the room in slow, sad strides.

"Why didn't you call?" Candace asked loudly, irritated.

The tall girl stopped and fumbled with the handle of the bag she carried.

"I–I tried. The line was busy the first time and then there was no answer." She looked toward them again, just avoiding their eyes and said, "Excuse me," and rushed into another room.

"I'm sorry, too," Candace said. "That's Marie and she almost never comes in from Sag until the end of the summer."

"That's all right," Mothersill said. "We weren't compromised and it is late."

"And I've got an early plane," she said. "To Chicago."

"I know," he said, rising. She rose with him and walked him to the door.

"Would it be so bad if you came to Chicago?" she asked.

There it was again, that insistence upon immediate ownership; he didn't like the feel of it.

"Let me call you when you get back, or you call me. That way there'll be no distractions on your job." He touched her bowed head.

From behind the latch-chain she puckered her lips and threw a kiss as he crept down the stairs. Behind his back, her eyes narrowed and her brows drew down. She thought, So, I'm not worth his making the trip to Chicago. . . .

Mothersill beat his way northward through the mocking coolness in the air. He began sweating after his first few steps. The summers were always so ugly in New York and they did ugly things to a man. If it had not been for the roommate, Marie, he'd be comfortable in an air-conditioned apartment. Strange kid, that Marie. Lovely, shy, but she was supposed to have been seventy-five miles away. Wonder what they're talking about now, the two of them. Maybe Marie was still apologizing. Maybe Candace was bawling her out. On the other hand, maybe they've said absolutely nothing about me.

Even at this hour the cherry bombs were going off, crackling between buildings like sniper fire, reminding Mothersill that in other cities the war still raged and that thousands of police sirens were slicing through the night instead of a couple of hundred. It was this condition that had brought him together with Candace.

An unusual kid, he thought, who so early had come to be filled with views that were sad; so young to feel so much, and most of all, too young to be in the hurry she was for shelter. But he believed he liked Candace. He did not know how to handle it, what to do with it and therefore would do nothing.

In his apartment he stood motionless in the dark before turning on the first light switch. Damn, he thought, the ramifications of Candace spreading, rippling quietly outward, like the rise of a fish at dusk, merging at last with some shore unseen, but there he knew, a truth pushed into his perception. Would he want to live here then, would she? The flames now singeing the night in other cities would be put out and "firemen" left in the areas to make sure no lingering sparks exploded into new blazes. But, under the house, almost two hundred years old now, the wiring was being exposed, the conducting copper unsheathed; fires could be expected with the regularity of weather.

Mothersill pressed the switch and his lights came on and he looked around with Candace's eyes. The room, the living room, tottered on the edge of being like the living rooms of the old-agers he had visited years ago; things, items, objects—all untouched in months. The fucking place is a museum, he thought. And I am nearly a mummy.

Part Five

DOROTHY NIGRO WAS the first to notice it.

It was not so much in the colorful shirts or the widening ties, nor the subtly fashioned suits nor the lengthening hair; it was more in the wintering of his gaze when he looked at her. Before, in those same eyes, there had been hints of spring, warmth, promises, as when the south winds pierce the northern squalls out of Canada.

She would be black, of course, Dorothy mused, and— My, God, she thought, for there was about Mothersill these autumn days a certain look she had seen captured in the photographs of aging personalities, singers, actors, senators, justices, and their new, young brides one of smug triumph not unmixed with a secretive guilt and pride, unvoiced September songs.

—that seventeen-year-old from Rochester, Dorothy thought. She could not know that Candace Cone was eighteen, by her own word, but she wondered just what a child could give a worldly man like her boss—beside some childish pleasures in bed. Even there how many pleasures could one hope to enjoy without having them repeated?

The long weekends: Philadelphia. A small knot of rage burned in Dorothy's stomach. There was not one official thing that'd passed her desk indicating agency business in Philadelphia, so the girl must be there. Dorothy blinked her eyes to shut out the image of Mothersill and the girl together. The girl would be pretty. And there were the times when she called him at home—on business—and there was no answer. That had happened before, of course, but never so frequently. As her calls to him had increased, his to her had become less frequent.

All of this she could have accepted, she thought, were it not for the obvious impatience he had with her now. He cut her off in mid-sentence, questioning, trying to hurry to points which could not be hurried. Often he stood with his door open waiting for her to finish what she was doing, angered that she had not come at his first buzz. If he had to stay in the office for lunch, he ate with his door closed, a sign that he did not want her to join him. There were no more jokes nor those moments of brushing shoulders and stopping momentarily to look at each other. No requests for opinions. There was nothing.

What, Dorothy wondered, would the girl's parents have to say about their daughter hanging out with someone old enough to be her father? She knew that if *she* were the mother, there'd be hell to pay. A forty-plus man knew a lot of things, could take great advantage of a chick who hadn't been menstruating very long, although they– Dorothy caught herself. *They*. Oh, no. He was not going to drive her into thinking like that. This was just a man and woman thing, and she was the woman scorned.

Odell ought to know better. It could be that he needed saving from himself. He could pick up a disease or something. Some of those chicks–oh, she'd seen them no more than fifteen or sixteen in Midtown doorways hustling. But Odell didn't go for that type. This one would more likely come up "pregnant," and hustle a few dollars plus expenses. Dorothy sighed. Maybe she was reading too much into things. They ought to get together and talk about–well–the office. She would be able to tell what was what over a couple of drinks, some place where they could relax.

She found, however, when she set forth the plan that she flushed and stammered with the result that Mothersill agreed more out of pity, it seemed to her, than any other reason. But it would be a private thing (he'd suggested dinner, too) and one of the rare times it had happened lately.

So a gray mood lifted that morning the day of their dinner. She came to the office, she knew, looking good. People who worked with you every day took your looks and your ways for granted until, every once in a while, a new perfume, a new dress or hair style, made them look at you two or three times instead of never, really.

Mothersill cursed. I should've got out of it, he told himself. But, he'd been feeling a little guilty. He hadn't been nice to Dorothy; he hadn't been bad, either. Just correct where they'd been so informal before, and moving toward an inevitable tryst, even when they'd agreed, without having said so, that it would not happen. With Dorothy, though, the sense of her waiting patiently, serving without complaint, first touched, then amused and now angered him. She had no right to wait, to expect, when he had so calculatingly tried to discourage her. There was no point in her waiting any longer.

She was a part of other things now: long days and longer nights, an old photograph in a new frame, a place one could visit with the tolerance of one who'd been there many times before.

But lately Mothersill had been anticipating the dawns, rising to meet them, feeling his energies at the ready, his mind overflowing with images of spring. Sometimes while holding the telephone on those mornings with the dawn sprinting up, like a kid in new sneakers, his hand trembled, and he grew erections at the sound of her voice whispering over the line like the soft rush of swallows.

Outside Mothersill's office door, however, sat another Dorothy. Her hair sparkled, matched the luster of her eyes, and she was something special in her short dress, the silk of which made small, lush sounds whenever she moved. Even though he was not matching her smile for smile nor quip for quip, she remained undaunted, her attitude like that of a long-suffering, wiser person tolerating the bad humor of another less wise and unscathed by the whiplash of time. And why not, Mothersill wondered. Make her as happy as he was; give to the deprived, as long as no questions were asked, no demands outside the bed made. She *was* looking very good.

It was just habit that he'd pushed her clothes back in a corner of his closet, clothes he liked to look at while selecting his own. They were her presence during the week when she was absent. He pushed them back so that if Dorothy (and he thought this was bothering her) snooped around, looking for traces of a woman, she'd find nothing. Not even the toothbrush or soaps and shampoos, the combs.

Had he been thinking all along that he'd take Dorothy to his apartment?

So he did Dorothy or, more precisely he felt, she'd done him. She had initiated the situation; she could have said no. It'd been sort of all right, handling that milk-white body (a porno term, but apt). The sun did not touch that body with its wayward, blue-black hair, a remnant of some "Saracen" rampaging over Calabria a few centuries ago. He had been a fool because he'd hoped that that was all there would be to it—two people together, satisfied, satiated and secure about feeling the same way at the same time concerning the same thing. Maybe it would happen again, maybe not.

Dorothy sat at her desk outside Mothersill's office. She was wearing the same dress she'd worn the day before, and her hair was a little less neatly arranged. She was aware of the glances. She imagined she could hear the girls in the washroom: "Dorothy gave some leg to some*body last night." Never mind that some of them hadn't changed dresses in a week; and what would they say if they discovered she had laid the boss? Now she thought she should have said no, should not have asked for the meeting. Except for those few moments of passion, she felt that he had been patronizing, that she had been boring him. Until she asked as casually as she was able, who he was seeing these days.*

"Nobody special," Mothersill had answered, his hand stroking her buttocks.

Then it was *true, there* was *somebody. Dorothy said, "Is that why you're so sharp these days? An Afro—" Feigning passion, she gripped one of his testicles hard.*

"Ow!" He had missed the teasing, taunting quality in her voice; had not even heard the hurt nor the anger.

"Sorry," Dorothy said. She did not have the right to be jealous, but she was. The danger was that it would leak out; he would see it.

Mothersill glanced at the little smile on her face. Being brave about who he might be seeing? She'd apologized when she squeezed that nut just a little too hard. In spite of her kisses and cooings, the pain, coming when it did, had alerted him.

Dorothy said lightly, "Well, one of these days you're going to settle down." Her smile hid her anger. She was already channeling it, her anger, into her love-making, when she asked, "Is she young and pretty?" And moments later, when they both lay breathing hard, "Am I as good as she?"

Mothersill had guessed there was only one way to change the direction of her thinking. He'd mumbled indistinct responses to her questions and hoped when they finished she'd want to go home. "Hey," he said now, after, in something like admiration, while shifting about and sitting up and generally making motions like it's-time-for-you-to-leave-baby.

"Is she?" Dorothy ignored his movements.

"Well, Dorothy, that's not the way to look at it. You've got your great thing going and she—"

It had been a foolish question to ask. What else would a man say in such a position but, Yes, you're the greatest? "Don't tell me any more!" There. It was out, strung down the length and breadth of his bedroom. Didn't know that old, faithful, quiet Dorothy could speak of such things, did you? Or that I wasn't as much a hedonist as you, or that I could care—get ready, Odell —if she's black or white. Then she said it: "Is she black?"

For a second Mothersill froze. Had he heard correctly? When did that matter to Dorothy? Or: Had it made the difference all along? "Hold it," he'd said. "Wait a minute." With something like pleading he said, "Hey, Dorothy, let's not get in to anything heavy. I'm sorry. I didn't want it to be like this, that's why—"

No, not Dorothy, too. We flee to that refuge in an instant; it was easy to get to because it confirmed half a millennium's existence. It was as if Dorothy had whipped off a mask and lying there in his bed had become another person. He had begun matter-of-factly and was now pleading and whining, insisting that they had the best thing ever, real attachments without the encumbrances, something not to be taken too lightly. In the dim light her eyes bored into him, lasers searing his innards. His words had not moved her; he returned to physicalities. She did not remove his hands. She did not speak.

She vacillated between boredom and suffering and felt him limply inside her. Still under his manipulations, scorn burned out of her. "Shit," she said. That was her verdict on his efforts, which she had discounted and despised from beginning to end.

It had been like coming into a mass of dough, Mothersill had thought. He removed himself, feeling her body giving under his weight. He smarted at her single word of judgment. She wanted to say something else or do something that would totally destroy him; he felt the shape of that desire in the room.

Dorothy, snapping the sheets, breathless from the fight to keep her rage under control, slipped out of bed. She wished she could say something kind, something good, but her mouth would not give the things issue. It was all too much, and suddenly she was overtaken by light-headedness. She raised a steadying hand to the bed, then dropped heavily to the floor, exhausted with loving and hating the man who lay in it; puzzled that she could care what he did with whom; afraid of her own possessiveness, more afraid of the next morning (today, at her desk), she dropped, and was sucked up in darkness.

For a moment after she got out of bed, Dorothy had stood, looking down at him, a figure of fury and vengeance, a victim of broken rules, and the next, she had dropped to the floor with a crash that shook the apartment. Mothersill was frightened. He flailed about for the switch to a stronger light, snapped it on and stared down at her. She had turned alabaster; her lips, cresting with foam, were bright red, a faint promise of life. Oh, man, Mothersill thought. A dead white woman nude in my bedroom. He moved quickly, anxiously, applying cold cloths, bent over her, his genitals swinging lightly inches from her face. An epileptic? Does she know?

Dorothy came to. Odell, a frightened expression on his face, was bending over her, wiping her brow with cold water. He'd looked so scared she wanted to kiss him, but she smiled instead and rested securely in his arms when he placed her in the bed.

"Okay now?" Mothersill's voice'd been hoarse.

She had nodded and drank from the water glass he held to her lips with one hand. With the other he stroked the strands of hair from her face. She had liked the feel of his hand that way. "I've never fainted before," she said. "I'll be all right."

"You'll stay the night," Mothersill said. "So I can keep an eye on you." He hoped nothing would happen. Even if it didn't, there would be tomorrow morning (this morning), and all those other days with Dorothy Nigro floating in the background.

Dorothy nodded and smiled weakly. She felt Odell pulling the sheets up to her chin. She had closed her eyes. She had been content.

"Dorothy, why don't you take a little time off that job. Go down to the Caribbean, a little sun a little rest, some play." Dr. Stang waited for some response beside the self-pitying shrug, then said, "I'll order that, Dorothy. You haven't had a vacation, a real one in years. The job'll keep. The poor won't get any poorer while you're gone—"

"But the rich'll get richer." Dorothy smiled at him. Murray Stang hadn't always had offices on Park Avenue.

"So they say." Dr. Stang watched her light a cigarette. He did not glance at the No Smoking sign on the wall. Dorothy was his last patient for the day, and he'd been seeing her for at least ten years. "How about it?"

She sighed. "Listen, Murray. It's really such a bother to go anywhere alone. I hate it."

"Why won't you see Ted Motola? He's a good shrink, Dorothy."

Dorothy's frequent topic, loneliness, embarrassed Murray Stang. Once in his old office, at about this same time on a winter afternoon when there were no other patients, they'd made love on the examination table; a discussion of loneliness had preceded the act.

Stang shook his head. "I've never understood it, Dorothy. You're good-looking, intelligent, loving, concerned. You must be seeing somebody. Hell, you don't have to be married to be happy. Go on down to the islands with a girl friend. Double-date all the calypso singers." He grinned. "Change your diet a little." Dorothy had changed; sometimes she sounded and talked and acted like the colored people she'd worked with for so long.

Dorothy ignored the innuendo; she was used to it. "For Christ sake, Murray. For you everything starts and ends with sex."

"What else is there, kid?"

"Something. Something in addition to that."

"You really ought to get yourself some rest," he said.

"Oh, I'm not working hard, just thinking hard. How about that fainting spell and the foaming at the lips, Murray?"

"The tests didn't show anything, and you said you were in a stress situation. Stop worrying. Except for your head, you're in good shape." Stang twirled a pencil. "How about a drink?"

"Here or in a bar?"

"Here, if it's okay with you."

"Murray, you're trying to take advantage of me—again." She stood, jabbed out her cigarette, and pulled on her coat. "There're too many people like you. But I guess I like you anyway or I wouldn't be here. How's your wife?"

At least there was nothing physically wrong with her, she thought, pulling her coat tighter around her. In spite of the cold, she decided to walk home; it might help to clear her head, and

Park Avenue was a good street to walk down. They cleared the walks on Park Avenue and there wasn't as much dog shit as there was on other streets. Spring and fall were her favorite times for walking along that street, but now it was January, a month she hated because it was so bleak, so abysmal after the long run of holidays had ended.

Since fall she had carried, she felt, the power to destroy Odell Mothersill. It had been easy enough to obtain: a call to Sociomatics to secure the home address and phone number of Candace Cone. There had been two; one in Manhattan, but that was disconnected, and one in Brooklyn. Her parents, which was the precise number she wanted. Dorothy had not called the Brooklyn number, not yet. It was obvious that the girl was back in college; that explained Odell's frequent visits to Philadelphia. If Dorothy knew anything about black families, and she believed she knew a great deal, she was sure that the girl's parents would do nothing less than draw and quarter the man—old man—who stood in the way of their daughter's career, whatever that was going to be.

There were times, however, when Dorothy stood apart from that self and in horror saw what she was doing, could understand and explain it and most times excuse it. Still, she had not made that call, her other self restraining, a thread still strong while others unraveled. Of course she had not told Murray her real problem, it was none of his business; but it had sent her begging Valium from him. How long, she wondered, could she hang in limbo, not making the call, but wanting to; wanting to, but not wanting to. How long could she insist to herself that she loved Odell, when she ground her teeth in hatred whenever he went to Philadelphia. But—if she hated him why couldn't she make the call?

Softly, like two Nerf balls, the words bounded around in her mind. They always did when she reached this point in her thinking. While she rejected them, she had to inspect their meaning first. Odell and these years of working with black people, for them, under them.

Pretending—her mind stressed every syllable—no. The sympathy, the empathy, were real. That sense of doing penance for being white, long gone now, left in its place the feeling that she was still doing penance for feeling glad she was not black. No, no.

But, couldn't she step out from under, accept some of the top-level jobs she was always being offered? Couldn't she appeal to the right ear, drop like feathered lead the suggestion of untoward behavior on the part of the black men who worked with her . . .

(She imagined Odell's face the night she fainted. What must it have looked like? Ancient black male fears suddenly carved on it? Trembling hands, rubber legs, a quaking heart and flaccid penis? Willie Best alone with ghosts?)

. . . wasn't he, weren't they, all dependent on *her* system however much it seemed to alter itself to accommodate their needs, forget the talk with its fevered imagery of bringing it crashing and burning down around everyone's head.

No. Beat back that thought.

Think of the kindnesses: to Kwame in Paris, so far from his home on the equator; of Dilip in London and his Kama Sutra antics melting before the gift of American whiteness, presented so lovingly in a hotel near Marble Arch; of Roberto moaning upon her in a turret of the Morro Castle, the sea crashing against the wall beneath, also chewing away Puerto Rico, spasm by spasm.

Her stride had shortened, become pretty, and her swinging arms shortened their arcs through the cold air. Her chin raised and a smile began to play upon her face. Dorothy was a fair princess, and she walked through fields of black-eyed Susans. She was supposed to have whatever and whoever she pleased; she was obligated to bestow her gifts upon those who hungered for them. Princess declined to Miss Ann.

"Power, more power to you," Asa McDaniels was saying. "You can't worry about what people will say, and, frankly, Odell, you're making sense for the first time since Eunice Potts. And she's a senior. You in good shape, man. That's really very cool. Twenty-five-year difference? That's sweet." Asa rose and refilled their glasses. "It doesn't hurt, man. See how fat and greasy I am? Got tired of so *much* pussy. You lookin' down and got it up, and they lookin' up darin' you not to put it down. It weakens the fibers, too much of it, Odell. You catch colds, changes your temperature, wears you out; you got to change your stroke for each new folk, and for some what raises so much sand, don't work for others a good goddamn."

Dr. McDaniels paused. "Yeah, this is okay. You've been out in the cold long enough."

Mothersill sipped his drink and looked through the venetian blinds into the street. He had never confided in another person; had never allowed himself to slip into the barroom, man-type exchange of confidences about sexual exploits.

And Asa smiled into his glass. This was a kind of breakthrough for Odell. He was talking about someone he seemed to care about, a woman-child. He envied Mothersill, remembering his own feelings when he believed he was in love. Asa sighed. It was late Tuesday afternoon. No more patients, and tomorrow he would be off. Maybe take the kids for a swim over at the hotel. That knocked them out in the winter, to be able to swim, while everyone else was thinking about Hunter Mountain or Scotch Valley or Mount Snow.

He said, "Bring her over when she's in town next, okay? If she's so boss Donna will like her." He winked. "People in your corner, y'know."

"Yeh," Mothersill said.

"The thing with Potts," Asa said. "Rare. I was sorry to see it fuck up your life for so long." He shrugged. "A shrink might've helped, but maybe not. Things run their courses."

"I didn't need a shrink," Mothersill said. "I just needed for things to stop happening to me."

"You were happening-prone, maybe. Some people are. They walk into the street and a cinder flies into their eyes. They open their mouths and somebody on the tenth floor spits into them, or a pigeon makes. They cross the street and get wiped out by a guy who's running the light. But, if things like that happen over and over, it's smart to remove yourself, one way or the other, from harm. Wear glasses, keep your mouth shut, don't cross the street."

"Well, I did go to Africa."

Asa chuckled. "Yeah, and African clapped all the way back. The lab said that was a strain they hadn't even *thought* of. Well, we whipped it. Didn't teach you much, though."

"It was out there," Mothersill said. "All that leg, like Everest. I got it because it was there."

Asa waved his hand. "Okay, okay." There was, Asa reflected, glancing at Mothersill, a change in the man, a subtle tension gone, a sudden growth from an arrested youth to manhood. An oversimplification. There were so many who never got over the hump; he himself had been on it for almost too long. Pussy, good booze, clothes, sports cars, pad. That was it, and thought I had it made. Wonder why it takes us so long, he wondered, to get everything in its place.

"Hey," Mothersill said, looking at his watch. "I've got to go." He rose and placed his hands on Asa's shoulders. "Thanks, Asa. I'll bring her around. Sometimes you want to be with other people."

"I can dig it," Asa said. "And listen." He looked into Mothersill's eyes. "If things don't work out, ain't no reason to lose your cool." His voice was light, but he knew Odell would know what he was talking about. There was such a thing as getting out before you lost and doing silly things over and over and over again.

The Church and psychiatry know that talking is good not only for the soul, but for the general health. Everyone fears in some degree the person who does not talk, who does not freely plumb the deeps of his being. "Strong" goes with silent only because it is assigned by those who are afraid of such types. If one does not talk, what can you know about him or her? Where is the Achilles tendon, or the jugular? They are revealed when we speak, revealed in subject matter, vocal cadences, inflections, choices of words, speech patterns.

The astute listener is thereby armed. The speaker is unburdened, or raised high, he hopes, in the listener's eyes. But the talker also knows, instinctively or not, that he seeks to frame out a reference for himself: Where is he? Who is he? What is he doing? An astute talker can guide himself between the shoals of indicated understanding—a nodding of the listener's head, the crinkling of a sympathetic smile—to a self-awareness.

Such was the case with Mothersill.

He even had moments of laughing at himself. There were many, many men who married women half their age; it was the thing to do, as ancient as its biblical references. He had worked with children too long. But now, he realized, he was in his prime; before, he, too, was a child. This was not a September song but a June ballad, a joining of the equinoxes at summer and spring. He liked the girl very much, and had been surprised that she liked him, too. Mothersill felt that he had arrived at a safe place, one where he could at last set his trust down and, catlike, flex muscle and mind, which had been held at maximum tension for too long a time.

Mothersill had talked more with her than with Asa, realizing with some surprise that talking, often like eating, was a part of loving. There were times, though, when, fearfully, they seemed to be talking too much. Shadows stalked through her words, darkening areas once filled with light, taking the shapes of old lovers and passions unleashed in bedlight. But those fears vanished when she spoke of her pregnancy, the abortion and her depressions. They live so much faster than I did, Mothersill thought. And she had expected him to have lived the way he had. There were, of course, things he did not tell her. There were always those things which he supposed she, too, kept in reserve. But they knew enough about each other. Things could work out. They had already surmounted one problem, both of them pitching in, and Mothersill had been impressed with her—*humanity*, he now described it to himself. For, since then, the scenes had played many times in his mind: the flow of a browning campus, the explosion of autumn colors, the three of them, a seeming black caucus looked past by white students and faculty, sitting sadly beneath a two-hundred-year-old maple tree, their baobab, their holy tree. There, nearly every time perhaps so their words could not be trapped by walls, stored up in pictures, trapped in the pages of books; their faces unshadowed by natural light, the scents of sadness, the twinges of pain blown lightly away, assuaged by the angle of golden light. Their voices filtered through their emotions and Mothersill thought of Lot and his two daughters who went up out of Zoar.

They had solved the problem.

And now he was, he thought, happy, a proper curb, age, on his lust, but his view extending far beyond the horizon of a bedsheet.

Dorothy, who had hung like a threatening gray cloud around the office, growing more pale each day, was going to take some time off, go to the Caribbean, she'd said with a wan smile. It was not that she was unco-operative or any less efficient than she'd always been; rather, it was the way she looked at him sometimes. It was a cold, measuring glance which seemed to accuse him of betrayal, and it vaguely threatened. But now she would be going, and hopefully the sun, rum and some judicious loving would clear the air. He worried about Dorothy; he did not like to think of her being alone.

Bathed, perfumed and packed, Dorothy Nigro sits on the edge of her bed dialing the number. Outside, the Murray Hill section hums with the early evening traffic. She knows the temperature is dropping, fast; the radio weatherman has said. The sky will be clear, the stars bright. Her plane leaves in an hour and she will be in St. Croix shortly after midnight. Dorothy bounces her cigarette against the ashtray as the phone is picked up at the other end. Good. A woman's voice.

"Mrs. Cone?"

"This is she speaking. Cohen."

"Cohen?"

"Yes, Cohen."

Dorothy is flustered. This, obviously is a Jewish name, a Jewish person.

"Hello, hello. What is it? This is Mrs. Cohen, Elisabeth Cohen, Mrs. Jonathan Cohen. Is anything wrong? Hello?"

Dorothy hears the names Elisabeth and Jonathan (spelled John, according to Sociomatics) and bungles ahead. "Have you a daughter named Candace?"

Laughter, but the relief is unmistakable. "Yes. Is this the school? Candace changed the spelling of our name. Too Jewish, she said. What's wrong?"

Dorothy both relaxes and starts being nervous. "She's all right. This is not the school. This is a friend, sort of." She pauses. "You might like to know that your daughter is sleeping around with an old man named Odell Mothersill. He lives in Manhattan." She hangs up, breathing hard. She mashes out her cigarette, turns out the light and picks up her bags. Outside, she trips the three locks on her door and rings for the elevator. The doorman hails a cab for her. Her tip is a smile; Christmas was not long ago. He will have to wait until the next one for his crisp, new five dollar bill.

She settles back in the cab, lighting another cigarette, and wonders what New York will be like in another two weeks.

"Who was that?" John Cohen asks. He sits before the television set. There is a special on the war and he might perhaps catch a glimpse of Jeremy.

"A wrong number, dear. Someone looking for another Cohen."

Elisabeth retreats into the kitchen and quickly thumbs through the Manhattan telephone directory. There is but one Mothersill listed and the first name is Odell. The voice, she thinks. She'd know for sure by the voice. She climbs the stairs of their brownstone to the second floor where, in the bedroom, with unnecessary caution, she picks up the phone and dials, wondering if the woman who called her felt the way she now did. No. Impossible. My God! she thought.

"Hello. Hel*lo*."

Elisabeth grips the phone and a dark dread winds around her heart. It sounds like him. Please say a few more words. "Hello? Hey, you ain't even breathin' into the phone—" A laugh moving away from the phone and it goes dead. She hangs up, plunges her face into her hands.

Lord, God. For just one afternoon, nineteen years ago, this? This, Lord? They wallowing in their ignorance, pleasuring in their innocence and this strange voice in the night, lighting it up to show its darkness, father and daughter.

Mrs. Cohen tries to think rationally. She cannot ask Candace. She cannot ask Odell; she doesn't trust herself not to tell them. She wishes for a blast of heavenly fury to destroy Mothersill where he stands or lies. Her daughter she wishes to save; she is from her womb. She is like Elisabeth Cohen wishes she had been or could be, the new black woman. Tough. Independent. Intelligent. And God knows she helped her daughter to be what she is, defended her against the worries of Jonathan, who—God, someone else to worry about. Content and proud that at last he had helped to make a baby. Oh, Jonathan. Worried sometimes, yes, but happy, too. Jonathan wished a pink-dressed cuddly girl, and Candace was that when she was small. He wished her to stay forever a little girl. But she grew, worried about the brothers and sisters in Mississippi and was sure marching and voter enrollment could help. "Go, child," Elisabeth had said. It had always been "Go child." Especially when Jeremy seemed to be faltering, staying out all night, coming home drunk or drugged, doing poorly in school. Maybe we didn't do enough for him, with him, Elisabeth now thinks; maybe in some way we treated him differently, being adopted, though you know, Lord, we tried not to show one particle of difference, not one.

A frigid fury fills her. Something must be done. The phrase—yes, it was a white woman who'd called—sleeping around, sleeping around—haunts her, takes her back quickly to the afternoon of the broken bed. Candace would be just the way she was, she thinks. Something must be done. This evil must be wiped out like the eye that needs plucking. She must return to Jonathan, but before she does, she wraps her arms around her body and squeezes it tightly, as if to force some poison out of it.

She is calmer the next evening, the gun in her bag. It is a small gun, a 6.35 Beretta automatic, and the magazine is full. Jonathan got it for her; he has a .38 Smith & Wesson. He simply said as he came home one night, black communities blazing from New York to California, "It's about that time, Elisabeth," and with drawn curtains taught her how to use it. Jonathan was that way; he *did* things people never thought him capable of doing.

Jonathan is working late; some securities have been discovered missing and tallies must be taken. Jonathan says the big shots themselves steal the securities. Elisabeth thinks of these things as she dresses carefully. A suit not too severe, a simple necklace, hat, gloves and coat.

The A train rushes her to Manhattan. She recalls the West Fourth Street stop, the coffee shop, Mothersill nineteen years ago. The conductors have told her to change at Fifty-ninth Street to a local, which she does, and emerges into the cold and walks quickly to the address clutched in her hand.

O. Mothersill, the nameplate reads. She presses the buzzer; it echoes before her, unlocking the door. She steps quickly and lightly up the stairs, having cocked the gun.

"Who is it?"

She almost smiles at the sound of his voice. "A friend," she says, muffling her voice with her wrist. The stair lights are dim. She sees him standing in the doorway of a fourth-floor apartment.

"Who?" he demands.

She sees him straining to see her better; she angles her head, comes up on the landing, turns to face him directly, the gun slightly behind her.

At that instant there comes recognition. But because he is completely unprepared for it, Mothersill discounts what he sees; his mind refuses to whisper her name. He stares. She approaches with that quick, dainty step, moving as in a dream because the carpet gives back no sound of the movement of her feet. She stops and smiles. Her hand moves from behind her and, almost hidden in her glove, the gun points at him. Mothersill is moving backward when he hears: "Candace's mother. You are her father."

Pain first, tracking here and there in his body, and then the noises rising up, hard-riding the crest of what remains of his consciousness, and looking up at his ceiling he hears in that fractured silence in which New Yorkers recoil, ponder and often do nothing, the soft thumping of her running down the stairs.

Part Six

CHAPTER ONE

A NICE DAY. Great. The mist is burning off already. I see the sun shining on the oak.

I slip out of bed and go to the window. One of my pleasures up here, seeing the days begin. Sometimes I watch them even earlier than this. Also, there are times when in the middle of the night I look out at the stars. They seem much closer to the earth here, and the Milky Way is scattered from one end of the horizon to the other. But I like mornings best.

I watch a woodchuck and her two children nibbling in the tall grasses, bending the daisies and blue bells and black-eyed Susans that grow there. A pair of barn swallows catch my eye as they curve away from their nest into the woods over by the lake.

I hear Marie groaning sweetly in her sleep, and turn to look at her folded softly, the sheets pulled up to ward off the early morning chill. I really love this woman, maybe all the more because it was such a long time coming. And so much pain, mental and physical.

I throw on my robe and limp into the kitchen. I'll limp for the rest of my goddamn life. Thanks, Elisabeth. That part of my stomach you ventilated so much that they had to cut away half of it has grown back, but the leg didn't do so hot. Never asked one fucking question, just bam bam bam bam bam bam bam bam.

I draw the water for the coffee and open the doors. The chill inside the house gets to my leg anyway. I like to see the grass all sweating dew, see the plotches of white spider webs sparkling like rhinestones dipped in water.

How the hell could I have known? I've asked myself that question for years. Elisabeth, like Isis: here's a reward (was it a reward, nineteen years ago? Twenty-two now. For what?) and here's your punishment: bam bam bam. . . .

Shit, Candace didn't even look at me good because I didn't go to Chicago with her. She didn't even want to see me, until Marie and I found something together. Two people with holes then. A hole in my heart and she had one in her belly, where they ripped away her child. More than sex, and sex was more than Candace and I ever had. Got blown half away for nothing. There was no way for me to have known that she was my daughter. Crazy Elisabeth, hat and gloves, and I've a daughter almost the age of my wife.

This mountain water makes great coffee. Maybe because there's no dog shit or cat piss leaking into the well, the way it seems to leak into the city systems.

Funny how nobody wants you until someone else does. Those afternoons on the campus, after we'd told Candace. Talking. Candace seeming to be upset, and maybe she was, maybe, maybe, and Marie telling her, like, some things just happen and they're so good nothing else matters. But it did matter. We wanted her to understand, to forgive us, to look kindly upon those nights we stole in Philadelphia hotels, the weekends in the Poconos and New York.

(Women eying each other, sunlight bouncing from the remaining leaves of a golden maple. They plumb each other's soul, disengaging from the secret things they know about each other—lovers, diseases, abortions, chippie-chasing fathers, nymphomaniac mothers, turned-around hopes.)

And Candace, the cool one, the lover of crippled young brothers, the marcher who like truth walking hard on the night had trespassed in Mississippi, looked at us, seeing what we, Marie and I, had come to feel. Perhaps she felt it too, however briefly, for her words had seemed to give that feeling shape one night, I believed.

Oh, Candy, don't be mad, baby. Try to feel glad for us, okay?

Silence. Hate and jealousy wrestling with a seldom-called spirit. A cyclist oozing past; voices just failing to intrude from across the campus, and I carrying then my forty-two years like

Methuselah at his last begat, watched them, saw their eyes starting to trickle tears; saw them stretching, leaning and clutching toward each other, their young firm hands fluttering like hawks taking a higher wind, about to soar across distances measured by the Commandments and the seven deadly sins; they cleared the abyss containing furies yet unnamed and fell, lesser goddesses, sobbing one upon the other.

I drew away, a great ease drifting over me, and I was filled with an immense pride in their age, a satisfaction with the race. I felt then like I do now, completely and overwhelmingly aware of the dawn, a fresh day washed clean by the horrors of the night. I had not found such a feeling in my own age.

I limp outside holding the cup of coffee to the acre plot turned and furrowed, ready for seeding, already late because I want the kids to do it. Tomatoes will go there so the plants in front won't be shaded later. Lettuce, beets, snap beans, potatoes, collards—the whole earth promises. The concrete of the cities is the final coating, promising nothing. Death runs faster on it, that is all. Ran right up to my house, it did, she did, then tipped up the stairs like a lady. Elisabeth, without so much as a "How do you do?" Why hadn't she let me know? I would've been cool; I'd have left Jonathan his fathership, been content to watch from afar. She robbed me! Elisabeth robbed me! Stole my seed and cultivated it; it rooted where there was thought to be no nourishment, then flowered. How she must have laughed sometimes. But even Oedipus at first took only his own sight; she didn't have to try to take my life. I was not a god to her goddess. I did not know; my senses told me nothing; my instinct slept. Even so, I never touched her, not where it mattered. Yes, I kissed her and felt her breasts, and yes, I wanted to, and yes, I would have, not knowing, but then Marie walked in and it was over. Elisabeth didn't know; I didn't know. Now she knows and now I know, and Marie. Dorothy must have guessed. But now we're all wrapped in our silences. Dorothy is where? Candace, we know is in Uganda, Elisabeth is where she was before she shot me. Shot me. Shot the shit out of me. I see the ceiling from a new angle; it is peeling badly, ten layers of paint flaking off, like stalactites. I touch all those places that do not hurt after the first second's pain, and feel relief that I am going to die, a deserved end for my sin. And I died. I didn't feel them probing and chipping and cutting, under some obligation or perhaps challenge, not so much to keep me alive, but so one intern could demonstrate to another how much he knew. Just one of those things. Nobody fucked up. Maybe I was a midterm examination. My death was temporary. I lived. I live. There was nothing to tell the police. *I opened the door and somebody shot me. Who? I don't know. Absolutely no idea.* They found Marie's clothes in my closet, of course, so I had to tell them we were lovers. And I had to tell Marie. She had to know. *Otherwise I'll always look for some bitch to be standing outside the door ready to blow your balls off.* So I told her:

I hear the truck from a mile away, gears growling, milk cans rattling and in a minute Mr. Gomes turns into the driveway and waves to me, his eyes widening. He believes city people sleep until noon. Farmers have that natural kind of prejudice against urban dwellers. Not only is he surprised to see me up; my legs sticking out from my robe amuse him too.

"What time they comin', Mr. Mothersill?"

"Noon." He's looking at my bare legs. Probably thinking how skinny they are. Mr. Gomes may be black, but he's like any other dairy farmer in these mountains.

"Well, anytime you want to show 'em how we milk cows, you just bring 'em on by; five-thirty afternoon's 'bout the best time."

"Thanks, Mr. Gomes." He's going to bring the milk every morning for the kids. Now he's hustling down to the cold cellar. He's pleased we're here. "Nothin' like havin' some of your own kind around, Mr. Mothersill. Don't know how a man can live in the city. Colored folks ain't natural in cities. They gets killin-slick an et out from the inside. You better off up here." He was curious as to how we would survive, but beamed with pride when

I told him I'd start teaching social science at the consolidated school in the fall. He thinks I'm an intellectual and that I sound like Dr. King. Maybe I am an intellectual, to have given up what we did. Which was, to give up the city, perhaps nothing. Or maybe it gave us up, and I'm not an intellectual, but a coward.

"Odell?"

Marie's standing in the doorway looking at Mr. Gomes's truck. She's smiling. The delivery of the milk is another sign of what's to come. She's wearing a short robe, long, fine legs showing; and she has that wondrously rounded, four-month pregnant belly. I limp toward her, pull up her robe and gown, expose her to the morning air, and kiss her belly, just as Mr. Gomes emerges from the cellar.

She pushes me away, grinning with embarrassment; she is all dimples and ten miles of white teeth. Mr. Gomes should have seen us two hours ago. "Morning, Mr. Gomes," she says.

"Nice mornin', Miz Mothersill." Mr. Gomes is flustered but he carries on, hustling to his truck, tipping his hat. "Good luck with the kids," he calls, going with a clash and grind of gears. We laugh, thinking of Miz Gomes and Mr. Gomes. I don't know what Marie is thinking precisely, but I can't visualize Mr. Gomes kissing his wife lower than her lips. I think of her pulling up the hem of her nightgown, and Mr. Gomes barely lowering his pajama bottoms. And there I was slobbering all over my wife's belly.

"Today's the day," Marie says. I see her eyes slide over the land, raise up to the hills and become satisfied.

I nod. My hand goes most naturally to her waist, then down to where her back starts to curve out behind her. She takes my arm and places it around her and we go in for breakfast. I marvel at the way I feel when she places my arm around her. No woman ever did it before, and it makes me feel, with all its random implications, the way I felt when Etta Mae would guide me into my parents' bedroom on those afternoons eons ago. So simple a gesture.

The sun is into the kitchen now and Marie has turned on the radio, and the world comes shouldering in, the newscasters layering the global troubles like stacks of buttered toast, for beyond these tree-strung mountains there is a dying, collective and so pain-racked that no opiate can work. We listen and I see our children, four of them, coming out with Asa's family, leaving the city behind as they rush up the highways through valleys and on the shoulder of mountains to here.

These acres will be silent no longer. The kids will romp across them laughing, crying, yelling. Two boys and two girls, culled from the foster homes that failed and the orphanages that can never succeed. They've been here before, but today they are coming home.

Pleasure and anticipation are etched in Marie's face; she's not listening to the radio. She is a mix, both mother and child, and wise and innocent, brave and fearful. After all, she will have five kids nearly all at once. Still, she can't wait.

I'm anxious. The responsibility impinges sharply upon the joy. It is easy enough to blame other people for the way they bring up their children, but who can you blame when the children are yours? But I have the kids to raise; there is nothing more certain than that, and that I will indeed raise them. (Raise: *To move or cause to move upward or to a higher position. To place or set upright. To cause to arise, appear, exist. To increase in size, quantity or worth. To increase in strength, degree or pitch. To begin. To arouse or stir up: raise a revolt.*

I agree.

"Thinking?"

I answer, "Yes."

"What?"

"Lots of things."

"The kids," she says, grinning, and I grin, too. We're both nervous.

"And us."

"Us?" she says.

I look around. Save for the radio the place is so quiet, so empty with all the unoccupied rooms. Lovers would grow bored here. We have certainly moved beyond that. I reach across the table and take Marie's hand, pull on it until she rises. Standing, I feel myself already. We go back to the bedroom, passing the boys' room and the girls' room and the room being readied for the baby. I remove her robe, her gown, as she stands with her eyes closed, a smile fluttering around her mouth. Her breasts are starting to swell and veins like tentacular embraces encircle her belly. We ease onto the bed, now golden with sunlight, the door of the room open and I am thinking, for the last time, with kids around, and listening to the sounds of summer—the screaming jays, the pigeons in the old barn, the peeps of the hawks, the distant barks of dogs, the hiss of young wind through the screens—when, rocking with the love-motion, we hear at the same time the brazen intrusion of a car horn and the voices of children and start, stop, stare at each other and say as we draw hastily apart, "*They're here!*"